without prejudice

Epic Tale of a Mumbai Bar Dancer

DEVASIS

olive turtle

NIYOGI BOOKS

Published by
NIYOGI BOOKS
Block D, Building No. 77,
Okhla Industrial Area, Phase-I,
New Delhi-110 020, INDIA
Tel: 91-11-26816301
Email: niyogibooks@gmail.com
Website: www.niyogibooksindia.com

Editor: Gita Rajan
Design: Nabanita Das
Cover Design: Misha Oberoi

ISBN: 978-93-85285-65-3
Publication: 2017

Printed at: Niyogi Offset Pvt. Ltd., New Delhi, India

To my family : Anjanaa, Dev and Dipayan,
without whom I am incomplete

Until the lions have their historians,
the tales of the hunt shall always glorify the hunter

– African Proverb

BOOK 1

- Initiation -

20th Century:
Last Quarter

Stepping into Womanhood

The sun was about to set. The orange glow from the fading sun would provide light for some more time. If only Kamala could find her niece and get started, they would be able to go past the ravines and reach the old crumbling fort, near the hillock, before sunset. A short distance from there was the desolate field by the highway. Once they crossed the field, they would reach the road leading to their village. If they wasted any more time, complete darkness would engulf them.

Kamala's throat was parched, she was dying of thirst, but she had to find the girl first. She set her rickety bundle of deadwood down and craned her neck to see as far as she could. She swallowed hard and called out to her niece again, in her already hoarse voice.

'Munia, *arre meri baachi,* where are you? It will be dark very soon. We should get out of the ravines now, Munia baby! Please Munia, hurry up dear, or we will be late.'

Further down, a group of women from their neighbouring village were trying to gather the firewood too. Some of them had already started loading the bundles on their donkeys. Kamala could see that the group was getting ready to leave the ravines.

The Chambal Valley – a maze of deep ravines and scrub forests which hides a large section of population defined by poverty, illiteracy, superstition and violence from the rest of the world, while urban India continued to be ever more modern, propelled by a healthy economic rate of growth.

Named after the river that runs through the central Indian provinces of Madhya Pradesh, Rajasthan, and Uttar Pradesh, the district of Chambal is in Madhya Pradesh, where a few-metre-deep gullies would suddenly give way to gorges with high walls of dirt and rocks, yawning chasms, and deep gaping extensive ravines – *beehad,* as known locally. A modest army could disappear into these ravines and not be found for days or might even be for weeks – the ravines are so truly deep and foreboding. Life for people all around is very hard. Wherever the valley had been a little flatter, even if over a small patch, the local people had tilled that land and planted mustard, wheat or gram or occasionally, Toor Dal, a variety of lentil.

'Munia!' Kamala called out again. Summer, harsh and unkind, had taken its toll on her. A film of perspiration coated her body. She wiped her face with her veil. Her armpits were soaking wet.

'*Aayi Mami,*' a soft, melodious voice replied in the affirmative from nearby.

Dressed in a torn and dusty green frock, partly tucked into a pair of khaki shorts meant for boys, held on to her tiny waist by a drawstring made out of torn rugs, a thin, very fair, undernourished yet pretty girl stumbled out of a gorge. Her shoulder-length hair, caked with dry yellow earth, framed her beautiful oval-shaped face.

'We need to start our journey home, Munia *beti*,' said Kamala. 'Others are also preparing to leave,' she gestured, indicating towards the group of women nearby.

'I want to rest Mami. My stomach is aching,' Munia pouted and shook her head firmly.

'I had asked you not to come with me. I told you to study your *angrezi abcb* that masterji gave you,' Kamala displayed mock anger tugging the girl along.

'Not *abcb,* Mami! It is A B C D,' Munia pronounced carefully and started laughing and clapping her hands in delight. Her skinny yet graceful figure started swaying as she started jumping in joy. Suddenly she exclaimed, '*Khoon*!'

Bewildered, Kamala glanced around. She was about to pick up the bundle of gathered deadwood, which she had set down earlier, to load it on the back of her donkey, when she heard the terror in Munia's voice. She saw a thin line of blood flowing down Munia's left leg, past the pair of khaki shorts and mixing into the dry earth, after kissing the girl's left ankle. Out of fear, by then, Munia had started crying loudly.

Without picking up the load, Kamala knelt down in front of Munia and held the girl's face lightly in her dirty, sweaty palms. 'Don't be afraid, *meri pyaari*. Nothing's wrong. You are not sick,' she reassured her scared niece. 'It happens to all of us. It happens to me as well,' and then she kissed the forehead of her little niece who had brought solace to her otherwise barren life.

The dusky, lissom, middle-aged woman, with sparkling kohl-lined eyes, tore a part of the bottom of the short petticoat she was wearing under her long skirt and wiped away the dripping blood. But she needed more help to make a protective shield for the blood. She was also not very sure if, under the circumstances, Munia would be able to walk all the way to the village. After hesitating for a fraction of a second, she called out to the group of women, who were nearby, for help.

Against the backdrop of the setting sun, in the ravines of Chambal, within the protective barricade of a temporary changing room formed by the chunris and dupattas which so far had covered the heads and faces of the women till recently – Munia stepped into womanhood.

Mangiram was worried.

He was squatting uneasily at the inersection where the crossroads from the highway met the road leading to their village. The glow of the lantern that illuminated the nearby makeshift tiny tea stall had given his gaunt face an ethereal appearance. He was worried because Kamala was yet to return from the *beehad.* With the evening setting in, convoys of trucks had started moving through the highway carrying heavy loads to far-off cities. In pitch dark, with heavy trucks plying, the highway around this locality was considered unsafe, accident prone. Mangiram was getting angry.

He had repeatedly told Kamala to return home definitely before sunset. In their village, the women did not stay out after sunset, as it was frowned upon by the village elders. And, today she had taken Munia too. He had objected to this, but his temperamental wife refused to pay heed. He regretted yet one more time for having been married to her. In his agitated mood, he sought out a bidi that he had kept tucked in the folds of his turban, and lit it up. He felt like slapping her. However, in his heart of hearts, he knew that it would forever remain in his imagination only. The poverty-stricken Mangiram could not afford to beat his wife, who was actually the breadwinner, lest she threw him out from their ramshackle shack.

Mangiram had no tangible income of his own. Nor did he look for a job to supplement the paltry sum Babulal gave him every month for sheltering Munia. He was not bothered that his wife had to go to the *beehad* in search of firewood, which she then chopped in smaller sizes to sell in the local market. Nor the fact that she had to augment the family's meagre income by selling the milk and the cow-dung cakes from their two cows which were gifted to her by her father. Mangiram was satisfied with his life so far, as long as he got two square meals a day and his quota of country liquor in the evening. He could not be bothered with any earthly matter except guarding Munia. She was Babulal's property and more importantly, a source of easy money for him.

Kamala was anxious. She was also worried because with each passing moment Munia was increasingly complaining of a greater degree of pain. Under her prevailing physical condition, Munia was finding it difficult to walk at a stretch, for a long time and they had to take repeated halts in between. For Kamala to manage the donkey with a load, as well as a sick companion, was becoming progressively difficult. Very slowly and after a considerable amount of time, the duo of aunt and niece reached the spot where Mangiram was waiting.

The moment Mangiram saw them he leapt to his feet and whispered hoarsely under his breath, '*Haramzadi*. Haven't I told you repeatedly not to return home so late?'

He threw down his bidi and quashed its flames under the sole of his left foot to display his anger.

Kamala hesitated for a moment. She knew it was necessary to let her husband know that Munia had reached womanhood.

Possibly, she could state the fact now. But she also knew this would trigger the process of her separation from Munia. Kamala felt sad. She did not react to her husband's profanity. She also curbed the sharp retort that rose to her lips. Instead, in a restrained manner, she said, 'Let's go home. I have something to tell you.'

'What is it, you bitch? Tell me now, right now,' Mangiram insisted, in a foul mood.

'I said we will discuss it when we reach home,' replied a dignified Kamala. She wanted more time to think about it; to weigh the pros and cons, decide how to deal with it. She held her niece's hand firmly and marched ahead.

Inside the decrepit shack on the eastern fringe of the village they called home, Kamala was busy preparing the evening meal. Mangiram was enjoying his usual quota of alcohol and Munia was sleeping on the earthen floor away from them. In a hushed tone, Kamala told Mangiram, 'Munia has become a woman today.' Mangiram looked at Kamala with a blank expression, not comprehending the nuances of her statement. Kamala paused for a while. Her stare was fixed on the reddish glow of the fire from the clay oven in front of her. With practised ease, she continued preparing the evening meal of dal and chapattis.

'Munia has bled today.' Kamala phrased her statement in a firm, matter-of-fact way. It never paid to be subtle with her silly and insensitive husband.

Mangiram's right hand, holding a steel-tumbler of country liquor, shook. Luckily, the glass was nearly empty, so the liquor did not spill. He put it down on the floor and looked at his wife balefully, for uttering the unutterable. He could see his main source of income drying up for no fault of his. He could see himself dying of hunger. His liquor-drenched brain frantically sought for some justification, using which he could at least plead with Dadua to let Munia remain with him for some more time. He narrowed his eyes, scratched his ears, and rubbed his forehead. Yet, he could imagine none. He realised how pitiable and vulnerable he was. It made him angry. He looked loathingly at his wife, the barren bitch. She could not produce even one daughter. So, for the rest of his life, he would remain a poor man, while all his brothers, cousins and other relatives had comfortable lifestyles. He could not eat. His stomach churned and heaved. He ran out of the shack and vomited. Rukmini Bai, the woman next door, cursed him at the top of her voice.

After some time Kamala came out of their shack with a jug full of water and dutifully cleaned the mess. She helped Mangiram, who was dozing off resting on the side wall, inside, and put him to bed.

The oven fire had been extinguished some time ago. Still there was the reddish glow from the embers. The flame of the oil lamp had been reduced to the minimum. In the flickers of these dim lights, Munia's face looked like that of an angel, the sleeping beauty, serene and divine. Kamala kept staring at that face unblinkingly. She knew it was only a matter of days. She would not see this face again, possibly for the rest of her life.

Tradition

Although Village Mirpura was only about a hundred and eighty miles away from New Delhi, the capital of India, it was a microcosm of rural India – ramshackle houses, narrow dirt roads, a hardly functional primary school, and an almost non-existent elementary health care facility. Electricity had arrived here, just a couple of years ago; however, its availability was totally at the mercy of the state electricity board and was severely rationed.

Even Shahgarh, the nearby town, was not any better, except for slightly wider roads, sturdier houses, and some quacks disguised as qualified doctors, practising medicine. The secondary school there was pathetic and lacked qualified teachers. The town had a restaurant – Moti Mahal, which mostly sold food by the fixed-menu thali system which usually included rice, dal, vegetables, and chapattis; pickles and papad were luxuries. In addition, the town had a small cinema hall, the Purnima Theatre – an apology of a movie theatre – which screened outdated Hindi movies with an old cranky projector that had run its course. Bharat Lodge was the residential hotel near the uncared-for Primary Health Care centre in the market square.

As with any hotel in small-town India, the telephone at Bharat Lodge was dysfunctional, the window curtains were faded and frayed, the concept of room service was not known, and bed sheets and pillow covers were changed only once a week. Cockroaches, bedbugs, flies, and mosquitoes were constant companions of the boarders. During high summer, ceiling fans or rickety air-coolers would provide visual comfort. The intense winter would be somewhat more pleasant under the protective cover of the quilts for those occasional guests, who had no option but to stay here.

Babulal was the head watchman of Bharat Lodge. He was the oldest member of the staff of the hotel and had witnessed more than half a century go by. He was perceived to be very close to the owner of Bharat Lodge, Bhupinder Singh, an empanelled civil contractor with the provincial government. Babulal was also the headman of his biradari, his caste-based community and controlled the *panchakala or panchganga* – the caste panchayat or the *Khap* of their biradari; the self-appointed custodian of caste traditions, customs, and cultural practices of the community in and around nearby villages.

The Khap headed by Babulal had no legal validity. However, in India's villages, it is the Khaps which rule the roost – a parallel forum of justice that lays down iron-clad rules and customs for the community, in addition to resolving disputes between members of the biradari, albeit at the local level. Most of the times, they pass judgements in an absolutely capricious manner; and always in favour of those who wield real power – social, economic, or political – to ensure that the status quo remains undisturbed. And, only because of this reason, the union government or the provincial state administrations are never willing to intervene to correct such situations. Villagers from his biradari, in deference to Babulal's age and also because he was the headman and leader of the Khap, addressed him as Dadua, the grandfather.

Babulal Dadua was involved in one other business. He was the main conduit for trafficking in women, mostly from his community. This was his hereditary profession, which he kept cloaked in secrecy.

The people from Babulal's community were originally village performers and 'camp-followers' – singers and dancers who had a latent tendency for practising 'concubinage' even prior to the British rule of India. When India came under British dominion, his people became victims of further social prejudice of the foreign rulers. Years of it made them gradually fall prey to the easy way of bartering their women to the rich and powerful for survival; all the more so because, when India was under British domination, most of the men of Babulal's or similar such communities had by then turned outlaws either as *Thugees* or as *Baghees*, and were hunted down by the British as criminals.

Babulal and many others like him were the debilitated and unfortunate progeny of these forefathers, who for circumstances beyond their control had started over a century ago the shocking tradition of trafficking in women from their own community.

It was well past noon when Mangiram reached Bharat Lodge. His eyes were blood-red from lack of proper sleep and continuous vomiting throughout the night. His face had over a week's stubble. He looked very sick.

Babulal was taking his bath. So Mangiram had to wait. In fact, he had to wait further. After taking his bath, Babulal meditated in front of the clan goddess, Matarani. Nobody was allowed to disturb him during this time. Babulal prided himself as a religious man. When ultimately he emerged after about an hour, Mangiram was seen squatting under a big shadowy banyan tree in the backyard of the lodge slightly away from the main building. With his tired back resting on the trunk of the tree, Mangiram was fast asleep.

Babulal made a young guard from within his staff place a charpoy under the shadow of the tree close to where Mangiram was asleep. Once he placed himself comfortably on his charpoy, he called out Mangiram's name in his loud rustic voice. Babulal, with his native cunning, had by now realised that Mangiram was in trouble. He was also very sure that it would be financial in nature and the problem would be so acute that Mangiram could muster enough courage to come and meet him directly at Bharat Lodge. All his contacts were strictly advised not to ever approach him directly, without prior permission taken through his older cousin, Snehalata, who looked after his network in the community.

Babulal was also annoyed with Snehalata. She was supposed to keep track of all that was happening in the twenty-four villages that were under his Khap. He concluded that with age she was losing control over her network. He thought of his aunt Mayarani, Snehalata's mother, who even at her age was a better organiser and networker of nayika*s*, or traditional familial madams, for his father, who too was the head of the Khap and was also involved in trafficking in women as per tradition till he died ten years ago.

Mangiram was still snoring. Babulal got irritated. He nudged Mangiram with his left foot. 'Look at the bastard, so filthy,' he said to himself. He regretted that some of the men of his clan would never leave their bad habits. Mangiram felt slightly disoriented and bewildered about the place and time of his existence, being forced out of his slumber rudely. Suddenly, Dadua's voice penetrated his perplexed consciousness. He got up hurriedly and paid his obeisance to the clan headman, and then, with folded hands, stood silently.

'What happened, Mangiram? What's so urgent that you came here directly without notice?' Babulal camouflaged his irritation and said in an apparently concerned tone.

'Dadua, I am in grave danger,' pleaded Mangiram.

'That I am sure of. Otherwise you would not have disregarded my instructions,' replied Babulal complacently, pleased with his intuitive analysis of Mangiram's sudden arrival. 'How is Munia? And Kamala?' Babulal tried showing his benevolent-self to this downtrodden rascal from his caste.

'Kamala is alright, Dadua. It's Munia I am worried about.'

'Why? What's the problem? What happened?' Babulal reacted very sharply. He could not afford to be casual or careless about anything related to Munia.

'She started having her *masik-khoon* Dadua. She is not keeping good health, crying continuously.'

'That's alright. Girls her age initially feel confused at such times because of the changes happening to their bodies. They get irritated. It is okay,' said Babulal, in a manner of counselling.

Staring fixedly at his own feet, Mangiram nodded his head in silent agreement.

'Why are you still worried, Mangiram?' Babulal asked coaxingly, 'What is bothering you? You have done your job. You have informed me about Munia. You and Kamala have looked after her and cared for her for the past so many years. You have served my father and me well. So, why worry?' With a hooded look and holding back a half-smile, he continued toying with him.

Babulal kept watching Mangiram. He could actually see the whirling of the grey-matter inside the scoundrel's head. The mental arithmetic the so-called village simpleton, with the facade of a gullible face, was trying to accomplish. He knew the answer instinctively. However, he wanted Mangiram to voice it. He wanted this rustic rascal from his community to plead for it.

Mangiram knew the tenor of the voice well. He hesitated, debating his reply, and then in wheedling tones said, 'Dadua, you know you are my God. You are my headman. You know I have lavished love on Munia. I treated her like my own daughter. Kamala has looked after her well. Without her we will not be able to live.' He looked at Babulal pleadingly.

'But she cannot stay with you forever, Mangiram. You know that. Don't you?'

'Yes, I know. But how will we live without her?'

'Why? What is the problem? Even if she was your daughter, she would have gone away, eventually.' Babulal quizzed cynically. 'All parents and family members have to forego their daughters one day. Others give them away in marriages. In our biradari, we give them away to the society. This is our tradition, our pride. Don't you know that?' The turn in Babulal's direction of thought jolted Mangiram unpleasantly.

Thinking that the opportunity was fast slipping away, Mangiram grovelled before the headman. 'Economically too, we are losers,' he sniffled pathetically. 'How are we supposed to live after Munia goes away? Had she been our daughter we would have had a share of her future income. Presently we cannot claim her income as she is not our daughter. But we raised her as if she was. We have no money Dadua, but we served your family faithfully. For over a decade we have protected her. We gave her a family. We need your blessing on that count.'

Babulal now had what he wanted. 'Don't worry, I will do something for you,' he said, as if his benevolence had nothing to do with putting Mangiram deeper in his debt. 'I will not be able to pay you the full monthly stipend I give you at present, but some gratuity will reach you every month once Munia is gone,' he said, assuring the poor man and knowing full well that this paltry act would be lauded by the community. Babulal wanted such publicity. It was good for his business.

Now that he had made his request and Dadua had acceded to it, Mangiram started crying unabashedly clutching his feet. He was weeping not because he was losing Munia, but because he felt relieved that he had some assured income for the rest of his life and would not have to work till his death.

After Mangiram left for his village, Babulal was in deep thought. He was worried because of the breach that took place in the age-old system. He was disturbed by the fact that a lowly mindless dolt like Mangiram could gather enough courage to access him directly, by-passing the community norm of first approaching the nayikas, who were at the front-end of his flesh trade and interacted with the villagers. He would have to take some precautionary measures to desist people like Mangiram approaching him directly, or else the power structure within his clan and the respect and fear attached to the position of the clan headman would gradually erode. Moreover, times were changing. People from the higher echelons of society and a part of the state administration had started forcefully despising their community norms these days. Such people, in their efforts to stop the despicable ancient custom, would be looking for similar lapses to connect him with the practice of harlotry and punish him, to make an example out of it. Moreover, he would lose the subtle patronage that he enjoyed with the political and administrative classes once he was tainted. Though, he also thought that God is merciful and, such upright and socially conscious people were still a minority; really miniscule in numbers.

Babulal contemplated calling for a meeting of the Khap. He thought of his father, Shankar Baba, and pondered how he would have reacted in a similar situation.

Babulal knew that he would deal with Mangiram's greed, but later.

The moot point was how to promote Munia's future? That entire evening Babulal was preoccupied with calculating the various permutations and combinations. He, once again missed the counsel of his aunt Mayarani, who had a razor-sharp instinct for assessing a girl's worth and the kind of training she would need to become a sophisticated and coveted courtesan. Her daughter Snehalata was completely devoid of it.

In the past few years Babulal had trafficked annually about hundred-odd girls from the villages under his Khap and placed them in the flesh trade. 'Munia is about thirteen, so I have roughly three years to train her,' he thought. Munia was also special. Unlike so many *Plain Janes* from his clan, Munia had pedigree. Babulal's father had taught him the importance of pedigree in their field of work.

Bloodline – the essence of appearance, wit, charm and personality. *'You could groom anyone, but the combination of all the four factors,'* Shankar Baba had opined, *'could only happen if you have a superior bloodline.'* The same set of factors gave distinction – and success – to both queens and courtesans. So potent was this combination in Munia that Shankar Baba had been forced to place her with an idiot like Mangiram to hide the bloodline.

Babulal made up his mind. He would personally take Munia to Bombay.

Training

That morning Munia woke up to an assault on her senses. Her introduction to modern India took place through the overpowering stench that made her feel nauseous. The train compartment she occupied was redolent with an odour much like rancid butter. She also felt the intense heat and humidity. The air in her village was so much fresher, even in the hot weather. Her next impression was visual: the frenzied crowds at the railway station. People, thousands upon thousands of them, moved, pushed and jostled their way to their respective destinations without complaint or protest.

The train had reached Bombay: the Victoria Terminus.

Munia overheard her co-passengers call the station *Vitty*. To her it seemed colossal, like a king's palace. With one small canvas bag and her bedding roll, Munia, escorted by Babulal, disembarked and fought her way out of the railway platform.

The street outside was even worse; a veritable hive of activity. Like giant bees, black and yellow taxis flew in and out of the station, disgorging their passengers and baggage in clouds of dust. Soon, Munia found herself whisked away in one such taxi, which just as quickly drove off from the station premises towards her destination.

While they were travelling, the very first thing that struck Munia was that she could never see the whole sky. However hard she tried by craning her neck in different directions and at different angles through the window of the taxi, the view was in patches obstructed by the tall and huge concrete buildings. Moreover, she was disturbed by the noise the city was producing. Cars honking, pedestrians shouting, the doors to the shops constantly opening and banging shut.

Mirpura, her village, was a very quiet place. She could see the whole sky up till the horizon whenever she came out of their hovel. However, she looked at Bombay with awe and amazement. The city seemed to enthral her. She looked at the various shops. She witnessed the vibrant colours of saris and dresses. Gold ornaments displayed inside the windows amazed her. She had never seen so many sweetmeat shops and grocery stores. Their village had only three shops. She looked bewilderedly at tall buildings, with cars constantly entering or exiting. Pace of life in Bombay seemed frenetic and frenzied. In comparison, tranquil Mirpura felt sleepy.

Dadua had told her that she would be staying in Bombay with some relatives of his: an aunt Madhuri and her daughter, Mukti. Their house was situated inside a large compound. The compound was inside a narrow lane, off a congested city main street. When the taxi was entering the lane, Munia could not imagine that at the end of the narrow lane, there could be such a large compound, accessed through a massive iron gate. Inside the compound, there were four buildings. At the other side of the courtyard, there was a large mosque. When she looked up, she could see that each building had four storeys. After staying in the compound for a while, she discovered that each storey had a long and narrow corridor. Each corridor had four or five single-room units. Each unit had a kitchen and a toilet attached to the largish room. The single-room dwelling at the extreme end of the third floor of the building, at the rear of the compound by the side of the mosque was her home. From the window she could see a portion of the near-by railway overbridge. Throughout the day she heard rumbles of suburban trains going underneath the bridge. Their full-throttle sounds were different from the sounds of the trains she had experienced in her village. Trains in Mirpura looked so romantic in comparison.

The first few days in the compound went by very quickly. Everything here was new and strange. People slept during the day and worked through the night. Most of the young girls, prettily dressed, went out in the evening and returned early each morning. When asked, they told her that they were going out to work, to 'office.' Munia remained unconvinced, curious. She remembered that Mangiram Mama used to always shout at Kamala Mami if she returned home after sunset.

She also heard music and snatches of laughter from some of the rooms at night.

Despite these strange ways, she was happy and soon made friends with three girls of her age: Namita, Mallika, and Jaya. All of them belonged to her community and came from villages in and around the Chambal *ghati* – Namita from Dholpur, Rajasthan and both Mallika and Jaya from Gohad, a small village in the Bhind district of Madhya Pradesh, close to Mirpura.

Soon Namita became her close confidant. To her, she confided one of her most difficult problems. Back in the village ... in Mirpura ... almost everyone from their community would visit the field, slightly away from the village, to answer nature's call. It was a very common sight to see groups of men, women, and children, squatting slightly apart – separately and not directly looking at each other to create a facade of privacy – while excreting the inevitable. The exceptions were the women, who for the sake of protecting their modesty, mostly covered their faces with either veils, or a part of their clothing, so that hopefully their faces could not be matched with their exposed bottoms, by casual or curious onlookers.

However, after listening to her friend's problem, Namita started laughing uncontrollably, and as a result a motley crowd gathered around her. When Namita described that Munia was missing the fields and that she had not been able to adjust to the privacy of a modern toilet, the crowd started laughing too. More so, when Namita said that Munia had asked her for directions to the nearby field. Everyone started shouting, '*Arre chutnike Girgaum chowpatty ja, tatti bhi hogi aur maal bhi milega*'... and continued taunting her. The reaction from the crowd made Munia angry, and she kicked Namita on her firm buttocks. Namita cried out loudly and fell on top of one of the middle-aged bystanders. For a moment, the crowd went silent. Suddenly, Namita mimicked a male voice and said, '*Abbe tatti saali tune meri gaand kyun mari, khud ki gaand samal*!' and the crowd cheered her loudly, to a round of applause for her wisecrack.

Someone went and narrated the tale to Madhuri, who was enjoying a cup of tea with one of her friends on the floor above. Madhuri sent for Munia.

Madhuri understood Munia's problem. She took the girl inside her room. She made Munia sit beside her on the vast mattress sprawled on the floor of the room and explained with great care that whatever problems Munia would be facing henceforth should be discussed with her first before sharing with others. Else, there could be similar kinds of embarrassing situations. People would make fun of her. She pulled Munia very tenderly to her bosom and held her there, stroking the girl's face, arms, and practically the whole body, with her very soft palms. Munia's face remained nestled between the soft and ample bosom. Munia could smell the sweet fragrance of Madhuri's body and could feel her extremely soft and silky skin. Madhuri then kissed Munia's forehead, and very tenderly moved her hand around Munia's thighs and lower abdomen. She lifted Munia's skirt and placed her soft and fleshy palm on the pelvic area and asked, 'Does it pain here?'

Munia shook her head.

Madhuri then closed the door of the room, switched off the harsh florescent light, and switched on a soft blue lamp. Slowly, she took off Munia's clothes and kissed the just pubescent girl gently on both cheeks. Munia was puzzled. Madhuri's touch was different from that of Kamala Mami. Mami's presence was very comforting and motherly, whereas Madhuri was enticing her with an unknown provocative feeling. She felt the urge to relieve herself. Madhuri took the girl to the toilet attached to the room. All through, Munia kept her face lowered, for an unknown feeling was building inside her so overwhelmingly that she could not look at the big evocative eyes of Madhuri. The lady then administered a glycerine suppository on the tender girl. The cold and slippery feeling inside her made Munia shiver and very soon she excreted as expected. Madhuri washed Munia's body with soap and hot water luxuriously, and then put her to bed.

Munia watched the object that fascinated her most, Madhuri's TV. During the evenings after Mukti didi went off to office, Madhuri would tune in the big box with blue screen for her and she would watch the songs and dances from Hindi *filums*. Madhuri said she should closely observe the dances. Munia kept on watching the dancing figures on the blue screen till all became a blurred haze as she went into a dreamless sleep.

While girls of her age played with their doll houses, went to summer camps, attended schools, were protected by their families against the ways of the corrupt world and were taught about the 'good touch' and 'bad touch', without even comprehending the process that she was going through, Munia's training on becoming a concubine started. She was slowly but surely tutored by Madhuri to love her body and gradually conditioned to love the excitement that physical touch could produce. She was being tutored on control mechanisms to subjugate men emotionally and physically. Unhurriedly yet deliberately, all the natural inhibitions that a girl would normally have about sexuality were stripped of her.

The lonely and defenceless girl, despite her natural instincts cautioning against the process she was made to go through, had to haplessly surrender to this wily woman as it was the diktat from her clan headman to follow the century-old tradition of their biradari.

She was put on a regimented life by Madhuri Ma. Every afternoon a couple of hours after lunch, she attended dance classes along with Namita, Jaya and Mallika in the ground floor hall of the building, under the guidance of Kale Khan, the dance teacher. After this, master Dayaram would coach her on diction, to pronounce Hindi and a smattering of English words properly. Slowly and surely, Dayaram polished her style of talking. Dayaram also taught her recitation of Hindi poetry to inculcate a sense of meter or rhythm in her speech pattern. Occasionally, he made her read out passages from popular Hindi magazines loudly so that she could speak in the chaste language, instead of her normal rustic dialect. She was encouraged to watch various musical programmes and news on TV so that she could converse on general issues. Once a week, he taught her simple arithmetic.

Madhuri Ma herself taught her *shringar* and *lasya*, the arts of make-up and enticement. An elderly woman from the building oiled Munia's hair and body every alternate day, during the early evening after her dance class and language lessons were over. She was served a high-protein diet and a ten-hour sleep a day was made mandatory. She was discouraged to go out in the direct sun. Once a month, chaperoned by the elderly ladies of the building, she and the other girls were taken to watch movies in the nearby movie theatre. Through casual conversation, Madhuri Ma and Mukti Didi started instilling in her a sense of greed for material comforts. Madhuri Ma let her play with real currency notes and allowed her to feel their supposed warmth.

Life for Munia flowed in predictable waves to its logical culmination. From an innocent teenager, she was cautiously and consciously trained to become a focused, materialistic, opportunistic, calculative, yet graceful concubine in a couple of years.

In spite of so much attention and physical comforts being lavished on her, at the core of her heart Munia still silently longed for that particular ramshackle shack in her village and terribly missed the motherly love of Kamala Mami. She knew that becoming a concubine was a certainty. Still, she refused to hear the drums of her destiny, and her heart longed for Mirpura.

Dev Deepavali

Three years rolled by. Around Diwali, Mallika's mother passed away, having contracted a sudden sickness, just a few days earlier. In deference to her last wishes her ashes were to be immersed in the holy river Ganga at Banaras. Madhuri Ma thought that it could also be an ideal opportunity for the young girls, especially Munia, to go out on a holiday after being trained rigorously for three years. If everything went well, this could be the chance for her to step into the real world and to be introduced to the mujra connoisseurs. The decision was made by Madhuri Ma in consultation with Babulal Dadua. They also knew that once Munia started her mujra it would be difficult for her to get time off in the initial years.

Nearly a fortnight after Diwali, on the day before the auspicious full moon of Kartik Poornima, when Dev Deepavali is celebrated, Madhuri Ma, Mallika and Munia were escorted by Babulal to Banaras. The city was ablaze with festive lights, in preparation for Lord Shiva's victory over the demon Tripura; the victory of good over evil. Fireworks boomed on the streets and all was madness and joy. Pilgrims, believing that the gods would descend to bathe in the Ganga on Kartik Poornima, were pouring into Banaras. Thousands of diyas were lit on the ghats of Ganga to welcome the gods. The banks were shining with a glow that could compete with the moon itself.

Babulal's family panda, the priest in Banaras, had fixed a propitious time early the next morning to immerse the ashes of the mortal remains of Mallika's mother near the Manikarnika ghat.

Babulal's presence was required for various reasons. Firstly, he was the only one who knew the priest. Secondly, a man from the deceased woman's family was required to perform the final rites. Also, very few girls, if any, in Munia's compound, knew the identity of their real fathers as required during performance of the last rites. Naturally, Babulal stepped in. Babulal also wanted to locate a girl from his biradari, who was allegedly seen in Banaras after running away from Bombay. She had defied the biradari customs and had supposedly married a customer. Babulal, as the clan headman, needed to discourage this practice. He truly believed that he should strictly enforce the rules of their biradari that disallowed girls from marrying. The girls were always tutored that even when they took up the role of a keep with customers, they must remain in touch with their nayikas. The socio-economic stability of his community would otherwise be at risk – the men of his biradari hardly worked. They, for all practical purposes, had lost the belly for physical labour and most of them being uneducated, could not find work. Since ages they had been living off the earnings of their women. Shankar Baba was ruthless on the issue of marriage. During his stewardship of the biradari, he would rather have had a girl put to death than allowed her to marry. In fact, there were unconfirmed reports that he had indeed killed a few girls during his time to put the fear of God into everyone so that a girl from their community could never ever think of getting married. Even today, nearing the end of the twentieth century, in independent India, the boys of their biradari could marry only girls from other communities or villages; girls from their biradari and from the twenty-four villages under Babulal were not allowed to get married and were coerced into the profession of harlotry, concubinage, and mujra. Because of the lure of easy money, luxury and comfort, and also because they had been conditioned to accept this lifestyle, the girls too, barring some exceptions, were mostly accommodating.

Madhuri Ma recalled Shankar Baba, Dadua's father, would always claim, '*Hum Rajput Rathod ke bansh hain.*' However, on closely questioning him on this, 'How come an upper class Rathod Rajput became a different and marginalised community over the years?' he used to get into a long lecture of, '*Hum zarur Rajput hai* – the warrior tribes. There is no dispute. History states that the descendants of kings, royal gentry and aristocrats used to visit our girls for many centuries; obviously they had children. We are the progeny of those children.' In some other situations he would say, 'Our ancestors had kept concubines of other castes.' The tenor of the claim was obvious: father determined the membership to a gotra or clan. 'Our girls were coveted and mated by upper-class men, and children were fathered by them, those royals. Though they were never married, but by association we belong to the upper caste, even if the offspring were born illegitimates,' Shankar Baba would rationalise.

The family panda Brijmohan, for reasons mostly economic, validated the claims by not disputing them.

Madhuri Ma, Mallika, and Munia fasted on Vaikunth Chaturdashi, the day prior to Kartik Poornima, the day they reached Banaras. Next day, heralded by a pale wash of yellowish pink light of the emerging sun, all of them took a holy dip in the Ganga at the precise moment of sunrise and immersed the ashes into the river.

Hindus believe that to die, be cremated, or to have your ashes at least immersed in Banaras gave you *moksha* – freedom from the cycles of rebirth. Madhuri Ma felt that certainly her friend felt peaceful in heaven.

That afternoon, guided by one of the younger brothers of priest Brijmohan, Dadua and his entourage set out to see Kashi Viswanath and Annapurna temples. Later, they took an early boat ride to see the arrangements for the illumination of the Dashashwamedh ghat, the main steps to the Ganga. Later still, Munia sauntered through the narrow and crowded lanes of the old city; past the old betel leaf shop with its rows of shining glass jars full of tiny pieces of betel nuts, cardamom, saffron, cloves, and scented tobacco known as zarda; past the oil-stained walls of the Misttanna Bhandar, the sweetmeat shop that smelt of ghee and smoke; past the shorts-clad, mineral water-drinking Caucasian tourists looking for instant nirvana; past the dilapidated old mansion where an even more ancient watchman dozed sitting on his rickety wooden stool throughout the day at the front gate.

She bought brass trinkets, colourful glass bangles, and sweet-smelling incense sticks. She bowed to passing ash-smeared sadhus. The sound of the ancient hymn emerging from various temples and the trade-cries of the street hawkers were sweet music to her ears. Losing herself in the surging sea of humanity, she felt liberated. Outside of Mirpura as well as the compound in Bombay, she was transformed into a normal free-spirited teenage girl. This was the first time ever in her life she felt happy, truly happy. This was the first time ever she felt part of the whole universe. Ever since she left her tiny home in Mirpura, she always had a faint feeling of being a truncated and an incomplete human being; though she could not actually articulate the thought till now, and it suddenly dawned on her.

However, in the process, she became unmindful of her companions and got separated from them inside the narrow and winding lanes of the city, amidst the crowd of thousands of devotees and locals. When realisation struck her, 'Madhuri Ma! Dadua!! Mallika!!!' she cried out loudly. She tried frantically remembering the name of the guest-house, where priest Brijmohan had put them up. It was somewhere near one of the ghats, the tall and old red building. There was a Banarasi sari shop on the ground floor of the building and a medicine shop on the other side of the street.

'Madhuri Ma!' She shouted at the top of her voice once again.

The crowd was closing in on her. She felt suffocated. Someone touched her bosom. A rough hand groped her from behind. She could feel someone's manhood being pressed into her bottom. Even though fully clothed, she felt being denuded in the crowd.

Despite trying her utmost, she could not get out of the human vortex. She felt being pushed towards an even narrower alley. There was hardly any light and the place was stinking of human as well as animal excreta. Someone clutched her dupatta and held it so tight that she could hardly breathe, let alone speak or cry out. She was enraged but could hardly do anything. The collective physical strength of five ruffians was too brutal for her to handle. Moreover, she hardly knew the lay of the land and the people around. Still, she fought.

The man chewing a betel leaf and reeking of alcohol slapped her face repeatedly. She felt herself being lowered on cold and slippery ground. She could comprehend what would happen next. She fought and fought and fought to try and delay what seemed inevitable.

One of the ruffians said, '*Saali ... matherchod ... himmat hai item me ... maza ayega ...*'

'Ha ha ha ha ...' the collective monstrous laugh was the last thing that her mind registered before losing consciousness.

Collateral Damage

'Masterji, Kinkar and his gang are forcefully taking a girl inside that alley besides that dilapidated mansion!' Pankaj Mishra came running to his teacher, Rajkumar, pushing past the vast crowd in his agitation. Like every year, Pankaj was one of the many NCC students of Banaras who along with their NCC teachers, were volunteering with the police force to maintain peace and order in the holy city during Dev Deepavali. During the current year Masterji Rajkumar and his students were supposed to look after the Gadhoulia-Pataleshswar area.

Rajkumar took a few moments to think through and then ordered, 'Go inform the police control room near the temple's main gate. Inform your father if you meet him too. I will tackle Kinkar.' He then called out to one of his other students, Balaram, to accompany him.

They took a shorter and narrower lane to reach the Misttanna Bhandar and cross over to the old mansion; even so, it seemed to Rajkumar that they were taking ages before they reached their destination. The overwhelming crowd made their movement slow and difficult. The evening had set in fully. Chants of Hara Hara Mahadev filled the air and bells of the various temples were tolling.

Rajkumar, his face determined, eyes set, and palms rolled into fists entered the dimly lit alley.

'Ha ha ha ha ...' the collective monstrous laugh was the first thing that his mind registered.

He could see the vultures, the shadowy figures, the 'bell-bottoms' and shirts with broad collars. He could feel their collective leer.

'Please release the girl, let her go,' Rajkumar said in his even baritone. In the narrow alley, the sound reverberated.

They turned around, glassy eyes and foolish grins on their faces. Senses numbed with alcohol, they could hardly balance or stand straight. The anticipation of sexually harassing and violating a beautiful girl had anesthetised all their feelings.

'You motherfucker! Fuck off!' Kinkar, the man who was repeatedly slapping Munia, retorted. One of his accomplices took out a *kanpuria*. The other three lifted the unconscious girl to carry her further inside the alley.

Rajkumar walked steadily and unfalteringly towards the man holding the knife. Looking straight into his eyes, without blinking, Rajkumar kicked the man in his balls with his heavy NCC boot; then put his NCC baton to good use. The man kneeled over as his *kanpuria* slipped from his fingers and both clattered noisily to the ground.

In a quick movement Rajkumar picked up the knife, walked over to Kinkar and slipped it under his chin. 'Kinkar Babu, I know you. I know that your brother is a very influential politician. However, I will not hesitate to cut your throat right here and now, if you do not let the girl go.'

Kinkar looked up in rage and growled, 'I will kill you, Babu. Whoever you are, I will find out and kill you. Nobody interferes with my businesses.'

Rajkumar pressed the knife a little harder against Kinkar's throat, 'Ask your friends to bring the girl back here, right now!' Without waiting for an answer, he slashed Kinkar's cheek with the knife.

'*Aargh* ...!' Kinkar screamed.

'*Abbe suwar ke aulad*, you can kill me later when you get the opportunity. Now you let the girl go.' Rajkumar hissed into Kinkar's ears.

The tactic he was following was to keep Kinkar engaged in conversation as well as unnerve him till either police or volunteer backup arrived. He could see the unconscious girl being brought back closer to where they were.

'Is she alright?' Rajkumar asked.

'Did you give us any time to do anything?' one of the boys retorted drunkenly.

While talking to Kinkar's companions Rajkumar felt the waistband of Kinkar's trouser to search for any hidden firearm, which goons of the province usually carried. Bingo! A .9mm was tucked in the small of his back. Rajkumar was puzzled, why didn't Kinkar fire it at him? At least he could have waved it in his face. Maybe he was too drunk to remember its presence. Quietly, Rajkumar slipped the revolver into his own pocket.

A beam of torchlight hit them on their faces, 'Masterji are you all right?' The familiar, tall and portly figure of Rajat Mishra, Pankaj's father, the inspector in-charge of the main police station, Banaras Sadar Kotwali, appeared in the silhouette. Sizing up the scene in the dark alley he added, 'Masterji, please go. I will take care of the rest.'

'But the girl, what will happen to her? Let me check if she is still alive.' Rajkumar knelt down and felt the girl's wrist. He placed the palm of his right hand on her forehead and the index and the middle fingers of his left hand on the side of her neck and felt her throat for a pulse. '*Well she is alive,*' he thought and nodded to the policeman. Just then, Munia opened her eyes and looked straight into Rajkumar's eyes.

'Have faith in me, Masterji. It is better that you leave the place right now. I will talk to you later tonight in the kotwali.' Rajat Mishra touched Rajkumar's shoulder lightly about the same time and then turned around to his son saying, 'Pankaj, leave now, accompany Masterji.'

Later that night, Rajat Mishra took Rajkumar to Prafulla Kumar Mishra, the veteran Gandhian leader of the city and main opponent of the young and brash Kamal Mani Singh, an erstwhile minister in the state cabinet and brother to the hoodlum Kinkar.

Word of the evening's incident had already reached Prafulla Kumar. Rajat had only to add that the minister Kamal Mani might try to humiliate Masterji or even harm him. He wanted Prafulla Kumar to help Masterji.

Surprised by this unexpected turn of events, Rajkumar intervened and, in a humble voice, he enquired respectfully, 'I am grateful for your kind thoughts but ... how come you are discussing my welfare without even consulting me?' Rajkumar looked at both policeman and politician with his incisive, calm eyes.

Prafulla Kumar said, his voice soft, 'We respect you Masterji, so we want to help you. I have heard about you from my nephew Pankaj. Oh, incidentally Rajat is related to me. I know that apart from being the in-charge of NCC, you teach history. So, I can make out your vision and empathy.'

Rajat interjected, 'Rajkumar Babu, people like Kamal Mani Singh and his brother are devoid of any sense of civility. For power, they will do anything. They are corrupt, shameless, and without any sense of justice. To them, sense of justice is merely to silence any criticism against them. I am sure they will attack you. I might not be in a position to protect you fully, at that time ...'

Rajkumar responded evenly, 'I am not afraid of death.'

Rajat, the seasoned police officer, patiently replied, 'Look at my position Masterji, I am a keeper of the law, yet, if I object to their activities openly, these politicians will either try and liquidate me or transfer me to new posts repeatedly. I can fight them but for a very short term, under those circumstances. Hence, I keep my cool and find strategic ways to thwart their obnoxious intentions and activities. I am doing that even now by soliciting help from Prafulla Kumarji.'

Prafulla Kumar summarised, 'You need to fight the system by staying within the system, at least for now.'

'What will happen to the girl and her family? How will we apologise to them?' Rajkumar enquired.

'The girl's family will file a case of attempted rape and outraging modesty. We will bring in the media. We will publicise Kinkar's misdeed. You will be our key witness against Kinkar. It will be a huge blow to Kamal Mani,' Prafulla Kumar commented indulgently, hiding a smile.

Rajat added, 'I have already made arrangements in the city hospital. The girl is there for physical examination and treatment. The hospital will give us the report shortly. With this and your statement, we will be able to prosecute Kinkar's gang. We are trying to trace the girl's family too. We have spoken to the girl and identified the family priest, so it shouldn't be difficult to locate the girl's family. I am sure by tomorrow we will have all the necessary information. For greater impact we can talk to the media tomorrow. As you can understand we in administration need to always calibrate situations carefully.'

'Do you think that this is the best option? Don't you think that the girl's reputation might be tarnished if not handled sensitively?' Rajkumar asked.

'There are casualties in war, Masterji. You teach history; I am sure you are aware of collateral damage,' with a very benign smile Prafulla Kumar Mishra made his concluding remark.

Unknown to them, even before Rajat and Prafulla Kumar could actually decide on the fate of the girl and manoeuvre it to their political advantage, lady luck and the astute Babulal turned the table.

Munia had been missing for a couple of hours. Babulal and his entourage had returned to the guest-house hoping against hope that she would be there. With every passing hour of the evening the congregation of pilgrims increased, making movement virtually impossible within the lanes of the old city. It was ultimately Brijmohan who came to know of the shameful incident through his chain of acquaintances. He rushed to the city hospital along with Babulal and his younger brother Rajmohan.

They found Munia on a makeshift bed on the floor of the crowded general female ward. Her salwar-kameez suit was soiled. Although she was fully conscious now, even to the untrained it was clear that she was in a state of shock. Her eyes were blood red and dilated. Her lithe, graceful figure was in shambles.

The head nurse objected to the three men entering the female ward. She shooed them back outside and requested them to wait there. After a brief consultation, Rajmohan was sent to fetch Madhuri Ma and Mallika. Priest Brijmohan left to organise a luxury air-conditioned taxi for immediate long-distance travel. And, Babulal decided to befriend the lone constable posted outside the female ward by Inspector Rajat Mishra to watch over the girl.

'Rajkumar, I have a problem and I need your help to sort it out in everybody's interest,' the mild-mannered and scholarly headmaster, Nandalal Sahay said without any preamble. Rajkumar stood mute waiting for Nandalalji to finish. 'Recommendations have been made to us to terminate your services. Or else, the school will face problems with its governmental grants and other permissions,' concluded Nandalal Sahay.

'What do you suggest I should do?' Rajkumar enquired, without showing any outward signs of emotional turmoil.

'As a teacher and a human being, you are exemplary. I don't even want to suggest that you resign. However, you know that we have thirty-one teachers and over two thousand students. This dilapidated building was given to us on trust some fifty years ago by the Maharaja of Rewa. If the government grants are withdrawn, we will not have sufficient funds to run the institution. Moreover, it will not be possible for me to fight the powerful politicians who have suggested this course of action,' sighed the veteran teacher.

'Do you suggest I speak to the police?'

'Do you think they can protect you?' the headmaster quizzed.

'Can you give me a day or two, at least, to think through the situation? This is so sudden, totally unexpected, you will appreciate,' Rajkumar requested.

'Of course, that is the precise reason why I am speaking to you in absolute confidence. You take leave of absence and think through. I also have a suggestion. If you want to work in Delhi, I have a very old student of mine working there as a general manager in a reputed bank. The bank has a few good customers. I am sure I can find you some employment through him, if not as a teacher, at least in some other field.'

Rajkumar nodded vaguely and left the headmaster's office deep in thought.

Inspector Rajat Mishra was reluctant to meet Rajkumar. But with persistent visits and requests, he softened his stance. Warning Rajkumar not to approach him at the police station or his home, he suggested a friend's house instead.

Rajat came directly to the point. 'Masterji, the matter is out of my hands now. I cannot help you in any way for the present.'

'But why so?' asked an annoyed Rajkumar.

'Because when I needed it most, you did not cooperate with me,' Rajat argued. 'You should have followed the advice of Prafulla Kumarji. But you didn't.' Rajkumar heard the hurt in the policeman's voice but was too amazed at his stance to acknowledge it.

'Mishraji, possibly I had erred about you,' he said slowly. 'My focus then was to protect the prestige of the girl and her family, which I felt was not very important to Prafulla Kumarji. Was I wrong in this? He was looking to score a political point using the girl as a pawn. How could I support the idea?' Rajkumar paused to gather his thoughts, knowing what he had to say next would be unpalatable to the inspector. 'Kinkar tried exploiting the girl physically in the heat of the moment; Prafulla Kumarji's cold and deliberate intent was to exploit her emotionally for the fulfilment of his own agenda, which is much worse.'

Rajat frowned but tried to remain non-committal. 'May be so Masterji, but he was the one person Kamal Mani would think twice before taking head-on.'

'Sir, why "maybe"?' shot back an exasperated Rajkumar. 'Look at the sequence of events. Next morning when I visited the hospital the girl was nowhere to be found. I tried reaching you. You were incommunicado, for days. Later, I saw newspaper reports on ruffians capturing the city during festive time and tireless efforts put in by Prafulla Kumarji and his supporters for preventing untoward incidents during the festival. Don't you think it is political opportunism? The moment he felt I might not play ball he completely forgot about me. He would have done the same thing with the girl once his purpose was served. And, the girl would have carried the stigma all through her life. You know deep in your heart that I am right. Don't you? Now Kamal Mani is after me. So what should I do?'

Rajat shrugged his shoulders, fleetingly looked at Rajkumar and turned his eyes away while answering to hide his emotion, 'What do you want from me now? If you do not value my suggestions, why do you want to meet me desperately?'

'Kamal Mani Singh has put pressure on the school authorities to terminate my services.' Rajkumar narrated what he heard from the headmaster.

Rajat Mishra kept quiet for a length of time. At long last he asked curtly, 'How much savings do you have, Masterji? Do you have enough money to sustain yourself for some time?'

Suddenly Rajkumar became alert. His instincts warned him of an impending crisis. A sense of doom dawned on him. He asked the police inspector, 'Are you suggesting that I leave Banaras? Why? What wrong have I committed?'

'I would rather say that you were at the wrong place at the wrong time,' replied Rajat. 'Life does not follow arithmetical logic most of the time. It has its own rigours. In any case, as far as I know, you do not have an immediate family. You had an aunt and she too has passed away. And, Banaras is not your original home. So going away should not be that difficult!'

'I am curious to know how you know that,' asked Rajkumar.

'Pankaj idolises you so much that I had checked you out long time ago, don't forget I am a policeman. So why don't you think of relocating yourself to a bigger and better city?' Rajat asked.

'I can, but if everyone deserts our smaller cities and villages, then what will happen to our country? I have some self-respect as well. How can I run away like a dog with my tail wagging between my legs? That too because of fear of some antisocial elements?' Rajkumar commented in a very soft tone. Yet his eyes radiated the steeliness of resolve.

'Rajkumarji, let me tell you point blank that I cannot protect you anymore. However much I like you and my son respects you, I too have limitations and can only manoeuvre within those. I suggest you do a tactical retreat. That would be sensible.' Rajat Mishra was now definitely irritated with Rajkumar's inflexibility.

'But sir, you mean to say that this is how we will run our country?' Rajkumar asked.

'My dear sir, do you have any idea how little an effort is required to eliminate one single individual? How do you plan to influence the course of the history of our nation, if eliminated?' Rajat Mishra mocked Rajkumar in his anger. However, the moment he did so, he regretted. He paused for a while. After taking a deep breath he continued, 'Did you know Masterji, the girl whose honour you are so concerned about is from a questionable background? I have checked out the panda and even interrogated him. His clients mostly come from communities of mujrawalis, the moneyed ones from Bombay, who even under the best of circumstances are of ill repute and social outcasts. Who knows – perhaps the girl enticed Kinkar to make the advance. That's why they fled the city after hoodwinking everyone on the night of the incident. That constable on duty at the hospital was an idiot. A member of the girl's family took him out for a cup of tea while others spirited her away. That's why you didn't find her in the hospital next morning. They are all bastards in the true sense indeed.' The inspector leered to ensure he was understood.

'How does this justify the rape or molestation, even if she is a bastard, a mujrawali?' He waited for Rajat's reaction, but none seemed forthcoming. So he shifted his stance and continued more amicably, 'By any chance, would you know the name of the panda?'

'Why? You want to meet such girls?' Rajat started laughing heartily. 'On a serious note, please think through my suggestions carefully this time.'

'Sure, sir. I will do what you have suggested. But look at the possibility that Kinkar Mani might also pressurise the panda to get to the girl and her family.'

'It is a possibility but a very remote one. And, if she was traced that would be for a different purpose, for the basic primitive desire, now that we know who she could be. Forget the girl. Kinkar's ego has been badly hurt by you, and you stay in this city. You have humiliated him publicly. He couldn't harm you initially because it took him a couple of days to find out your identity. Since the matter was in high public visibility, physically harming you would have had a direct fallout on him and his friends, who were in custody. If my understanding is correct, once he gets to settle scores with you, I don't think he will carry his vindictiveness forward,' Rajat said.

'That's precisely the point. If he fails to settle scores with me, then he might harm others. The school is in danger if I remain in the school. I can leave the school and start working elsewhere. I have no problem, but he will find it out and the same problem will recur. If I go underground and not be found, it could be harmful for the girl and her family. As you know of the whereabouts of the panda, he too, I am sure, knows about him. And, can reach the girl's family. So, either he exists or I. Hmm ... and you suggested the best possible option is to surrender to Kamal Mani Singh and ask for reprieve so that the threat of Kinkar is eliminated?' Rajkumar with an apparent earnestness put forward a poser.

'Now you are talking sense,' a visibly relieved Rajat Mishra fell for it.

'That's right, sir. You have made me realise, once again, how little an effort is required to eliminate one single individual,' Rajkumar replied.

Initiation

Madhuri repeatedly cautioned Munia and Mallika not to discuss the incident that took place in Banaras with anyone, ever.

On return from Banaras, both Babulal and Madhuri wanted to initiate Munia's transition into the real world as quickly as possible, as decided earlier, through the religious as well as biradari traditions. Madhuri was concerned because even after a fortnight Munia could not sleep properly. Madhuri thanked Goddess Matarani a thousand times for protecting Munia. She was immensely relieved to find out that Munia's virginity had not been breached.

She could not take any more chances. Before something could go wrong further, she wanted to have the feast and Munia's 'initiation ceremony' as quickly as possible. In a hurried manner, the feast for the ceremony was planned at Snehalata Mai's house in Ambe village, close to Mirpura.

The evening before the week-long ceremony started, the priest of the nearby Krishna temple was requested to narrate the scriptures. The elderly women of the community were invited for the occasion. Before the crack of the dawn next day, though it was the beginning of the cold weather, both Munia and Mallika took their baths and attired themselves in new clothing. They then set out to visit Matarani's temple led by Madhuri Ma and accompanied by an entourage of other women, a village brass band, and a few village urchins.

They covered a distance of more than six miles through the dusty and uneven village roads by successive prostrating to show reverence to the Goddess, the resident deity of the community. The group of middle-aged women, who were accompanying them, washed the road ahead of them by throwing bucketful of water, fetched regularly from either nearby public wells or even from some homes, who willingly donated the water. Initially, the two young girls stood straight with their hands by their sides. Then they knelt down. Next, they bowed low on the surface of the road, their faces directly touching the ground, their bodies bent. They stretched their bodies full length and extended their folded hands in unison in front of their heads as far as they could reach, and drew an imaginary straight line ahead on the surface, on which they would then stand for the next prostration. They continued to repeat the prostrations until they reached the temple.

With each drawn line, the accompanying women shouted, '*Jai, Matarani ki jai,*' seeking blessings of the Goddess. The village brass band increased the tempo of its devotional music. Flowers and coins were thrown into the air, as offerings to the Goddess, and the motley crowd of village urchins, even so early on that winter morning, fought to pocket the small change.

By the time the team returned to Snehalata Mai's house after offering the prayer to the Goddess, which was a very elaborate ritual of chanting and Aarti, evening was about to set in. Under the keen supervision of Madhuri a separate group of elderly village women applied a mixture of white sandalwood and turmeric paste over the entire body of the exhausted girls.

They were then bathed by Madhuri herself. Thereafter, brand new bright red silk saris were draped on the bare bodies of the girls. They were made to sit cross-legged in the open courtyard of the house, surrounded by the elderly women of the biradari. Madhuri placed a handful of dry earth on each of the girl's lap. An elderly woman put a handful of rice on top of the dry earth. Accompanied by the sound of *dholak* and ululation by all the women, who were present there, Bari Dai, the venerable community matriarch, placed two apples and a ripe banana on each of the girl's lap as the symbol of *Purush,* the man, on top of the dry earth and rice grains, symbolising land and sustenance, to complete the ritual. Thereafter, she brought her mouth very close to Munia's ear and recited an even more ancient biradari lore, –

> '*O sun re mona, ghama, chona, saj devala,*
> *e hoi thommniata, biav.*'

The girls and the invitees were then given a meal of sweet curd, soft rice and ripened yellow banana followed by gajak, a sweet made with sesame and jaggery, and pede, made with khoya – the milk solids, and sugar.

The girls were so exhausted from the journey and the ritual that they slept like logs throughout the night until next afternoon.

'Munia! Mallika! Wake up, babies,' Madhuri slowly coaxed the girls out of their deep slumber.

'Yes, Ma.'

'Both of you go and take your bath. Motirani *nain*, the lady barber, will arrive in half an hour. She will take off your silver nose studs and will put new gold nose rings instead.'

'Madhuri Ma, I have a request,' said Munia.

'Tell me my girl, what do you want?'

'Please invite Kamala Mami from Mirpura. I want to meet her.'

'Munia, my girl, we cannot invite Kamala. She is infertile, a *baanjh*, and considered to bring ill-luck during festive rituals. Even if we invite her, she knows it and will not attend,' said Madhuri and continued in a conciliatory manner, 'When you return from Bombay, next time, I promise I will personally invite her to meet you. But right now you have to let it go my girl. The last few weeks since Banaras have been very strenuous. You need to relax now and enjoy the good life. Please baby, listen to me!'

'Okay Ma, as you say.' Munia's large limpid eyes tried to conceal their disappointment.

That very night, the police informer attached to the village kotwali informed Babulal that Gopal Chhari, the elderly maverick reformer from their community, who was fighting the traditional community practices singularly for a long time, was planning to raid Snehalata Mai's house and release Munia and Mallika from their clutches. The raid was being delayed by the local Thanedar, the man in-charge of the kotwali, on the pretext of manpower shortage. Meanwhile, he sent word to Babulal so he could transport the girls out of the village, without any incident. The police chief did not want to rock the boat, neither did he want to attract undue media attention through community rivalry. After all, he was on Babulal's payroll.

Anticipating that the reformer might visit Snehalata's house even without any police help, Babulal quickly gathered a few trusted gang members from within his community for his own protection as well as to fight against Gopal Chhari and his small yet dedicated entourage, if it became inevitable.

Gopal Chhari was a pious man. He had little support for reform either from his community or from the provincial administration, for what many considered his very rigid puritanical social outlook. Yet he fought relentlessly and single-mindedly against corruption within his community. He had also been working tirelessly to educate the underprivileged and make them realise the folly of thriving on corruption. To Babulal and his followers, Gopal Chhari, even at his old age, was a dreaded name. Without wasting any time, in the wee hours of the dawn, Madhuri woke up Munia and Mallika, 'We have to leave immediately for Bombay.'

'But why so, Madhuri Ma?' questioned Munia, 'What is the hurry? You said that we will stay in the village for at least two more days.'

'Oh my dear! We have to arrange for both of you to step into the real world and dazzle it with your maiden performances. Thereafter, we should find real good suitors who will take excellent care of you,' said Madhuri with an apparent outwardly cheerfulness, though in her heart of hearts she was dreading the imminent raid instigated by Gopal Chhari. She was restless. She wanted to leave this damn village as quickly as possible for Bombay. She had already planned along with Babulal, for the last couple of weeks, about the additional rooms that they would require in the compound and the process of rejuvenating and operating their traditional mujra-mehfil, the soiree of dance and music, with Mukti, Munia, and Mallika. Madhuri Ma, once again, had started dreaming of reigning in the compound after a gap of nearly seventeen years ...

Mehfil

With her native efficiency in managing things, upon return from Ambe to Bombay, Madhuri immersed herself in starting a unique mehfil that the compound could never have imagined before.

She shifted their dwelling to the upper floor, to the room where Mallika's mother used to live previously. She got the huge room converted into a comfortable unit of a bedroom for four with an attached bath, a modern kitchenette, and a tiny living room. The unit below, where she used to reside along with her progenies earlier, was converted into a compact dance hall with strobe lights, music system, a built-in bar, and an anteroom with attached washroom. With ingenuity she connected the rooms on both the floors through a private stairway, just like a duplex.

She started dreaming big to revive the old glory of her erstwhile familial mehfil.

The city of Bombay had just passed through massive riots and communal turbulences during that winter, yet the inauguration of the mehfil was planned without any deviation from its schedule. The competition was fierce. There were at least four other established mujra rooms in the compound, similar to what Madhuri was planning. She however had the advantage of Munia and Mallika's freshness and Mukti's networking capacity among the patrons of the upcoming Bombay dance bars to sustain her mehfil.

Madhuri toiled diligently so that the inaugural day of her mehfil became a celebrated talking point among mujra connoisseurs. From her experience, she knew that mujra, like other adult entertainment businesses such as pubs, discothèques and nightclubs, operated on one simple logic: crowd begot crowd and word-of-mouth publicity worked best. Secondly, she had decided to regulate customer access to her mehfil, based on quality of association and the capacity to spend from the very beginning. She scrupulously avoided using the so-called pimps and panderers as go-betweens, those who hovered around the compound, to lure walk-in customers against commission. She brought in experienced bouncers from Babulal's network to regulate entry to and exit from her mehfil. She, with her hereditary business sense in this field, wanted to establish a differentiation from the already existing mujra rooms and very rightly wanted to create a mehfil with tradition, class, sophistication and elitist aura.

She also enlisted the support of some of her old customers with whom she had kept in touch through thick and thin over the years. One of them was Sukumar Divakar Shah; a very wealthy, middle-aged diamond merchant from Surat, who in his youth used to visit Bombay with his father on business trips and invariably frequented the earlier mehfil – that of young Madhuri and her mother Sushila Bai. The other one was Akhram Khan, a film financier well-known in the Hindi as well as South Indian movie industry. Madhuri also invited Bhupinder Singh, owner of Bharat Lodge at the behest of Babulal. Mukti's boyfriend, her pagadwala from the dance bar, Pushkar Gupta, a well-known

Mumbai builder agreed to attend the mehfil along with some of his friends.

Simultaneously, Mukti, though she was not keeping well for some time after the birth of her daughter, Niyati, took over glossing and further enhancing the *looks* of the new entrants, Munia and Mallika. They were sent to a beauty parlour for thorough grooming. New wardrobes consisting of chania cholis, ghaghras, and lehengas were stitched by Hanif mian, the master tailor and one of Madhuri's favourites from Foras Road.

The new mehfil was ready to roll.

Madhuri received summons from the nearby police station to meet the Inspector-in-charge a day before the inauguration of her mehfil. She was fortunate that Babulal was in town as he wanted to supervise the opening of the mehfil; moreover he had accompanied Bhupinder Singh.

'You should stop your dirty work here,' the police inspector asserted the moment Madhuri and Babulal met him in the evening.

'Saab, we are hereditary mujra artists; we do not do any dirty work,' politely Babulal replied.

Madhuri chipped in, 'Saab, we have our own room in the compound for more than thirty years. The earlier inspector, Khadye saab, knew me very well. The room has been with us since my mother's time. Everybody in your police-chowki knew my mother, Sushila Bai. She was famous for her singing and dancing. My cousin sister was also a craze in her time in our mehfil. I will not encourage anything improper. You can ask ACP Godbole saab too.'

'You have two minor girls. You are putting them in the trade,' the officer replied.

'Minor girls? What are you saying, saab! They are my sisters' daughters. How can I do such injustice to our children? They are of legal age to start working. We are *khandani*, pedigreed dancers, saab, not fly-by-night operators. My children have ration cards, sir. If you want, I can bring those. They also have certificates from the village school where they studied,' replied Madhuri politely.

'You plan to sell and serve liquor in your mehfil? You do not have the license to do that,' the Inspector retorted.

'Saab, if you have guests in your house and you serve liquor to them, do you obtain license? They are my guests, Baba. I do not sell liquor. I am not a liquor shop owner. But if you insist, they will carry their own permit. And as for my mehfil, maybe you can suggest to me how to go about getting the license, if any,' Madhuri cajoled the inspector.

Studying the drift of the discussions, Madhuri was, by now, pretty sure that the police had no objection to her operating the mehfil. It was possibly the competition that was provoking the chowki. She was sure that with adequate impetus, the controversy about age and liquor could be amicably settled.

'Saab, we plan to inaugurate the mehfil tomorrow. We would be honoured if you would come and grace the occasion,' said Babulal.

'Are you trying to bribe me? You are inviting a respected police officer to get involved in nefarious activities? I will put you behind bars, right now,' he retorted. Babulal's smile did not waver. 'Okay. If what you say is correct, I need to see the age proof. I will send my constables tomorrow morning,' the Inspector reiterated and looked pointedly at Madhuri.

Madhuri was ecstatic. After seventeen long years, she could finally accomplish her ambition, her own mehfil.

After consulting Babulal she had brought in three *laachhi* girls as well to add to the joie-de-vivre. Madhuri thought that the *laachhi* girls – the girls who were bought by Madhuri, through Babulal, at birth from other communities and were used mostly for baser entertainment needs of the clients, would be nice background dancers while introducing Munia and Mallika. Moreover, if for any reason whatsoever, one of her guests became restless, these girls could tackle it. Madhuri, under no circumstances, wanted to rush *nath utarna* of Munia and Mallika until she approved of suitors not only in terms of solid economic potential but also of pleasing presence as well as personality. The bloodline—as Shankar Baba would say, was very important. *Nath Utarna*, literally 'removal of the nose ring' and *Sar Dhakna*, literally 'covering the head', are in reality the symbolic gestures of a girl being betrothed or deflowered and sexually active. The nose ring of a courtesan signified her virginity. Betrothal, being the most important aspect of a girl's life in their community, needed to be handled very delicately, as well as the choice of a courtesan's patron or pagadwala for her initial years. Madhuri did not want to repeat the mistake that took place seventeen years ago.

Sukumar Shah was the first to arrive exactly at the appointed hour of nine. Madhuri could immediately recognise him. He had gained a few kilos. His skin looked very healthy and was glowing. He was wearing a midnight blue suit and a pink shirt, but no necktie. The black shoes were shining. Hair was stylishly cut. Nails were nice, long, manicured. She smiled at him. He smiled back. No betel nut stains in the teeth. Excellent. Pass marks! Money he would be having, thought Madhuri.

'Shah saab, it is a real honour for us that you could make time, despite your busy schedule and grace the occasion,' Madhuri welcomed Shah.

'Madhuri Bai, you said that Munni's daughter is going to give her inaugural performance, so how could I not come? That son of a gun, that *Dilliwalla,* pushed me out of the race seventeen years ago. Today is my day of revenge, if for nothing else but to see her daughter dance in this mehfil.'

Madhuri became visibly alarmed with Shah's attitude. She did not anticipate such a sharp reaction from the amicable Shah after a lapse of so many years. She knew that she had to nip this feeling of revenge in the bud. However, she could not afford Shah to comprehend her vulnerability on the subject. After swift deliberation within herself, she sat down beside him on the gadda, the cotton mattress, and in a very solicitous tone implored, 'Munia baby is very tense. This is her first performance. Please do not openly compare it with her mother's dance. Her mother was an exceptional dancer and you saw her when she had already performed over some years. The comparison will be unfair to Munia. Moreover, Shah saab, if you take such an emotional stance, it will not be fair to her as well as to you. If you bring her mother in between, Munia would appear to be like your daughter. In fact, you have a daughter too, don't you? Possibly Munia's age?' Madhuri deliberately winked at Shah and quickly added, 'Do you think you will be able to interact with Munia with such a mindset? So, relax! If Munia comes to know that you wooed her mother, do you think she will look at you as a friend? So, forget the past and enjoy the present. As far as that bastard you mentioned, he is a nonentity. You know *na* that my cousin was playing truant; she became fat-headed and arrogant; Shankar Baba, my mama, gave her away to our local Zamindar as a gift and thereafter she died. Bad luck, what to do!' Madhuri looked at Shah with her large evocative eyes; after a while, when reality dawned on him, she asked, 'What would you like to drink? Black Label? I suppose on the rocks? Am I right?'

'You are absolutely correct. You are a marvellous nayika, a gracious hostess, and *aadab, kya dimag hai aap ki* ... the poise and grace,' Shah accepted his drink.

Akhram Khan, Bhupinder Singh, and Babulal came in together. In fact, Babulal had gone in a hired car to pick up Bhupinder Singh from a nearby hotel. They met Akhram Khan at the compound gate where he was alighting from his BMW.

Akhram had aged. The lines on his face had hardened, but his height of six and a half feet, lean body, and golden skin compensated everything. He too had retained his trademark smile. The moment he saw Madhuri he uttered, '*Meri jaanu*' and landed a very deep passionate kiss on her left cheek.

Bhupinder Singh was the regular businessman type, not much air, not very different from any other of his clan. In a safari suit, he looked calm and composed. He said, 'Namaste' to Madhuri and sat quietly on the gadda that was covered with a spotless white sheet, with assorted pillows and bolsters strewn around.

His task accomplished Babulal quietly disappeared from the mehfil.

Shah and Akhram were past acquaintances and were catching up on old times. The sweet smell of flowers kept on silver trays mingled with the fragrance of incense and permeated within the cool air of the room. The musicians – the sarangi player, the tabla player, and the harmonium player – took their respective seats. Assorted snacks and tidbits were placed before the guests in silver bowls and plates.

Three *laachhi* dancers came and sat opposite the guests. With professionally done make-up and hairdos as well as with their natural confidence in handling men, they were looking very attractive. Madhuri praised herself silently for her good sense in choosing them as the prop, the wallpaper, for the inaugural show.

It was half-past nine.

Just as she was thinking of inaugurating the mehfil without waiting for the remaining guests, the door opened; like a gust of wind the fat and pompous Pushkar Gupta invaded the room along with four of his friends. He went straight to Madhuri and hugged her very ceremoniously. Thereafter, he introduced his friends. Madhuri with her sharp business instinct tried remembering all their names: Rajan, Mustafha, Walter, and Aditya Narayan. The last name stuck with Madhuri. The name as well as its owner had an unusual dignified appeal.

While the newly arrived guests made themselves comfortable and the drinks were being served she looked at Aditya Narayan once again. Very fair, medium height, and medium structure, but what attracted Madhuri's attention was his very long and artistic fingers, like that of a painter.

'Mommyji, why don't you inaugurate the mehfil? Are you expecting anyone else?' Pushkar asked Madhuri impatiently.

'No, not really; we were all waiting for you,' Akhram Khan replied instead. He was slightly annoyed looking at this relatively young and supposedly wealthy group. He didn't mind the competition, but what irritated him was the lack of courtesy and the apparent arrogance. He was a seasoned and experienced hand at the game. He also had money. However, age was not on his side and he knew it. And, it bothered him.

Madhuri could feel the tension in the air. The moment was just right. She signalled with her eyes and the *laachhi* girls immediately took their positions on the floor. The musicians took the cue. Madhuri went to fetch Munia and Mallika.

Transformation

Munia was sitting in one corner of the bedroom, with her costume and make-up on. She was deeply immersed in her thoughts. Tonight she might be betrothed as per the community tradition and would possibly earn a lot of money. The highest bidder could take her away for the night. She tried remembering her mother's face at this important juncture of her life. As usual, she could not remember the face. She felt angry. Why was it that there was no photograph of her mother? Why was it that Dadua and Madhuri Ma always avoided discussing about her? Munia's eyes filled with tears. Nevertheless, she prayed for her blessings.

'Munia baby, we have to start the mehfil,' Madhuri Ma said as she entered the room and softly touched the girl's chin. 'Get a hold on yourself. Tonight is the night of celebration.'

Munia had tried delaying her entry to the mehfil as much as she could. However, neither could she muster enough courage nor had she the support system or financial resources to defy the community tradition. She closed her eyes once again and paid her respects to her mother and sought her blessings. She also thanked that honest, keen, and piercing pair of eyes and those manly set of hands, the stranger who had protected her honour from the goons in Banaras. She often wondered who that could be and whether she would ever get an opportunity to meet him again and say thank you for being so kind and courageous.

At long last, she realised she could not delay the inevitable any longer and got up. Moving with heavy steps towards the dance floor she silently vowed to herself that one day she would accumulate so much wealth that her community would bow down to her wishes. As she entered the mehfil, the collective encore of the audience greeted her. She flashed an automated smile and made eye contact with each person in the audience while acknowledging their appreciation as she was repeatedly tutored by her dance master Kale Khan.

With the *laachhi* dancers surrounding her, and in consonance with the music, she started pirouetting at the centre of the floor. The mehfil came alive. With that began the transformation of a sensitive, introvert, and lonely teenager Munia to the worldly-wise, graceful, and coveted courtesan, who would be known henceforth to the world by her stage name Pallavi Singh.

In a deliberate and sustained manner, Madhuri started thrusting Pallavi towards the depraved customers who visited her mehfil during their nightly prowls to look for opportunities for satisfying libidinous activities. Pallavi was dangled as a carrot to Sukumar, Akhram and Aditya Narayan, among other exclusive guests, every evening, with her cultivated 'touch-me-not yet come-hither' look and attitude. Predictably, each one of them behaved as modern Tantalus, the archetypal and proverbial character with temptation without satisfaction and frequented the mehfil ever more vigorously to pursue her every day.

Madhuri made Pallavi behave as a flirtatious young woman, a naive and willing participant, in construction of the eternal fantasy within the established narrative frame of suppressed male sexuality. And, as Madhuri and Babulal knew from their collective past experiences, with each passing day, Sukumar, Akhram and Aditya Narayan started throwing more and more and more money, as well as expensive gifts, at Pallavi, to attain her. For the debauched connoisseurs, it became their obsession. For Sukumar, it was the suppressed desire of cohabiting with the mirror-image of a girl he had failed to attain in his youth; for Akhram, it was to reconfirm his vigour and vitality, possibly for one last time; and for Aditya Narayan, it was fulfilment of his lecherous desire to make love to an exquisite uninitiated teenager.

All through the enactment of the entire event Babulal and Madhuri waited patiently in the wings. For over a very long period both of them had invested time, money and energy on this girl and now they wanted to continuously reap the benefit of their labours.

In a very short time, due to her looks and dancing skill, Pallavi's reputation grew. It was further heightened because of her conversational skills and ready wit. People were drawn to her. A number of very rich businessmen, patrons who frequented the other mujra-mehfils in the compound, started keenly pursuing her with continuous offers. She manipulated their feelings expertly, with steadfast encouragement from Babulal and Madhuri in a very focused manner. By then, she had become an expert in the game of enticement and deceit. Moreover, she started to make her mark on the subterranean adult entertainment industry of Bombay with her grace, poise, charm, beauty and determination. Babulal and Madhuri were ecstatic because their prized goose started laying golden eggs for them as they had thought she would.

They bought and refurbished a small dwelling unit in Guruji Chawl in Byculla away from the compound in a mixed-community, lower-middle-class area and shifted their residence. The rooms in the compound continued to be their mujra-mehfil though.

A number of high-end dance bars of Bombay, which had started operating a couple of years or so before and were getting recognised practically world-over for the unique adult entertainment they had started providing to both the international and domestic visitors, leave aside the rich residents of the city, practically went head-over-heels to have Pallavi in their roster of dancers.

Soon Pallavi became the centre of attraction in the city's dance bar circuit and well-ensconced herself in Magnet, one of the city's topmost and internationally known dance bars.

Sudden Twist

Sometime after his encounter with hoodlum Kinkar and his brother Kamal Mani, Rajkumar drifted away from Banaras and had also arrived in this city, which was still known as Bombay and was in the process of being rechristened Mumbai. He knew not a single soul in the city at that point of time. He did not request anyone in Banaras to put in a word for him. On his own, he looked around for the job of a teacher but could not get one readily as he did not have any formal training from any recognised institute nor did he have a degree. During his tenure as a teacher no one in Banaras had asked him for either a degree or any kind of teacher's training, but in Bombay the degree and the formal training were pre-requisites to work as a teacher in a school. Since he had learnt driving in Banaras it provided him with an alternative. He took a test and procured a licence for driving commercial vehicles. By dint of sheer perseverance, dogged determination and communication skill, he landed the job of a chauffeur in a well-known travel agency, and started life afresh. On that particular Saturday he was driving a company car to meet Babulal whom he had finally traced through panda Brijmohan. After much persuasion, a very reluctant Babulal had agreed to meet him near Grant Road station.

Rajkumar was driving his vehicle to reach Babulal. He was near the *agiary* at the base of the street, where the road leading to Nana Chowk met Tardeo. He wanted to reach the nearby destination as quickly as possible. He had decided to touch base with Babulal before Kamal Mani could find him and eventually find the entire family and abduct or murder them. In the past one year, Kamal Mani had repeatedly tried tracing the girl responsible for his brother's death but could not do so effectively as all the trails were getting cold leading up to Babulal, the master of deceit. However, one could not be vigilant enough. And, as for himself, though Kamal Mani was on the lookout, Rajkumar was confident that he couldn't be traced by Kamal Mani. He had no trails. No family. Not connected to anyone in this world. He was a ghost.

Immersed in his thoughts, Rajkumar was driving at a high speed. He was also under time pressure as he was running a bit behind schedule. Possibly, it was destined that the particular day would be different from other days and his life was to take a sudden twist for which he was totally unprepared.

While his car was at the crossing of the junction, all of a sudden without any warning another vehicle with a learner's plate swerved down the crossroads towards him. He could see that an adolescent girl and her young trainer were trying their best to avoid the collision. It struck him that by speeding up more he would be able to avoid the hit, but it was already a bit late by then. And, instead of the front door, the other car hit the rear of his car. The impact made his car skid and it grazed past a scooter driven by a rotund man. He heard the screechy sound of a bus stopping very abruptly, somewhere behind him. He also heard the cry of an anguished person.

He saw from his side of the window, a portly old man lying coiled foetus-like on the road near him. The Contessa car with its learner's plate was now stationary at an awkward angle beside his car. A bus stopped short of kissing his car's backside. A couple of onlookers were staring curiously at the scene. However, none was making any proactive move to help the old man. Possibly, all of them had written him off. Rajkumar too was momentarily confused. Fortunately, there were not many vehicles on the road; hence the old man did not have much threat of a second accident or a runover.

With a few more seconds passing by it became clear to Rajkumar that the fault, if any, for this unfortunate incident would rest partially on his shoulder. While speeding up to reach his destination he was unmindful for a small portion of time about his bearings. He overlooked the possibility of a vehicle coming down the crossroads. He was oblivious of his surroundings and even for a moment did not remotely consider the chance of such an untoward incident occurring.

Before the victim could fully regain his composure, one of the few men passing by the *agiary* could identify him, and started shouting at the top of his voice, 'Farokh Mistri had an accident.' The shout propelled Rajkumar into action. Without thinking twice he forced the door of his vehicle open and got out, scooped up the body of the old man from the road, and made a dash to the nearby general hospital. It was a matter of great luck for Rajkumar that the general hospital was at a stone's throw from the site of the accident. He considered himself lucky because the hospital was so close and it had an emergency wing for casualties too. He could manage to impress upon the doctor on duty to take charge of the old man. By this time, the screaming gentleman from near the *agiary*, with a few more on his toes, arrived at the hospital. The doctor had already started attending to his patient who was regaining consciousness. The hospital security by then had secured Rajkumar on the doctor's order. In addition, the police was informed of the incident.

Sometime late in the evening, the Senior Inspector of the police station called for Rajkumar from the remand room.

The moment he entered the Senior Inspector's room Rajkumar could smell a beautiful fragrance. Even though he was in despair, he could still identify the source emanating the smell – the profile of an oval face partly hidden by layered shoulder length neatly brushed brownish hair.

'*Tuzha nao*?' Senior Inspector Pawar asked Rajkumar for his name.

Without hesitation he replied, 'Raja Mallik … it is there in my driving licence …'

'*Kuthey Rahte?*' He was asked for his address.

He replied in chaste Hindi, 'Sir, I don't understand Marathi so well. Can I speak in Hindi please?'

'Where have you come from?'

'From up-country, sir.'

'How long have you been in this city?'

'Over six months, sir.'

'Why have you come here?'

'To earn a living, sir.'

'Don't you have anywhere else to go? Why all of you have to come here?'

'We can get a living here, so we come here, sir.'

'Look at this idiot. Giving lecture,' the inspector told the pretty face in his thickly accented English. 'What is happening to this city? God alone knows why all these idiots are spoiling this city.'

In his cultivated high-handed manner to give this criminal a bit of a nervous jitter and to show-off to the pretty woman sitting in front of him, Pawar continued, 'What do you do for your living?'

'Sir, I drive a luxury car in a tourist company. I am sure you know of it, sir. Your people must have towed away my car to the police station after the accident and must have put the description of it in the case diary.' Without blinking an eye and with a straight face, he replied evenly.

He could sense that the pretty face was trying desperately to suppress laughter that threatened to erupt. And, in the effort to do so a peculiar gargling-like sound came out from within her throat. All this because of the exhibition of foolish and empty bravado of this police officer and the polite yet sarcastic replies he had received in turn.

'You idiot! Keep quiet, don't talk back to the senior,' the constable couldn't resist displaying his supreme loyalty to his superior in such a humiliating situation.

'Kunte, *thamba*. Don't lose your cool. These are poor rustics. They have no manners. Just let it go.' Pawar tried retaining control over the situation. 'So, for how long have you been driving the luxury taxi?' he asked languidly.

'I've been driving the car for about three months,' Rajkumar replied evenly.

'And within three months you caused this serious accident? Who gave you the licence? From where was it issued? Up-country?' Pawar mocked Rajkumar.

'The RTO in Tardeo, situated practically next to your station, sir. But, yes, I had an up-country licence on the basis of which they took my test and gave me a fresh one,' he replied.

'*Chop*! *Shana banta tu*? *Haan*?' The constable slapped Rajkumar on his face. 'Do not answer back to the senior, you swine!'

For a fraction of a second, he had felt enraged and wanted to kick the asshole, that dim-witted constable, but restrained himself. He realised that there was no point escalating the tense situation unnecessarily.

The pretty face reacted very sharply to the constable's unwarranted behaviour though. She said to the senior officer very emphatically, 'Mr. Pawar, you can make out from his uniform that he is a chauffeur, and in any case, this is not what I have requested for.'

He could immediately make out her American accent. He looked straight ahead without showing any sign of comprehension of the verbal exchange the people around him were having. He could not afford to let these people know that he could jolly well understand what they were discussing in English. He already had seen enough problems in Banaras. Kamal Mani was looking for him. If this police inspector got to know that he knew the Queen's language so well, he could, in all probability, land up in Arthur Road Jail as a very suspicious character.

'Kunte, hold on. Restrain yourself!' Inspector Pawar spoke indulgently to his subordinate and then addressed the pretty face, 'Madam, you do not know these elements. They could do untold mischief.'

She shrugged. 'Look, let us not get into all those arguments. As I have said, we are not pressing for charges against this man, as my father is out of danger. We have no complaints against him. I would be grateful if you release him.'

'Sure, madam. Still, I have to look at the case legally. There was an accident. Your father could have died. One more vehicle was involved. The occupants of that vehicle blamed this man for the accident. God forbid, if some untoward thing had happened to your father, possibly you would not have been so charitable. The tourist company will make an insurance claim. So, investigations are required.' Inspector Pawar's ego was hurt but he camouflaged it well and replied with an artificial magnanimity. He did not like anyone encroaching upon his area of authority, above all, he hated high-society women and this high-society lady had put pressure on him through one of his seniors. So, just to delay the process of release, he was coming up with as many obstacles as he possibly could.

Rajkumar intuitively had a clue about the thought process of the cop. He decided that he should not waste anymore time. Moreover, he was feeling genuinely sorry for the old man, though he knew that he was not really and singularly at fault for the accident. Yet, he was ready to do anything to mitigate the old man's discomfort. The suffering of the old man had actually brought to the surface of his conscience a very painful memory of his young adult days, which he had kept buried deep inside him with great difficulty; about his incompetence of not being able to help his foster father a very long time ago.

Getting entangled in a law and order situation for a silly mistake was the last thing Rajkumar wanted to be in. His past experiences of interaction with police authorities had honed his intuition and prompted him to say to the police officer, 'Sir, please believe me. Why would I hurt that old man; he did me no wrong. But, if you feel that by punishing me the gentleman will get better or recover quickly, then by all means, please punish me.' Rajkumar made the statement with a very straight face, with his hands folded and looking apologetically towards the inspector.

Before Rajkumar could complete his comment, the pretty face turned towards him and said in a very soft yet firm voice, 'Thank you. My daddy is out of danger now. Thank you very much for admitting him to the hospital. I do not have any complaint against you. You did not run away but stood by my father in the hour of crisis.'

She then turned around, looked at the inspector and in a very stern voice said, 'Mr Pawar, will you order the release of this poor man? Look, Daddy was probably not paying attention to the traffic ... my mother passed away only a few months ago ... even today ... he pines for her. He must have prayed for her and was thinking about her while he left the *agiary*. Mr Pawar, don't you understand? He was also rushing to the *bhaji galli* to buy vegetables for our restaurant. I do not think the incident is anything other than a pure and simple accident. And, in any case the quick thinking of this man has probably saved Daddy's life.'

Mr Pawar glared at her.

Unmindful of the resentment she was causing, she continued, 'What about the other car? Why aren't those people here? Some of my well-wishers, who were present at the accident spot told me that she was an underage learner! Please release this innocent man,' she said, pausing to take a breath. And then, as though the thought had just occurred to her she said with her head held high, 'Or, I can call my uncle Soli in Delhi once again and request him to speak to your Commissioner this time.'

A quick glance at Inspector Pawar's face and Rajkumar knew that both the pretty face and he himself had made this police officer their lifelong enemy.

'Daddy wants to meet you,' said the pretty face once she and Rajkumar came out of the police station.

'*Ji. Bilkul,* yes,' he replied nodding in agreement.

'Oh! We are extremely sorry that you were harassed by the police.'

'*Koi baat nahin,* madam. It happened because of my carelessness. I should have been more vigilant,' he said with earnestness.

'Will you come and visit Daddy after a few days?' The pretty face asked him and continued, 'He has just been operated on his right elbow and may need a few days to stabilise. He is over sixty, you know.'

'I don't gain much by not coming. You have bailed me out literally. I will definitely visit him.'

'Can I ask you a question?' she asked and without pausing for consent, looked at him, and stated in a very matter-of-fact manner, 'Are you sure that you are a *taxiwala*? I mean, you know, the inspector is possibly correct suspecting your true vocation. Your way of communicating, body stance, and something else to which I cannot put my finger ... my instincts tell me that you could be somebody else.' Then she started fumbling for appropriate words to express her doubt. 'Never mind, but I don't think that you are a taxi driver. You do not fit the type,' she did ultimately express herself.

'Madam, I don't understand what you are trying to say and why would you say so,' Raja Mallik alias Rajkumar was almost pleading.

'Surely you understand. You are different,' she said and offered a hundred-rupee note to him, 'Incidentally, in case you have forgotten, it is Mr Farokh Mistri and he is in room number six on the third floor.'

'*Namaste ji,* madam, welcome to you,' he tried playing the part of a villager flaunting supposedly perfectly smart English learnt in this city. In his effort to resolve the suspicion he also accepted the tip like a true proletariat which he thought might fit into her perception of a very common person.

'Oh, by the way, could you tell me your name once again please. I didn't catch it properly at the police station. Did you say Raja Mallik?'

'Yes. My name is Raja Mallik,' he reconfirmed promptly.

'Are you a Muslim?'

'What difference does it make?'

'No. Nothing actually. And, what did you mean by up-country? Where are you really from?'

'I have come from Banaras,' he replied after a slight pause.

Even as he mentioned Banaras the face of the vulnerable girl started haunting him again. He cursed himself that he missed touching base with Babulal. He had to start the loop once again to contact him through the third parties and the resultant delay.

In the meantime, out of his natural sense of responsibility, he went to visit Farokh Mistri six days later.

Dikra

An old man with a serene and smiling face, a pair of deep brown eyes, and a mop of white hair crowning his head greeted him. He was clean-shaven. Flashing a Santa Claus smile, he extended his left hand and said very softly, 'I am Farokh Mistri. I am so sorry to have caused inconvenience to you. I am sorry about you being harassed by the police.'

'Please don't say sorry, sir,' Rajkumar earnestly said. 'I was not at all harassed by the police. They just did their job.'

'Anyway, it is over now. I am very happy to have met you. All credit goes to my daughter, Ayesha. It is she who traced you with the help of Burjor Patel my friend from the *agiary*, and Dr Ranade, who was on duty when you took me to the hospital.'

'Tell me Raja what made you say to the doctor that you were responsible for Daddy's accident? I have been told that you literally threatened Dr Ranade with physical abuse when he was dithering a bit and refused to admit my father immediately. Why did you act that way? You do not know us. It is a simple case of accident. Why did you get so worked up and took it so personally? In fact, most drivers would have fled the scene,' said Ayesha in a very easygoing manner and looked straight into his eyes.

He took his time before replying. He hesitated and debated within himself. In the end he preferred a politically correct answer to the actual truth. He decided that the truth about himself would have to wait in the wings for some more time and said, 'Madam, of course, I am responsible. I should have been more careful on an apparently empty street. I should have been more focused while driving. I am very lucky nothing more happened. As far as Dr Ranade was concerned, he needed to be pushed as we were losing precious moments because of his indecision. I couldn't let that happen.'

'Daddy too, I am sure, was unmindful. In fact, I am so angry with him. Since my mother passed away, he is the only family I have and he is not listening to me. I had requested him earlier a number of times not to ride his scooter any more. I had told him that he should always use the car now. He does not pay heed. I want him to come with me to the US and he is not willing. What should I do?' she said, her face intense.

'My dear Raja, possibly if I had died, I am sure, she would not have been so generous. A fracture at my age is indeed painful but the fact remains that my injury is not of a very serious nature. Yes, I am lucky to have escaped so lightly without a multiple or a compound fracture or a hip dislocation, as the young doctor was suspecting initially. Moreover, the fact is that you brought me to the hospital on time. It is also true that you have spent some time in the police custody without protest and without trying to justify your side of the story. Both Ayesha and I feel that justice has been served. So, you do not owe us anything,' said Farokh Mistri. He looked exhausted and pale after his long monologue. 'Oh, I would be delighted if you visit us again,' Farokh said displaying his disarming smile once more.

For the next fortnight, Rajkumar was a regular visitor at the hospital. He went to meet Farokh Mistri in between his duties. During those visits Farokh introduced him to Bombay's history. He told him stories from his childhood and youth, of a gentle unhurried life in a Parsi family. Farokh was nostalgic about the trams running on tracks from Fort to Sion and Pydhonie to Gowalia Tank on a north–south and east–west axis. He also shared stories of various soirees, society lunches, concerts, dinners, art and culture. He held on to those cherished memories of the genteel time gone by.

As he grew closer to the mild-mannered Parsi gentleman, Rajkumar couldn't help feeling that his cover was no longer as secure as he had wanted it to be and slowly Farokh Mistri was giving him hints that it was time to reveal the truth. In fact, he could vividly remember one such story.

– The movie *Frankenstein* was released in Bombay in the 1930s. It was an instant hit. People flocked to see the *Talkie* in the theatres. It became a talking point in society gatherings. The title role in the film was played superbly by one Boris Karloff. During a lunch break at the Bombay High Court, a few days after the release of the movie, the honourable judges were speculating about the nationality of Boris. Most of the judges felt that he was a German. One particular judge categorically stated, to the surprise of all the others, that Boris was an Englishman. After the debate had continued for some time, the solitary judge who claimed that Boris Karloff was an Englishman closed the debate with the astonishing announcement that he would know best, as Boris Karloff was related to him. Finally, the mystery was solved when the learned judge, Mr Justice Pratt, pointed out that Boris Karloff's real name was William Henry Pratt. –

Farokh Mistri's uncle, Soli Rustomji senior, was a practising lawyer at the Bombay High Court during that time and had narrated the incident to Farokh later on. While concluding the story, Farokh had obliquely referred to the fact that names could be misleading and the real identities behind names could be so different.

Rajkumar could not make it in the afternoon to meet Farokh the day prior to his discharge from the hospital. He was away on duty in Alibaug. He returned to the city in the late evening. He hesitated to visit Farokh Mistri so late. But deliberating again upon it, he decided to meet him because, in all probability, this would be their last meeting. Farokh was to go home the next day and he was to attend to a very early morning duty. He felt that for the last time he should meet the fine man. He had much solace interacting with him during the last fortnight; though he could always sense that the people around Farokh, his friends and relatives, with the exception of Ayesha, were really getting uncomfortable with this recently brewing friendship between an upper-middle class, moderately successful Parsi restaurateur and a lowly Banarasi taxiwala.

He reached room number six on the third floor of the hospital. As he had been a regular visitor for a number of days, the hospital security guards let him in for a quick visit. He had expected that by now Mr Mistri would have had his dinner, the room lights would be dim, and probably Mr Mistri would be preparing for his sleep. Even before he could step out of the elevator, loud angry voices from the room reached him. To his astonishment, the lights inside the room were blazing in full glory. He could also see two tall and muscular clean-shaven men with well-oiled hair and dressed in safari suits guarding the door of the room. As he approached the room, they blocked his path. He looked at them. They simply looked back at him and tried pushing him back to the lift. Without losing his temper, he said in a very even tone, 'Kindly inform Mr Mistri that Raja has come. I am sure he will want to see me.'

'Mr Mistri busy. Meeting,' replied one of the men in peculiarly accented English. The other one chipped in, 'No disturb now. Tomorrow come.'

The voices from inside the room were getting louder by the minute. He thought that he heard Ayesha screaming a 'No.' Just then, the doors were flung open. A fair, tall and large man wearing white kurta pyjamas came out. Possibly as an afterthought he turned around at the door and said in a wrathful and edgy voice at the semi-reclining figure of Farokh Mistri, 'Please don't forget ... I will come to the house tomorrow ... keep the documents ready. Even if you cannot sign the documents because of your fracture, Ayesha can. I want to settle this amicably. *SahebJi*,' the man then did a cursory salute, turned back, and without even acknowledging Rajkumar's existence started climbing down the stairs followed by his two faithful chucker outs, who brushed past Rajkumar deliberately.

Rajkumar looked intently at the downwardly receding figures for a while and then entered the room softly. 'I am sorry ... possibly I have come at the wrong moment,' he said very courteously.

Farokh looked very sad and distressed. Yet, he nodded his head in understanding.

However, Ayesha shot back irritatedly, 'No point apologising just for the heck of it. You have already disturbed us. You have made it a habit to be at the wrong place at the wrong time, always. Now, if you do not have anything specific to discuss, we have noted your courtesy visit and it is time for us to say good night and goodbye to each other.' She was high-strung and dismissive. He did not mind at all her uncalled for rude behaviour. He understood very well that the anger was misdirected because of her frustration of not being able to say anything to the man who had just left. Deliberately, he provoked her further, 'Why are you taking out your anger on me? I did not insult your father ... the other man did. If you are so capable and sure of yourself, then you should have objected to that buffoon for his presence and not mine.'

'Please leave at once and take your wisecracks with you,' Ayesha retorted loudly.

A nurse appeared from nowhere and sternly asked Rajkumar to leave the room.

He quietly looked at Ayesha's flustered face and downcast eyes. After some quick thinking and with a calculated risk he spoke to the nurse authoritatively, '*Aap kahan the*? I didn't see you intervene when that rascal came and was trying to physically abuse your patient.'

The nurse looked unsure of herself, yet as a last ditch effort she said, 'Please leave, else I will call our guards.'

Unperturbed Rajkumar said, 'Please *security guard ko bulaiey*. I will also request Mr Mistri to report against you for not doing your duty properly.'

The nurse replied nervously, 'Mr Mistri himself had advised us not to disturb him while they were having a family discussion.'

'What family discussion?' Rajkumar rolled his eyes. 'Do you actually mean that it was a family discussion, sister?' he taunted the nurse nastily.

Farokh Mistri, by now somewhat settled and composed, waved and excused the nurse out of the room and said, 'That was Adil, my nephew. He runs a permit room-cum-dance bar, Magnet, near Grant Road station. I do not approve of that but can do nothing about it. He had inherited a huge restaurant from my brother-in-law and converted it to a permit room earlier for selling beer and subsequently to this dance bar, which has become very successful, of late. He also has developed a relationship with the Pathan gang which I do not like. He wants me to give up my restaurant too. It is in a very attractive location. But why are you standing, Raja? Pull up that chair please.' The old man sincerely wanted Rajkumar to relax.

Ayesha tried to intervene, 'Daddy, you need rest.'

'No my dear, I need to discuss and seek resolution. You cannot fight your cousin. He is a brute. But, never mind, come my darling and sit beside me.' He extended his arm towards his daughter.

Rajkumar, after a long pause, said in a very soft voice to Farokh Mistri, 'I am not very conversant with the businesses of the permit rooms and dance bars you are referring to sir, but I understand one thing; that you should not succumb to pressure,' and then enquired politely, 'Do you want to give up your restaurant?'

'Well, what do you think, mister? I thought by now the answer was evident,' Ayesha interjected.

'Ms Mistri, I can assure you that at times it is better to keep your trap shut than open.' For once he just let his irritation override his cultivated restrained behaviour. 'I don't think your cousin can bulldoze your father by sheer brute force and wrest control of the restaurant. I can assure you of that.'

'How, pray, would you guarantee it? And by the way, who the hell do you think you are to talk to me like that, you charlatan?' She laughed with nervous excitement anticipating that Raja Mallik would get unmasked very soon.

He looked steadily at the nervous yet anticipating hazel brown eyes and, without much ado said, 'Allow me, Ms Mistri to give you an excerpt from an ancient Egyptian book of instruction written by the wise vizier *Ptah-Hotep* more than five thousand years ago which I used to oft quote to my students in Banaras. This quote was taught by my teacher when I was in school. Translated roughly it says: *"If you seek responsibilities, make yourself perfect ... If you take part in a council, remember that silence is better than an excess of words"* so, in other words, just keep quiet and pursue your goal and you will succeed.' He calmly made his statement. He then turned around to Farokh Mistri and looking at the old man he said with intensity, 'If Adil is a businessman, he will listen to my logic. I am sure of it. If you don't have any objection, I will request you to give me his phone number and the likely location of your nephew, where he will be available tomorrow for discussion.'

'You will be able to contact him only around late afternoon because he sleeps very late. Ayesha will give you the number. But are you sure of ...' halfway through his utterance Farokh Mistri looked at Rajkumar's mystic yet steely eyes and suspended his comment. He then simply nodded his head and said, 'Do as you think best. I have full faith in you, *dikra*.'

After Farokh addressed him as *dikra*, son, and gave his consent, Rajkumar took the soft left palm of the old Parsi gentleman in his calloused hands and looked up directly at Ayesha. In a measured voice, and clear English he said, 'You have been absolutely correct in your suspicions, Ms Mistri. I drive a taxi yet that is not exactly my vocation. I came here from a comparatively small town, but I am not a simpleton. I could be a maverick, but not a charlatan. I try to be a human being and act like one. I don't like to be pushed or be a victim of prejudice or injustice. And, of course, I resist situations where others might become one.'

Ayesha smiled victoriously all through the night, even in her sleep ...

Rajkumar had made a phone call to Farokh Mistri's nephew Adil Powvala, owner of Magnet, the next afternoon. Without a preamble he started off, 'Adil seth, if you want to legitimately grow in the long term, behave like a businessman. Not like a rogue. You are really one of the most foolish businessmen I have come across; one who is fighting with his family to destroy an established well-run business.'

Adil thundered, 'Who the fuck are you? Don't threaten me *matherchod*. Come face-to-face and I will teach you business.'

Rajkumar remained calm and replied evenly, 'Let your dance bar run. Let the restaurant of your uncle run too. Two different business verticals, two different profit centres. Why do you want to destroy it? It is doing well. If you want to start new projects take over other badly managed dance bars, permit rooms or restaurants. It's downright silly, fighting with your uncle and cousin instead of protecting them.'

Adil shouted, '*Abbe chutiye*, stop your lecture and get lost.'

Still Rajkumar persisted, 'We don't know each other but force will get you nowhere with me. In such a scenario either of us can get hurt. It means you have as much chance of dying as I have; even if you know the Pathan gang. Think it over. Mr Mistri will know where to find me, if you ask him politely. Have a good day.'

Messiah Complex

In the budding stages of their romance, Ayesha and Rajkumar were inseparable, as was to be expected with lovers. Physically, they were a perfect match; possibly too perfect a match. To Ayesha, who had led a protected and sheltered life being an only child within the confines of South Bombay's reasonably affluent social circle, the bohemian and maverick lifestyle of Raja Mallik was a deep attraction. However, like all young, emancipated city girls, she wanted to participate in every aspect of her husband's life. Rajkumar was not very comfortable with that. He needed time to open up, needed his private space and was averse to sharing all facets of his life at that point. Ayesha did not display enough maturity to understand it. After her initial euphoria wore off she could not comprehend his complex nature, could not tolerate the thought that he had secrets from her, secrets he refused to share. Within a short span of time, Rajkumar understood that he had perhaps rushed in too early into the marriage without giving himself and Ayesha the time to understand, appreciate, and respect each other's nature and differences in their respective personalities. He acknowledged that it was his fault, not Ayesha's, for she was after all not mature enough to know the vagaries of life and the nuances of relationships, having led a protected life thus far and never having been exposed to the harsh realities of life. And fate, which had never been kind to Rajkumar intervened yet again in its peculiar way. During this turbulent period, sometime after his marriage, he met Babulal and Pallavi. The accidental meeting took place in Magnet in Adil Powvala's office, of all the places.

'Where are you going, baby ?' Ayesha had purred like a satisfied cat after a torrid love-making session during the early hours of the evening. It was a Saturday, the promise of a relaxing weekend waiting in the wings.

'I am planning to meet Adil,' he replied.

'But why would you want to do that?' Ayesha questioned impatiently. 'He is no longer a threat. He can't bulldoze us anymore. So, why bother?'

'I want to meet him. He is your family. Why shouldn't we keep good relations with him, now that he honoured our request and no longer wants to disturb Mr Mistri's business?'

'Why do you always address Daddy as Mr Mistri? You should call him Daddy.' Ayesha shot back.

'Now don't start throwing tantrums again. I have already explained it a number of times. I like calling him Mr Mistri. I always addressed him so. I am not being disrespectful.'

'But why not Daddy?' she shook her head and questioned back.

'Because, I am not comfortable.'

'Why are you not comfortable?'

'Because, I have never called anyone Daddy ever.'

'I have heard this argument before. Can we just go past this silly behaviour and have some real justification?' Ayesha spoke in a very cold voice.

'This is the real justification. Anyway, let me have a shower and go and meet Adil.' Rajkumar's reply and body language were detached and distant.

'As you please,' Ayesha too replied nonchalantly. 'In a while I will be going out to Cricket Club, plan to have dinner there with Daddy, and meet my friends at Gymkhana Club later. I will be late. If you want to join in, you are welcome, I would like it,' she moved away to the other side of the bed.

'Hmm ...,' Rajkumar was non-committal and started heading off to shower. Mid-way, he turned around and said in a measured voice, 'I don't mind joining you and Mr Mistri for dinner but I don't like your silly friends. They have no sense of reality; just big talks, false bravados and show-offs.'

'Oh really! What are you? The Messiah? Hah! Actually yes; you suffer from the Messiah Complex,' She said very sarcastically and turned her back towards her husband.

It was really unfortunate that two genuinely nice people, in love with each other, who made torrid love just a short while ago, could become so insensitive to each other over a trifle argument.

'What do you think of my proposal?' Rajkumar asked Adil even before they were seated in the small spartan room Adil Powvala called his office, behind the ground floor lobby of the dance bar. It had an old rectangular yet well-maintained wooden table placed at the centre of the room, with wooden chairs placed on its four sides. Photographs of deities of various faiths decked with fresh garlands were adorning the walls. An antique grandfather clock placed at one corner still kept time faithfully, and a huge floor-to-ceiling Belgian mirror fixed on one of the walls was providing the smallish room with an illusionary depth.

While he was waiting for Adil's answer, he could see the reflection of a beautiful girl who had tiptoed into Adil's office very quietly through a side door, in the mirror. The girl looked familiar.

Adil reacted sharply to the girl's presence, and said in an irritated manner, 'Not now Pallavi. Don't you see I have a visitor? Come back later.'

The girl nodded her head. While leaving, she looked at Rajkumar through the mirror intently.

Rajkumar too noticed the intent look from the girl but ignored it. He thought that possibly she was upset as she could not pursue her business with Adil. As a matter of courtesy, he enquired, 'Am I interrupting something?'

'No, you are not. These girls don't have a sense of propriety. Her grandfather would arrive soon to collect her pay packet so she was in a rush to remind me about it,' said Adil waving his hand dismissively, and resuming his discussion with Rajkumar. 'Anyway, I think starting a catering business is a very good idea. You already have a kitchen. People are aware of Uncle Farokh's restaurant and they do like the food there. I think you should put up some nicely decorated notices on the restaurant windows announcing the catering service. May be Uncle Farokh can also request the priests of a few *agiaries* to allow announcement signboards near their gates. Not much of an expense, a lot of impact. There is no pressure on you as you are not dying without the catering orders. So, you have time on your side and over time the business will grow. You just need the staying power,' Adil winked and smiled.

'I like your idea, minimal expense, maximal impact. Much appreciated,' Rajkumar nodded his head.

'How come you are not with your lovely wife on a weekend night and are sitting instead with a fat, middle-aged, cynic dance bar owner discussing business prospects?' Adil asked very politely, by way of conversation.

Rajkumar smiled again and did not respond.

Adil looked at him with his hooded eyes and smiled back.

A burly young bouncer appeared from nowhere and whispered something in Adil's ear; he listened to him and nodded his head. The bouncer left. Adil looked at Rajkumar and said very softly, 'I just need to take care of this payment thing, will you please wait for a while?'

Rajkumar quickly reacted to Adil's comment, 'Please go ahead. I should get going myself. You don't really have to be polite and formal with me.' He stood up.

Adil impatiently waved his hand, indicating Rajkumar to stay put, 'Just relax. Why are you leaving? We will have *Irani chai* together. Did Uncle or Ayesha ever offer you one?' As Adil was speaking, the young bouncer returned with a dhoti and kurta clad man of indeterminate age. Looking at the man, Adil said very curtly, '*Bolo* Babulal ... *kaise aana hua*?'

As Adil uttered the old man's name, Rajkumar craned his neck and looked at the man addressed as Babulal. All of a sudden, it struck him that the girl he saw sometime ago in Adil's office would definitely be the girl from Banaras and that was possibly the precise reason why the girl looked intently at him. He held on to his breath, kept a very neutral disposition and looked away from Babulal in an uninterested manner. He did not want Adil to become unnecessarily curious. He did not want Adil to know that he was in search of this man and the girl for nearly a year now; that if the freak accident had not taken place on that fateful Saturday morning involving Farokh Mistri, by now Rajkumar would have been able to meet this man and the girl. The more he thought about it, the more he became convinced about this man being the same Babulal who he was supposed to meet near the Grant Road station, as the station was located at a stone's throw from Adil's dance bar. It made sense.

While Rajkumar was pondering over all his options keeping an expressionless poker face, Adil and Babulal concluded their business.

Thereafter Adil turned his attention back to Rajkumar and said in a jovial manner, '*Damadraja,* let's have tea? What say?'

Suddenly Rajkumar became overtly epicureanistic and said, 'You call me *damadraja* and offer only tea? Where is your fabled sense of hospitality, Adil? You are not even inviting me to step into your famous dance floors? What a *kanjoos, saala*.'

Adil burst into a loud laughter, looked at Rajkumar and said in an easy voice, 'So very well said Raja ... *damadraja ka kanjoos saala*. Go, go, see some dances ... go ... go ... *mood thik ho jayega*.' While Rajkumar was preparing to leave, Adil uttered very softly, 'By the way, women are unpredictable, I am sure you know that. Now that you are married to Ayesha, you need to be aware of it, constantly. *Baap ki ladli hain* ... handle her delicately. Now scoot.'

He then turned around, looked at the bouncer who was standing just outside the office door and thundered, 'Why the hell are you standing there like a bloody moron, escort Rajasaab to the mujra hall, and ask the hall manager to speak to me.'

She was dancing at the centre of the floor. Rajkumar sat on a sofa very quietly away from her; even before the young bouncer Manoj could alert the hall manager about his identity. He could see that a reasonably decent looking, middle-aged man in a midnight blue trouser and pink shirt with a couple of diamond-studded rings on his fingers was randomly selecting either a fifty or a hundred rupee note from the wad of currency notes kept in a silver tray in the glass table in front of him, squeezing them into paper balls, and continuously throwing them, aiming at the buttocks or the breasts of the girl, in tandem with the beat of the song being played on the DJ system. He abhorred the activity and looked at the man distastefully. He was highly irritated by the man's behaviour. A couple of waiters were squatting on the dance floor to collect those currency-balls. Some were re-filling his wine glass and he went on gulping down the wine quickly. The man called for more money. He went on drinking more wine. Rajkumar did not like the atmosphere. He looked at the girl. No sense of joy there, a plastic face holding a listless professional smile.

He also felt bad that he had stepped into a dance bar just because he was in disagreement with his wife.

He was momentarily distracted as the hall-manager came to greet him.

And then it happened. There was a very loud crashing sound. The man in the midnight blue trousers had thrown his wine glass aiming towards the girl's face, she ducked it. The wine glass crashed into the glass-panel mounted on the wall, behind the dancer. The man was abusing everyone around, the waiters, the other customers and the dancers. No one was able to control him. Everyone around was handling him delicately. He was constantly trying to grab the girl's body parts and she was constantly evading his touch; an influential customer in all probability. Rajkumar became agitated, in an ideomotor action he stepped in between the man and the girl and gave a high-power tight slap on the midnight-blue's face. The slap had a devastating physical and emotional impact on midnight-blue, he fell on the floor. Rajkumar went on kicking him repeatedly on his butt. He cried out in pain, and out of fear for his life soiled his trouser. In reality, the man would have possibly been killed had not the dancer stepped in front of Rajkumar and started shouting, 'Stop hitting him. What did he do to you? Who are you to beat him?' She then turned around to the waiters and bouncers and continued screaming, 'Who the hell is this man?'

Rajkumar suddenly heard Adil's booming voice from behind, 'What nonsense is this, Pallavi? Why so much commotion? Why can't you tackle your own pagadwala? It affects my business.'

Rajkumar turned around to Adil to justify the girl's behaviour but even before he could speak, Adil said, 'Come along, Raja.' While leaving the dance hall, pointing to the man sprawled on the floor, he instructed bouncer Manoj and the hall manager, 'Escort Sukumarbhai to the Guest House. Clean him up and put him to bed. I will speak to him tomorrow. Clean up the hall, send the dancers and customers to the disco-hall for sometime and start the music again. *Chutiya saala,* collection should not get affected.' He looked back at Rajkumar and signalled him to follow.

'Mr Messiah ... how are you doing?' Rajkumar was greeted at the breakfast table by Ayesha with a sarcastic smile, accompanied by an edgy comment. 'How was your evening at Adil's? Did you enjoy it to the fullest?' Some more sarcasm. Rajkumar kept his cool and went on sipping his lukewarm nimbu-pani with honey. He thought for a while and surmised that Ayesha did not know about the incident that took place at Adil's dance bar. Her comments were a throw-back of their last evening's argument. He smiled politely. However, Ayesha was relentless. She wanted to make peace but was hoping that her husband would propose it. When it did not happen, she became aggressive.

'What did you do at Adil's last night?' she asked with a poker face. 'Nothing? So sad! Why did you go then? I had so much fun at the *disc*; never danced so madly lately. All the boys went crazy watching me.' She looked slyly at her husband to trace envy while making those comments. There was none. She got up from the dining table, went to the bedroom and returned with a big white envelope. Standing close to Rajkumar she handed over the envelope to him and said, 'Open it.'

Rajkumar slightly leaned away from her. Instead of asking what was inside the envelope, he commented, 'You are reeking of alcohol Ayesha. Go have a gargle. We will discuss about the envelope later.'

Ayesha shot back, 'You don't simply care anymore? Do you? You only smell alcohol on my breath. Horrible man. You disgust me.'

Nonchalantly, Rajkumar took out the papers from the envelope. They were acceptance letters and accompanying brochures from Ayesha's university in the US admitting her to the Master's degree. He looked up at Ayesha and said in a non-committal voice, 'Great. Congratulations. I am happy for you. You need to prepare for your journey,' and walked away from her.

The moment he walked away, he felt instinctively that he should have behaved differently. He had the advantage of wisdom and experience. He should have been more conciliatory in his approach; his behaviour should have been more even-tempered. However, he felt cheated that Ayesha had applied for Masters without even letting him know. Alas, if he had asked that question he would have known that this application was pending for the last three semesters and Ayesha was not very keen to go to the University at this point of time. She only wanted to use it as an ice breaker in their stagnated conversation and was seeking his attention.

Both of them remained boxed within their own squares. As the night set in, Rajkumar headed for Adil's Bar.

It was Farokh Mistri who remained the rallying point. His love for his daughter and trust in Rajkumar kept the thread of the relationship alive among the three of them. Ayesha's love for her 'Daddy' was eternal. Rajkumar's devotion to his father-in-law was beyond reproach. So was Farokh's belief in Ayesha's goodness and Rajkumar's honesty in conducting and managing his restaurant – 'Queen's Necklace'.

In the meanwhile, time flew past. Rajkumar kept on procrastinating and waiting for the right moment to apologise to his wife; he kept his relationship with his wife on hold. On the other hand, his visits to Adil's dance bar became more frequent.

BOOK 2

- Impression -

21st Century: First Decade before
The 59th Independence Day

Dilemma

Kumudini Sharma, Executive Editor of The India Post magazine, was feeling agitated. Her Deputy Editor—Roy, was having a difference of opinion with her on reporting on the unique dance bars of Mumbai. She said to Roy, 'I had been following the Mumbai dance bar stories very keenly. Paucity of time for further research is stopping me from taking this up.'

'So?' Roy did not show much enthusiasm. His response was monosyllabic and he continued looking at the data-sheet given to him by his junior on the weekly market trends.

'It is an interesting and topical issue. I think you should do a feature on it,' she suggested.

Roy was not moved by her arguments. He looked at her, smiled politely and declined, 'The subject might be interesting and topical but I don't know anything about it at all. Never followed it. In any case, Freny wrote about it in the last issue.' His answer was indifferent, almost dismissive.

Kumudini replied evenly, 'Yes, she did. And, made a mess of it. You know that. We have discussed it at the edit meeting.'

Post *Chandni Bar*, the Hindi movie made on the life of a Mumbai bar dancer, the hoi-polloi of the country became interested in the goings-on inside the Mumbai girlie bars. Sensing the undercurrent of resentment running through a section of the population against such entertainment, an influential politician took it upon himself to eradicate dance bars from the province. The move provided the politician and his party a very encouraging response from a sizeable slice of the electoral base which reacted favourably to this action. Once politicians across various other parties also adopted the issue, Kumudini felt, the subject of dance bars of Mumbai, rather than being a complex social issue of concern, became a focused political agenda. Editors of newspapers and magazines jumped at the opportunity to comment on such a contemporary social situation. Some started claiming the moral high ground while others supported the dancers. Readers were treated as emotional media junkies. Coupled with visuals of dancers' exposed deep belly buttons, smooth midriffs, and undulating hips, yellow journalism was at its best. Television channels were having a field day!

While trying to pursue Roy to write on the subject, Kumudini commented, 'Be honest and different.' Roy, an analyst and a consummate business correspondent, had the mettle to be insightful. A diligent researcher and a responsible corporate journalist, his world-views were very complex but never conceited. With the ban on the dance bars coming into effect in less than a month, Kumudini wanted her magazine to make a decisive statement. She wanted Roy to write this article which he was reluctant to pen.

From the very beginning Roy said to her, 'I find the subject of dance bars abhorrent. Though I am new to the city but being a journalist covering corporates and markets, I have received enough hints from my acquaintances from the "Dalal Street" to visit dance bars for "relaxing." And, I don't condone illicit relationships, so I will be biased while writing the article.

In any case, a lot has already been written. There's nothing special left.'

Kumudini knew that Roy would not play the circulation game by treating this subject only through the softer lenses of lifestyle reporting with pathos, melodrama, and a bit of flesh sprinkled into the story, which was actually what Freny Merchant, the Features Editor of The India Post, did in her previous article when Kumudini entrusted her to do a meaningful and investigative story, a story with a difference, on Mumbai dance bars. So, she stuck to her gun of Roy writing the article this time, till a reluctant Roy burst out, 'Why glorify prostitution? It has its space within the society but this is too much.' Kumudini had a different take on the subject. Her native instinct prompted her to ask Roy to take up the assignment. She knew Roy would look at the subject differently. She also knew that Roy would treat the subject with dignity, sincerity and utmost honesty. Slightly over a year ago, she had read an article written by Roy on the destitute children of Delhi in the features section of the newspaper where he worked prior to joining The India Post. 'It was so insightful and emphatic,' she remembered. So, these were the precise reasons why she requested Roy, but he was reluctant. When he wanted to relinquish the responsibility by not wanting to do the dance bar article, predictably, she was angry. She had no option but to use her authority as his boss to push him to accept the assignment.

She told Roy, 'If a dance bar is a decoy for plain and simple prostitution, why do the *tamasha*, the pretext of the dance shows? There has to be a reason for having a thousand dance bars with thousands of dancers ... go and find it out, and let's talk after that! Again, by closing the dance bars will prostitution go away? What is the guarantee that the same dance bars will not erupt somewhere else in some other form? Indulge me, I am in a dilemma.' Kumudini looked straight into Roy's eyes, once she finished saying what she wanted to say. She wanted to be certain that her message was understood well. He looked back. She could apparently see no rancour or animosity, but only a pale shadow camouflaging his thoughts. A little sadness! With not much time in hand, Kumudini had no other option but to do the sequel as a damage control exercise to the mundane feature of Freny Merchant. She was on the mission of rebranding The India Post, and she knew that she would not be able to achieve her objective by publishing hackneyed stories.

Dance Bar

As Roy entered the hall, foot tapping, heart-thudding rhythms from the latest Bollywood hit-list split his eardrums. Winking psychedelic lights assaulted his eyes. He saw a dozen or so lithe, young, stunningly beautiful girls gyrating in the middle of the large dancing hall of Magnet, one of Mumbai's most popular and infamous girlie bars. In contrast to the music and the lights, the interiors seemed tastefully done. The pink Italian marble floor was complemented by a large chandelier hanging suspended from a high ceiling. The walls were done in panels of polished mahogany, alternating with Belgian mirrors and pure silk drapes. The last soothing touch was the perfect air-conditioning; a tangible contrast to the sultry weather outside. Roy was mildly surprised. This did not match with his preconceived image of a dance bar – a dimly lit place, garish and shabby, somewhat smelly and sleazy.

Only the panel of discotheque lighting, the sound system and the under-current of sexual tension gave away the fact that this was not the drawing room of a high society ultra-high-net- worth, jet-setting, flashy lifestyle individual. Under the winking lights, it seemed as if a private party hosted by a naughty millionaire was in progress.

As he absorbed the atmosphere, he could feel twelve pairs of beautifully made-up eyes, appraising him with feline keenness. He could also sense the anticipation among the customers inside the hall. They were getting ready for a perfectly rollicking weekend night. The early-bird customers had already occupied nearly half the couches that ran along the three sides of the hall. The remaining wall was dedicated to the bar. Two young bartenders dressed smartly in black-and-gold uniforms were mixing drinks, while a large, tall, fair, middle-aged man in white kurta-pyjamas was furiously punching on a calculator on the counter and scribbling in his notepad.

Roy wondered, looking at the casual and carefree attitude of the people inside this dance bar, who could possibly imagine that only a couple of days ago the city's infrastructure was dealt with a crippling physical blow by a flash flood. A large number of people had lost their lives. The weather could still throw some more challenges at the inhabitants of the city. The dance bar proved to be a world far removed from this human tragedy.

Feeling most uncomfortable, Roy looked around for a place to sit. He waited patiently near the entrance of the hall, for an usher to escort him to a seat. He decided strategically, not to attract any untoward attention; to enter the bar quietly, observe its life, and exit without much ado. In a place like Magnet, if you were a newcomer, you might want to observe before you rush in. He thanked his prudence. And, right at that juncture from the corner of his eye, he saw a smartly-attired steward in a black suit coming towards him with his right hand outstretched.

'Hello, sir. Myself Manjunath, sir. Welcome to Magnet.'

With his weather-beaten and experienced eyes, middle-aged Manjunath tried to evaluate Roy's worth as quickly as possible. While shaking hands, Manjunath realised that the guest's grip was firm. One quick shake and the guest immediately withdrew his hand as if he would rather avoid body contact. Manjunath sensed aloofness in the touch. His experience told him to be cautious. Roy looked at him inquisitively.

Manjunath had been working at Magnet for nine years, and felt certain that this customer was new to Magnet. A tall, handsome figure like his, with such white skin like *firangs* and with aquiline features would be hard to forget. For certain, this man was a newcomer at Magnet; whether he was new to the DB, the dance bar circuit, Manjunath had to find out. He asked politely, 'Sir, how can I help, sir? Will you like to have a seat, sir?'

Roy looked at the man and noted: middle-aged, average height, darkish skin and dyed hair parted at the centre. No facial hair. Pearly whites in his mouth. Specimen of an everyday Indian male; he was holding a pen and a small notepad in his left hand, and looking expectantly at him. However, the pair of eyes gave him away. They were far too alive, as if he had had an overdose of life while dealing with the lovers of the night.

'Yes, I believe so,' replied Roy, struggling to suppress his discomfort with a very dry and *propah* English baritone.

'This side, sir. Please. Let me show you your seating place.' While speaking rapidly as he always did, Manjunath guided him to a corner seat though two seats were empty in the middle of the same row. The customer obliged by taking the corner seat indicated to him without any hint of protest.

'Yes!!!' Manjunath thought triumphantly and congratulated himself. He had predicted the customer was a novice and now he was sure. Experienced customers found corner seats inconvenient for interacting with the dancers. Dancers too generally discouraged their regular customers to be in the corner, as they did not get enough floor space for dancing in front of them. Of course, there was the chance that this man belonged to that rare breed of the shy, hesitant customers, or that more common unwanted breed, the impecunious one; but Manjunath was prepared to bet his shirt on these odds.

Justifiably, Roy was unaware of these mental calculations. However, the moment he saw Manjunath's triumphant expression, he instinctively knew that he had committed some kind of a blunder. He let the feeling of bewilderment within pass and decided to wait for an appropriate moment to find out from Manjunath what exactly he had done wrong.

Manjunath felt confident of Roy's worth. For the first time that evening, he felt confident of pocketing a hefty tip. In the past, he had usually extracted a reasonably good tip from novice customers. The trick was to behave like their guardian angel. Therefore, he turned on his charm by paying undivided attention to Roy and placed the beverages menu on the low glass table that was in front of the couch. 'Sir, menu, sir? Whisky, beer, rum, vodka, wine, sir? What do you want?'

While browsing through the neatly designed and printed pages of the menu, Roy enquired, 'How about a Coke?' Though he was not very certain whether Magnet would be serving Coke to its customers.

'Sir, yes, sir. Coke yes. You like juices?' Manjunath counter offered suggestions. 'Orange, pineapple, watermelon, mango, apple?' Manjunath, by offering more choice for selection, tried to be helpful to his new customer to make him comfortable.

'Are you sure about the juices served being fresh?' asked Roy.

'Sir, everything fresh-fresh, sir,' Manjunath replied with a double entendre that went unnoticed by Roy. After a moment's pause and slightly leaning towards his guest, he repeated in a theatrical, hushed voice, 'Garden fresh.'

At this juncture, Roy looked up sharply. His abhorrence for the place swelled. Deliberately ignoring the comment, he asked, 'Can you bring me a watermelon juice please, with some ice? Do not add any sugar syrup. Oh, by the way, how much will it cost?'

'Sir, really it does not matter, I mean the price, sir?' Standing erect, Manjunath replied with softness in his voice and a disarming smile. He was trained to show deference to the wealthy and handle their smallest of tantrums, 'Only three hundred rupees.' With apparent nonchalance, an inwardly stunned Roy nodded his head in an affirmative to place his order.

Manjunath, on the other hand, failed for the first time to read Roy's reaction correctly. Believing he had offended the novice by dismissing the freshness of juice in favour of other attractions, he spoke with real earnestness, 'Please, take watermelon juice. It is really good.'

'Fine,' Roy replied quickly, masking his own tentativeness and naiveté.

As Roy tried to settle down after ordering his drink, the music stopped and the disco lights suddenly went off. Two powerful spotlights lit up the centre of the hall, as the general hubbub died down. Roy felt the mood change. Through the door by the side of the bar, emerged two exquisitely beautiful girls. The taller one was decked in a black-and-gold midriff-showing ghaghra-choli. Her figure was slender and shapely and her skin tanned. She held herself with great confidence. The other girl in a golden yellow silk sari with heavy embroidery and embellishments, and a sleeveless, backless choli exuded old world charm; she was refreshingly innocent-looking. With her smooth golden skin matching the heavy sari, she looked just like a traditional Indian bride.

Both the girls bowed low to greet the audience with aadab and namaste. That age-old trick used by women to show off their cleavage and soften up the men. Predictably, there were a few scattered drunken applauses. 'The warming-up round,' Roy thought.

Slowly the dancer-duo straightened up, took a few steps back, and on cue, the melodious opening notes of an old Hindi song reverberated through the hall. The girl in the sari turned towards Roy. Their eyes met and held each other's gaze. Her almond-shaped eyes had the colour of clear blue seawater and were dazzling like sapphires. With precise coordination, both girls began dancing to the song as it had been choreographed in the movie but, Roy observed sarcastically, laced with a bit of an addendum of wiggling of their much-defined butts through their dresses.

As he watched, Roy felt questions rise unbidden in his mind. How did such beautiful girls land up in a dance bar? Popular belief held that most of these girls had been forced into the profession, owing to physical threats or economic compulsions. But what compelling circumstances made them stay? While interacting with so many customers everyday, they could reach out for help. Did they do that? What was the pattern of trafficking? How did the supply chain work? Roy was not convinced that brute force alone could be the reason why the girls adhered to the system. The reason had to be a far deeper one. He reasoned that if dancers in bars were not in the hard-core flesh trade, then why would there be coercion or fear at all? He knew the statistics ... 'with more than one thousand dance bars scattered over this city with nearly a hundred thousand dancers interacting daily with more than a million customers in open audiences'... the traditional route of force could not possibly work to make these girls dance, he thought. In fact, the use of force would have been counterproductive as the entire circuit would have known about it and more so because these girls were not quarantined tightly at one place under surveillance. So, what held them in these glitzy pens? Roy kept on analysing. His train of thought was interrupted when Manjunath came hurrying up to him, 'Sir, your juice.'

Roy looked up at him, distracted.

'Sir! Are you comfortable here, sir?' Manjunath asked very politely with a straight face to become friendlier, with a hope that he did not upset the new customer further.

'No. Not really. What about those high cocktail tables and chairs you have kept at that corner in the alcove?' Roy asked.

'Well sir. Those spaces are for a few select guests but you are welcome to sit there, in case you want to.'

'Great,' replied Roy and shifted to the alcove. 'Till what time do you keep your shop open?' He knew this question would expose him as a newcomer, but he felt certain that Manjunath had already categorised him as a novice. Displaying his vulnerability subtly might help Roy's cause. He would be able to ask questions without tipping off his real purpose, and might even be able to cultivate Manjunath as a source.

Looking at his watch Manjunath replied, 'Dances will get over by one thirty. Two hours from now.'

'So, Cinderella doesn't disappear at midnight anymore?' Roy remarked, displaying his magnificent smile.

'What sir?' Manjunath felt totally lost.

'Ah! Never mind!' Roy waved it away dismissing the joke that he wasted, made himself comfortable on one of the high cocktail chairs and took a sip of his drink. 'This is really garden fresh! Well, the juice, I mean. It's good. I wouldn't mind having one more.' By now, he was beginning to understand what made Manjunath tick. So, he played along the line opened up by Manjunath initially.

'Sir! Just one question, are you visiting the city on business or pleasure?'

'Why do you ask?' Roy countered with a straight face.

Manjunath's polite repartee was, 'You are new to Magnet. And, you don't look like us, I mean Indians.'

'Well, I am an Indian. I live in this city. Believe it or not, you are correct; I have come to your bar for the first time. Anything else?' he asked Manjunath, quizzically making a face.

'No. Nothing sir,' Manjunath bowed and muttered softly, 'let me place the order for your second glass of juice.'

Suddenly Roy realised that the room had filled to its capacity. In fact, a few men were even standing on the passageway leading to the hall. Men of all shapes and sizes were present among the audience. The quantum of money the crowd was showering on the dancers was sizeable. More than three dozen girls were dancing on the floor, in tune with Sting's *Desert Rose*. Just to be precise, Roy actually counted the number of dancers present in the hall intermittently. The floor was practically covered with ten, twenty, fifty, and one hundred rupee currency notes. A few bearers were busy gathering these notes, putting them on silver trays and depositing them on the cash counter where a few men were counting them with the help of cash counting machines and posting them in some kind of registers.

Roy was curious. He looked for Manjunath. He saw Manjunath entering the hall through the make-up room behind the bar counter, and he waved at the steward. When Manjunath came closer, he asked, 'What's the point of showering money on the girls?'

'It's called daulatzada. This is the traditional system of showing appreciation to artistes for their dance and beauty.'

Roy thought that Manjunath's reply had the poise of a classical British Butler. Still cynical Roy said, 'Is that so? But, in the West, I mean abroad, in London, New York, and other places in striptease or table-top dance bars, showering of money or the practice of putting money in the dancers' garter belt is a request for sex or a display of nudity.'

'*Chhi chhi chhi,* sir! No! Very bad, sir!' Manju exclaimed and vigorously shook his head in disagreement, holding his earlobes with his long index and middle fingers crisscrossing his chin. 'I have not gone to London, New York. No knowledge. In Mumbai, in Magnet, no such bad things are allowed. This is not our culture, sir.'

'Culture? What culture are we talking about and that too in a dance bar?' Roy mocked Manjunath.

Manjunath replied, 'Yes, sir, daulatzada is a part of our culture. Maybe you do not know!' Manjunath held his head high. He felt proud working in Magnet, one of the finest dance bars in this part of the globe. It had its own traditions and rituals, and surely not vulgar or cheap. Roy could sense that Manjunath's pride had been hurt. On the other hand, Manjunath was getting increasingly perplexed by the behaviour of his new guest. So very handsome. Sober. Polite. So inquisitive. Very down to earth in his attitude and not throwing any tantrums at all, had not made a pass at any of the girls. Though, Manjunath realised that all the dancers were waiting for a chance to pounce upon this prized prey. Had it not been Magnet, with Adil seth's strict instructions that a dancer should not approach a customer until the customer showed interest, Roy would have been mauled by these cats by now.

In an effort to convince his guest, Manjunath continued with an elaborate clarification, 'You must have noticed that during marriage processions garlands made of currency notes are offered to performers, musicians, and brass bands. That is called daulatzada. The older, traditional people, at times, wave currency notes over the heads of the bride or the groom and offer that money to the performers, a variation of daulatzada.' Manjunath held his ground.

'So, if I don't do daulatzada, in essence, if I don't pay money to the girls, they will neither stand in front of me nor will they dance for me. They will abandon me for a more appreciative customer doing daulatzada. Am I correct?' Roy asked mischievously.

'Well sir, you are right. You surely know that for every relationship, there is some exchange. If you want the dancers to dance for you, only for you, you need to pay them,' said Manjunath, polite yet unmoved. 'Sir, look at the situation like this; when you go to watch a movie or a play, don't you have to always buy tickets?'

'Of course, if you say so,' Roy shrugged his shoulders. 'Well, I am paying for my drink, which incidentally is exorbitantly priced; so the ritual of dance, I suppose, should be included in it.'

'Sir, the sitting arrangement, the dancers around you, the music, the total atmosphere in Magnet, even some small snacks and eats like wafers, cashewnuts, and fruits, are on the house. However, a dancer to dance for you specially is not covered. That is a separate payment, that's gratuity, that's how the dancers earn their money.'

'You mean I have to buy the company of a dancer by throwing money at her, right? What would she do for me then?'

'Dance and only dance,' Manjunath replied with a very straight face.

'Only dance? Nothing else? Rubbish, then why should I throw money uselessly? I am told I can pick up girls from here. They go out with customers. Don't they? I am told I can take any girl out from here and you will organise it, for a price of course.'

'Dancing is a performance, sir. She is entertaining you by dancing for you specially. If by any chance you are pointing at dirty doing, possibly that happens elsewhere. In Magnet, we do not encourage those. Impossible.' Manjunath paused for a while, thereafter in a last ditch effort he tried one more sales push at Roy, 'Sir, you look lonesome; maybe you are becoming bored talking to me. In any case, I have to go. Do you want to talk to any one of our dancers? I am sure you will enjoy the experience; a good time-pass. Most of our girls speak good English, like me.' He looked expectantly at Roy for a favourable response.

Roy's upbringing tussled briefly with his journalistic fervour. Then he said, truthfully, 'I have not yet seen a dancer whom I would really like to request for a dance or feel like speaking to. Maybe I need some more time.'

Manjunath slightly leaned forward towards Roy and tried once more, 'You want me to call Raima? She is a very good dancer, good height, intelligent, good English. I am sure you will like her. She was that tall girl in black and gold dress during the first duet dance. You remember her?' When Roy didn't respond, Manjunath continued, 'Or, I can call Praveen or Namita or Nisha – smart girls. Or, even Pallavi, our lead dancer, who danced with Raima in the duet dance. But she will maul you; very costly dancer.' Solicitously he offered the information to Roy trying to be friendlier. However, when he saw Roy unmoved, he resigned saying, 'I know you will like her, everybody likes Pallavi.'

Roy remembered Pallavi; something in her presence and carriage had stirred his interest.

Even before Roy could very emphatically decline Manjunath's barrage of continuous requests, he saw her – the girl in the golden-yellow silk sari, with a diamond dazzle in her eyes. Casually, she strolled into the hall from the other side of the bar counter. The girl was looking around, as if she was searching for something, someone, and then she looked towards him and their eyes held once again. She stopped in her tracks. She gave him a spectacular smile; wafted over to him in a wave of Davidoff's Echo for women and said liltingly with her right hand extended towards him, 'Hello stranger, how is Magnet treating you?' She paused for a few moments for effect, and quipped, 'What? Cat got your tongue? Nothing to say?' She started giggling; inclined her head sideways and asked, 'What's your name?'

Roy had been cornered, literally. He accepted the extended right hand. Her grip was firm unlike that of most other women in Roy's experience. He responded, 'I am Roy.'

'Hi, I am Pallavi Singh.' She replied with a smile and paused.

She smelled fabulous. Her heaving breasts, inside her designer choli, were taut and pert. Her stance was erect and elegant with a flat belly and wide and curvy hips. Her dense black silky hair was flowing like the poetry of the night. Her nose was cute and small, though her lips were slightly on the heavier side. He also remembered the distinct way the girl had deftly turned her slender neck while looking at him earlier and the way she carried a half-smile and the deep, focused look of her diamond-dazzling eyes. She had a significant presence. He did not show any outward reaction though, and kept all his thoughts to himself, except carrying a formal and polite smile to encourage the girl to carry on with her conversation, in case she wanted to.

'Roy? Nice, smart name. But Roy what? What is your full name?' She made a face, raised her symmetrical eyebrows in unison towards her forehead and kept staring at Roy, an over six feet tall, broad shouldered man; straight longish black hair; large black eyes with a very slight bluish tint, long eyelashes, aquiline nose and curly, heavy lips. He had long ears with nice earlobes, definitely made for wearing studs, she thought, mentally noting down his facial and outward personality traits.

'People just call me Roy.' Cryptic, he volunteered no further information.

'Hmmm. Problem. Are you afraid to disclose your identity in a dance bar? Will it tarnish your image?' Pallavi asked, keeping her tone casual.

'No. Not really. But I don't feel the need. I may not be socialising with the crowd here.' Roy replied honestly.

'So, why are you here?' very naturally, she followed him up on his reply.

He answered truthfully, 'Heard a lot about Mumbai dance bars. Thought of checking it out since you guys would be closing down shortly.'

'You want to check us out?' Pallavi asked, her face sombre.

'Yes, I do. Any problem?'

'No. Why should there be a problem?' Pallavi shook her head and continued, 'But what exactly do you want to check and what are you ready to offer in return?'

'Why are you dancing here? You can earn your livelihood otherwise too!'

'What is the problem if I dance here and earn?' Pallavi asked, in a soft tone still holding on to her smile.

'Do you feel that the audience comes here for the aesthetics of dance?' asked Roy in a curious tone.

Pallavi did not flinch for a moment, and indulgently replied, 'Roy, you and I both know why people are here. Still we dance because no one can dishonour us without our consent. As far as the place being dishonourable, that's purely a matter of perception. Anyway, the income is very good. So, no complaints, no regrets.'

He was completely unprepared for a dancer of a Mumbai dance bar to be so perceptive, candid and unassuming. Even before he could reply, she asked categorically, 'Where are you from?'

'Delhi.' Roy replied truthfully.

'And you are not an Indian? Of course, you don't look an Indian. You are a foreigner, a *firang*, right?' she guessed.

'But I am an Indian,' Roy insisted. 'My father is Indian and my mother British. I was born here. So, I am, like you, an Indian,' he paused, thought for a while and counter queried, 'Where are you from?'

'Today you are the hero. So, we will speak about you only.' She side-stepped the question adroitly. 'You know, I saw you during my first dance,' she said softly. 'You indeed look like a *firang*, a *gora*, but the colour of your eyes and hair are like mine – black. So, I was curious. And, now I know the reason. I agree with you that you could be an Indian, but a very handsome Indian. What do you say?' She made a face and addressed her last sentence very pointedly at him.

Roy felt uncomfortable but with his natural genteel self managed to say, 'Thank you for your compliment, you are extremely good looking yourself.'

She continued confidently, 'Yes I know that. But we are now talking about you ... I could not contain my curiosity, you know, so I came to ask you directly. Of course, Manjunath said that you worked in some foreign bank. Are you from a foreign bank? So where is your khazana, the treasury? Show that to me, please? I need my collection,' she asked mischievously, looking straight into Roy's eyes.

Momentarily Roy thought of lying but at the end he decided to go with the truth, 'No, I am not from a foreign bank. Manjunath is wrong. Does it really matter what I do?'

'You hesitated yet again,' she said matter-of-factly, without being judgemental. 'So you do not want to tell me what you do? I am okay with that. I will not force you.' Then she asked him bluntly, 'Why are you sitting so quietly? Not throwing any money, not asking for a dance ... what's your problem? Don't you like any of us? Not even me?' She narrowed her eyes mockingly and giggled.

Roy took the chance to be consciously direct and said candidly, 'I don't like throwing money at a girl. She is not some commodity.'

Pallavi's soft voice took on a slightly hard edge, though still she held on to her smile and without any malice uttered, 'Roy, I respect your sentiment but this is a place where you pay to see a girl dance. That is how we earn our living. So, if you occupy a space and not pay, we lose our collection. At the end of the night, we are responsible to the bar owner for the revenue. Please do not misunderstand me; I am not requesting you to leave, but each coin has two sides. You need to respect others' points of view as well. This is not some charitable organisation; moreover, we don't force anyone to come to a dance bar. Those who are present, they are here because they wanted to be.' She shrugged, still smiling.

Roy was amazed, once again. He never expected that a Mumbai bar dancer could stand up to his argument and counter it so accurately and aggressively.

A group of six belly dancers had, by then, taken over the floor. At the same time, a group of Middle Eastern men entered the hall, possibly searching for some action, and on witnessing the belly dancers, immediately went berserk. They began clapping their hands in tune with the music and started throwing currency notes in abundance at the dancers. Some of them even joined the dancers on the floor. One particular middle-aged man wearing traditional white robes and a red-and-white *keffiyeh*, came directly to Pallavi, gently took her by her forearm and coaxed her to accompany him to the centre of the dance floor. Before moving away from Roy, she turned her neck in her trademark delicate way and silently mouthed the word 'collection' towards him and winked.

Magnet was fully alive and kicking.

It was way past midnight. The Cinderellas did not evaporate but were busy. Roy was shocked at his behaviour that he lingered at a dance bar for nearly three hours. But for what? What made him do that? He was not prepared to delve within his self to find the true answer.

At least, not at that point of time.

Roy nodded his goodnight to Pallavi and made for the exit.

At the end of the day all humans lay their bodies down, close their eyes, and surrender to sleep and the world of dreams. They give up active control and surrender to darkness. In his deep sleep, Roy was dreaming about an enigmatic Mona Lisa smile.

On the other hand, Pallavi could not wait any longer to call her best friend in the world to talk about Roy, once she reached home. It had been their ritual. It had always been their time. Undisturbed and uninterrupted by the world at large to discuss about the day they lived with vigour, when the rest of the world was fast asleep.

Different Dimension

Kumudini was busy talking over the phone when Roy walked into her room on that cloudy and rainy Saturday afternoon. She gestured to him to take his seat at the usual place, an antique wooden rocking chair kept by the window.

With her high-cheekbone and chiselled face tilted, her slender shoulders slightly hunching over the round antique work table, Kumudini was taking down notes at a furious pace keeping the cordless telephone receiver nestled between her left cheek and shoulder. Simultaneously, with an articulated by-play of the slender and artistic fingers of her left hand and an apologetic face, she indicated to Roy that it would take a few more minutes to finish this discussion. By overhearing her side of the conversation, Roy could guess that she was talking to one of her sources on the ongoing tussle for the control over the business empire between the two sons of a departed industrialist, which had engulfed the city as well as the country. The Saturday afternoon weekend edit meeting of The India Post was to start in some time.

Last night's experience was still haunting Roy, though after a gap of nearly twelve hours he was not as irritated or intrigued as he was earlier. His reluctance to handle the assignment resurfaced the moment he woke up late in the morning and surprisingly the first image that invaded his consciousness was that of Pallavi and her enigmatic smile. He felt disturbed. He was not prepared to admit that the personality of a dance bar girl whom he had met randomly to complete his assignment had affected him so much. Why? He was not very clear about it. By itself, that was even more disturbing. He knew instinctively that such girls would behave in such a manner with vivaciousness to attract customers. Yet ... he liked remembering her smile.

When he entered The India Post building, he was still deliberating how he would request Kumudini to excuse him this time. To add to his irritation, the dreadful situation which he was hoping to avoid, took place: he met Freny Merchant in the corridor leading to his cabin.

'Hi, Sherlock Holmes. How ya doing?' drawled Freny, arching her already pencil-thin arched eyebrows with a sardonic smile.

'Hello, Freny!' Roy greeted her and gave her the customary peck on the cheek, for which Freny had already half-closed her eyes, and angled forward her left cheek towards him, practically demanding her pound of kiss. Spinster Freny Merchant was notorious for demanding both attention and affection from her eligible male colleagues. She was equally famous for throwing tantrums and making life miserable for everyone in the magazine. Being sexagenarian managing editor Ashok Mahajan's trusted friend, and, as per insider information, by having his balls literally in her clutches, she always acted like a diva and constantly expected attention from everyone in the magazine. So, everyone tried to be on Freny's right side, if not for anything else, at least just to avoid her unnecessary histrionics. Freny was unhappy that this follow-up article on dance bars planned by Kumudini would not have her as the author. For Freny, who lived by her 'by-lines,' this was a major setback.

Kumudini finished her telephone conversation, at long last.

She gave him her famous dimpled smile, touched his shoulder and came and sat in a chair in front of him, 'How was Magnet last night, Roy?' she enquired.

Roy narrated his experience.

Kumudini questioned him very directly, 'Are you intrigued by this girl? Do you think she is the prototype of an average bar dancer? My intuition says – No.'

'But Magnet is not the average bar,' Roy replied thoughtfully.

'Agreed.' Kumudini accepted Roy's argument and continued, 'Hence possibly we need to examine the entire episode of Mumbai dance bars from a few different dimensions.'

Roy nodded his head in agreement and handed over a slip of paper to Kumudini, 'I think this could be interesting,' The slip read: Mahendra Goradia, Senior Managing Partner, Goradia, Bengzon and Lall, Attorneys & Counsellors-at-Law, Ninth Floor, Tower Chambers, Nariman Point. He continued, 'This man represents the Bar Dancers Action Forum legally in various courts in India. I have made an appointment with him through Commerce Bank's Executive Director at 11:00 am on Monday. He should be able to give us some insight.'

A couple of weeks ago, Kumudini had discussed the same story idea with Freny Merchant before she had involved Roy. After the discussion, Freny and the staff photographer, Shiva, went in for a recce of the situations in a couple of bars. The first problem they faced was that cameras were not allowed inside any of the high-end bars. In fact, it was a revelation to them that at these high-end bars almost all the door attendants, bouncers, and musclemen were completely clued-up about the bags photojournalists carried and so unfailingly made sure that Shiva's cameras were kept outside, before the two of them could enter the dance halls. In one-on-one conversations, some of them admitted to Shiva that ever since the deadline for closure of the bars was nearing and political pressures mounting on the dance bars, the owners had given their bouncers strict instructions to not allow any kind of camera inside the dance halls. Even inside the dance halls, strict vigil was kept on customers taking photographs on their mobile phones.

Without his equipment, the photographer was handicapped. He, however, managed to take a few photographs with his small yet powerful Sony digital camera in one of the smaller bars situated at the outskirts of the city after bribing the waiter. Obviously, the pictures had to be shot without using the flashlight. Freny was not happy with either the quality or the compositions of those frames – she had wanted to capture the grandeur of the bigger and high-end dance bars.

Being the 'odd woman out' in a predominantly all-male bastion, Freny faced other problems too. In the high-end bars the door attendants routinely stopped her from entering. '*Ladies no allow inside*,' unequivocally they uttered in their cool Queen's language. And whenever she managed to enter the bars, especially the medium and low-end dance bars, she got curious glances from the dancers as well.

She also had problems interacting with male customers. Some of them simply refused to talk to a woman, sitting beside them about their dance bar frequenting habits. She categorised them as male chauvinists. Whatever they were, the fact remained that Freny failed to make a dent into their citadel. On top of all these follies, in a suburban medium-end DB, she was mistakenly pursued by a somewhat inebriated customer as an 'over the hill walk-in call girl.' The customer inevitably took his chance making a pass at her, 'Hi sweetie! Wanna go?'

Freny was terribly offended and haughtily shouted back, 'Fuck off, motherfucker!'

Next day Shiva let this information out inadvertently while having a casual conversation with some of the junior staff during their regular roadside late afternoon *cutting chai* session, '*Abbe, kal raat aunty ko ek customer ne raand samjha.*' The gossip spread like wildfire. So, without much more deliberation or research, just to conclude the report, Freny took the easy way out; of focusing her story around the two middle-aged bar dancers with whom she had barely managed to strike conversations in one of the smaller bars on the fringes of the city.

Kumudini had wanted a more analytical and credible story but because of pressure from Ashok Mahajan gave that sentimental and hackneyed report a reluctant go-ahead for the last week's edition after much chopping and changing. Then and there, she decided that Roy would do a follow-up story on the dance bars as the principal writer as well as the researcher and Freny would be, if necessary, the co-writer.

Mentoring

'Hello, Rajababa! Why didn't you come to Magnet last night? I was waiting for you! I even called your mobile last night, but it was coming unreachable. I have not seen you for more than two months. Yesterday was my first day at Magnet after a gap of two months, and you were not there. Are you still angry with me?' said Pallavi, very softly and pleadingly to Rajkumar over the phone.

It was around five o'clock in the evening on that rainy and windy Saturday. The inside of the master bedroom, situated on the South-East corner of the ninth floor apartment of Gulmohur Tower, was shadowy and cool. Heavy drapes were drawn across the tinted glass floor-to-ceiling windows. The cloudy sky further accentuated the darkness. The temperature inside the room was comfortable, courtesy the newly installed air conditioner. Lying on a king-size bed, Pallavi brought the phone receiver very close to her mouth, collected her thoughts, and very softly continued, saying in her liltingly husky voice, 'Say something! You have all the right to rave and rant and scold. You know that. Please talk to me, *na*.'

Rajkumar knew Pallavi and her family for more than a decade now, since the time an adolescent Pallavi had visited

Banaras, along with her family to immerse the ashes of her friend Mallika's mother. It was he who had intervened with the powerful local ruffians led by gangster Kinkar when they tried molesting young Pallavi. Sometime later, Kinkar, the younger brother of the minister was found dead, shot by a .9-mm revolver at a point-blank range. That particular incident became so far-fetching in the local politics of Banaras that ultimately Rajkumar, as a strategic defence, had to leave the holy city quietly and relocate himself, for the second time in his life, in the city of Mumbai.

Currently, when Pallavi called up, Rajkumar was in the small office room of his specialty restaurant, Queen's Necklace, on Marine Drive promenade, along with his Master Chef Arianna Ferranti. Both of them were scrutinising the menu and discussing last minute details for the big private party catering they were supposed to handle the very next day for about one hundred guests at industrialist Kishan Mittal's residence at Breach Candy. For Rajkumar, it was a chance to make a statement to Mumbai's A-listers. He made a coup of sorts when he got Arianna to agree to work with him leaving the Executive Chef's job in *The Marriott*. In the last six months, Rajkumar's move had paid rich dividends. From a fairly accepted Parsi restaurant serving continental food on the Marine Drive promenade for the last six decades, it suddenly became the talk of the town for fine-dining, and business increased by leaps and bounds.

Rajkumar was experimenting with various permutations and combinations for long to make this restaurant a craze. It became an obsession with him, more so as he drifted apart from Ayesha. Possibly he wanted to provide Farokh and Ayesha with such amount of revenue that would provide them with a grand lifestyle. He possibly thought it would compensate his insensitive behaviour towards Ayesha. Anyway, to cut the long story short, Queen's Necklace had received a few invitations to cater to the parties covered by page three of city media as well. Rajkumar made plans to expand the franchise of Queen's Necklace through a specialised outdoor catering wing and he also wanted to open a branch in Bandra, one of the hot spots of the city for fine dining and nightlife. He nourished a secret desire to open a branch in Delhi too. He wanted to make this restaurant a 'must visit' for gourmets as his tribute to Farokh Mistri. A number of private equity funds with specialisation in the food and beverages sector had shown interest to fund him. The only hitch was the technical problem of ownership of the restaurant which was coming in the way of his plans for expansion. Technically, his father-in-law, Farokh Mistri, was still the owner and there was no power of attorney in favour of Rajkumar to carry on the aforesaid activities. Rajkumar recently wrote to his estranged wife about his plan and sought her opinion on it.

Frankly and candidly, he wrote to Ayesha that he was tired of running a moderately successful restaurant for an indefinite period of time, when he had no sustainable relations with either his father-in-law or his long estranged wife. This was taking a toll on his spirit, but because he felt a sense of responsibility towards them, he was continuing with the operations. However, he expressed that he would feel happy if the actual owners could take charge. He also outlined his plan of expansion and requested Ayesha to visit Mumbai so that while the business was thriving she could come and take charge and relieve Rajkumar of his responsibilities.

In her short reply, Ayesha requested Rajkumar to bring over all necessary documents and meet her father in Philadelphia. Rajkumar had told the Private Equity firms which showed interest to invest in the business as well as Farokh's solicitors to provide the necessary papers and, had applied for his US Visa.

Rajkumar could ultimately return Pallavi's call, around eight o'clock in the evening. By that time, Pallavi had already reached Magnet and was sitting inside the make-up room gossiping with her fellow dancers Namita, Nisha, Dolly and a few others. She took Rajkumar's call on her mobile and went out of the make-up room, to the adjacent toilet to seek privacy for their conversation. Unlike calls from her customers, Pallavi never exposed or revealed Rajkumar's calls to anyone – she had always considered him a family member as well as a very dear and close friend. Had she been well accustomed with the nuances and meaning of mentoring, she would have obviously considered him to be her mentor. So, whatever catty remarks the girls would have had previously made, Pallavi never dithered to keep her interactions with Rajkumar as closely guarded a secret as possible.

It had been two months and they had not met. Now that Pallavi was back in town, Rajkumar seriously wanted to resolve the issue with her – he wanted Pallavi to marry and settle down in life, so that he could, at least in his mind, be relieved of his responsibility of rehabilitating her and integrating her with the mainstream society, where she could reside with her head held high as any other girl of her age, and did not have to hide her profession or carry the stigma of it. Rajkumar was a man in a hurry. He needed to definitely start discussing with Pallavi about her future plans. In slightly more than three weeks, the dance bars would close and the thought of how Pallavi would want her life to pan out after that had been nagging him.

Resolving issues related to Pallavi was very important. Rajkumar had already decided that he too needed to correct his follies and the mistakes that he had committed in his personal life by getting separated from his wife just because of his very keen concern about Pallavi. No doubt Ayesha behaved impulsively during the early days of their marriage, but he too had been headstrong. Looking back, Rajkumar always cursed himself for being so engrossed in his own self-serving mode; to be so self-occupied in restoring balance in others' lives, overlooking the principle of charity begins at home and literally ignoring his wife. He should have had frank discussions with his wife explaining his position on Pallavi, clarifying that he was protective, a kind of father-figure, and had no romantic or other undesirable interest in the girl or a liaison with her. He should have stopped Ayesha from going to the US for higher studies, more so when it was clear that it was just a pretext on her part to seek attention, to provoke his reaction. He should have shown a far greater maturity, understanding the issue, and not allowing it to snowball to a prolonged relationship crisis. He should have changed his lifestyle when Ayesha took up a teaching assignment after completing her Masters. The fallout was that his father-in-law had to move to the US to protect his daughter from the terrible emotional disaster she was rushing headlong into – with prolonged estrangement from her husband whom she continued loving, and who loved her truly. Farokh Mistri's decency, his understanding of both his daughter and son-in-law and their characters, of their love which they cloaked in their own peculiar ways, his maturity and deep-rooted conviction in their innate good nature and his belief that Ayesha and Rajkumar were made for each other had kept their marriage alive. Otherwise, both Ayesha and Rajkumar had let their relationship deteriorate; a chasm they were not sure how to bridge, separated them.

Hence, Rajkumar's current two-point agenda was to see Pallavi settled in life as soon as possible and to sort out issues with Ayesha. He had neglected Ayesha for far too long, for nearly a decade to be precise, and wanted to seek her pardon. However, he could not and did not want to seek absolution from Ayesha, with Pallavi still being an active part of his life. He, for sure, wanted to see a positive turn in Pallavi's life before he took a bow from it. Whether Ayesha would take him back in her life was a different proposition altogether, but he could not approach Ayesha for the second time to become a part of her life with Pallavi still in the foreground.

However, the problem he had to face in the case of temperamental Pallavi currently was that instead of trying to build a reserve fund for her rainy days, by working hard during the last months before the shutters finally went down, she had dashed off to Mirpura to supervise the completion of the construction and furnishing of her village home before the monsoon. She wanted to do so because she thought that during the forthcoming *Navraatri*, which was about two months away, she would do a *havan,* and would formally enter the house she could call her own home finally. Rajkumar nodded his head in amusement because people at large always had a feeling that cold-blooded Pallavi was devoid of any emotion and was a very calculative and scheming bar dancer, a mujrawali, who would make them empty their purses completely every day, day after day, yet remain elusive and untouched; but had they known her personal life, as intimately as he did, they would have found a sensitive, perceptive girl full of gentleness, affection, emotions and sacrifices.

As soon as Pallavi entered the toilet, she pulled down the seat cover and sat on the commode using it as a chair without a second thought, and in a hushed voiced, said, 'Baba, please forgive me. Don't be angry. I feel miserable when you get angry with me and don't speak to me. What have I done to deserve such behaviour from you this time?'

The answer from the other end in a staccato baritone was crisp and clear, 'You know that the government would close the dance bars by 15 August, yet you chose to remain in your village for the last two months. Fine, don't earn anything. But why have you invested all your savings in a real estate that would not appreciate fast? By doing so, you have locked all your liquid funds. What kind of mature thinking is this?'

Pallavi was quiet for a moment, and then in an even softer voice replied, 'Aap *hain na*. If I am in trouble, I will take money from you.'

Rajkumar retorted, 'Over my dead body! I have never given you any money in the past nor will I give you any in the future as long as you continue with your profession. I have been asking you to get married and settle down. If you can't do that, I am sorry, I am not there for you anymore. Get married and I will bear the cost of your marriage.'

'*Toh aap mujhse shaadi kar lo na?* If I marry you, I will get a father, a husband, and a friend ... three-in-one!' Pallavi started giggling.

'What utter nonsense are you blabbering? I told you in the past that never ever talk such rubbish.' Rajkumar was really angry. She knew the problem he was facing with Ayesha, despite that such a joke. 'Do you have anything important to talk tonight? Else, I am really busy. I have a huge catering contract for tomorrow and I need to work.'

'*Arre* Baba, you have a lot of people and on top you have appointed the *firang* woman, they should take care of your office *ka* problem *na*! When there is a big rush of customers in our *office*, can we bring in *Adil seth* to dance on the floor? No *na*. We only take care of our customers, Baba.' She put forward her impeccable logic. And, on a serious note she continued in her own way of creating a resolution, 'You are my best friend. You saved my honour from those goons in Banaras, even though you did not know me. You gave me your love without any reservations despite knowing that I am a mujrawali. You are the best man to be in my life.'

Pallavi had missed Rajkumar's company, his concerns, his no-nonsense, easy-going attitude for the past two months and so wanted to hang on to this conversation as long as she could. This was the man who had saved her chastity, who till now had always treated her as a fellow human being and never a commodity, and who was always there with his good counsel to help her better the quality of her life, even at the cost of his own marriage. He had never complained to her that his own marriage was crashing, never ever. On the other hand, he wanted her to get settled, to live a life other than that of a mujrawali. Where would Pallavi get such a friend?

He was about to hang up because he could understand that Pallavi had called only to say sorry, which she did in her unique way, and was just about hanging on to the phone to have some utterly inane dialogue. But he had to go. He was really required in the final planning of the morrow's party. It was a make or break situation and he could not let this opportunity slip by. If he succeeded, in the long run it would be good for Ayesha and Farokh Mistri. He owed it to them.

Just when he was about to hang up, Pallavi chose to drop the bombshell, 'Baba, I have seen a boy. I want you to see him.

He is very handsome, Rajababa. You know *na* that I like good-looking men. All the girls have gone bonkers over him. The good news is that I think he has good habits. *Mast hai ladka, ek dam film-star jaisa.* I did not see him drinking or smoking or throwing money on girls. I spoke to him and tried to flirt with him, but he was very decent and aloof. I quizzed Manjunath too. You know *na* how information flows in our bar circuit. Please Baba, if you can, find more details about him. I have seen him only once, yesterday. He was very secretive, reclusive. You know *na* Baba we can make out men easily. We can pick out the good from the bad. I know there are too many "ifs," but what to do, I have to take that much risk in any case, to find a good boy.' Pallavi felt relieved, and excited at the same time, after she could share her innermost secret with her Rajababa.

Rajkumar Mallik was ecstatic. *Pallavi has become serious about leaving the age-old practice. She has decided to defy her* biradari *elders and norms. What an achievement that would be for that girl.* This would be the most blissful experience in his entire life. What a fantastic evening it was turning out to be, he thought.

Decisive Day

Even for Roy, this Saturday was decisive. He was determined to wrap up the assignment as quickly as possible. He had tried cajoling Kumudini to let him off, but she had been adamant and determined that she wanted the feature from him and only him. He called up Chirag Shah, director of a well-known stock-broking firm in the city, whom he knew through past interactions. Roy's calling Chirag was not as random as it might have seemed. Following the prototype of audience he had sampled at Magnet last night, he felt wealthy stockbrokers, diamond merchants, builders, investment bankers, and not so surprisingly, politicians and such people belonging to particular socio-economic strata of the society had a higher chance of patronising dance bars. And, especially DBs like Magnet. Well, there could be possible exceptions. He understood that much through his maturity. So, at first, Roy was hesitant to bring up the topic of the dance bar with Chirag and was beating around the bush for some time discussing the trend of the Sensex. It being a Saturday early evening, Chirag was relatively relaxed. However, after some prolonged discussion on the market, Roy sensed restiveness in Chirag's voice. He felt that he could not take any more time and that he needed to bring up the topic. At the same time, he did not wish Chirag to misunderstand him. As such, he plainly stated the fact that he was ordered by his boss to write about the dance bars, but he neither had any knowledge of that industry nor any contact with it, and so thought that possibly Chirag could help him out with some connection or tip. He profusely apologised if Chirag felt scandalised by his request. However, Roy did share the information that last night he had visited Magnet alone. Contrary to his apprehension, Chirag, making a quick U-turn, warmed up to him like a long-lost friend and dispelled his uneasiness.

'You bloody fool! Why are you so apologetic about a visit to a DB with a friend? Be my guest. We shall visit a DB this evening but only after 11 o'clock. I have to visit a relative for dinner with my wife. We can meet after that.'

After having a further customary tête-à-tête on the equity market, Chirag excused himself.

Roy felt a bit confused after he hung up. He was not very sure whether he did the right thing by enlisting Chirag's help to visit a dance bar. Roy would not want to be indebted to Chirag, the stock broker, for entertaining him in a dance bar. He made up his mind to make it very clear to Chirag that he wanted Chirag to only get him an insider look at the world of DBs and not entertain or fund him there.

As far as the basic background information was concerned, Roy had been looking up the Internet and was also assured of a briefing by Kumudini. By now, more or less, he had an understanding of the current situation, the viewpoint of the authorities and why they wanted the dance bars to close. He had also gone through the statements issued by various non-governmental developmental agencies and support groups in favour of keeping the bars open. What he felt most perplexing in the jigsaw puzzle was the behaviour of the owners. Firstly, he had a feeling that the bar owners were not united, or at least, they did not appear to be so in their efforts to fight the 'ban.' Moreover, the dancers were used as puppets and were being dangled before the media and the mass as the victims by the owners. In the meantime, the authorities were, surely and steadily, in a planned manner, keeping the pressure on. Roy was not interested in such overused information and he did not intend to repeat all this in his article – 'like old wine in a new bottle' – by simply adding a new introduction in a flowery language. The analyst in him was saying that there would be more to the problem of the dance bars than could meet the eye. He must have missed something. The socio-economic and socio-political ramifications had to be much larger and deeper than only the loss of jobs of the dancers and waiters, and the loss of revenue for the bars and the state. He was sure that the genesis, initial incubation, and further augmentation of the genre held the answer to his question. In fact, a few not-so-important websites and blogs carried certain critical information on the administrative and economic reasons for the dance bars coming into being in Mumbai and not so largely in any other cities of India. These threads were not followed up by the mainstream media. They had possibly considered such information as mundane and irrelevant. He made a mental note of checking out those suppositions. He made a further note of researching on the revenue generated by these bars through entertainment tax, performance tax, sales tax, and excise duties on beverages for the state. How much could be the gratuitous earnings of the police from such kind of a night life, he thought? It would be naive to deny existence of some such arrangements. He was absolutely sure that he should study the supply-chain-management of this typical business. He knew that there had to be a key issue that triggered the whole system.

He was in search of that key.

Pallavi was having her evening chai in the first floor make-up room when one of her mobiles rang. She was in a very good mood after having spoken to her Rajababa. She looked at her mobile. It was Madhuri Ma calling her. She was surprised. Madhuri Ma rarely called her around this time of the evening when she was busy in her office. It was only after 2 o'clock in the morning, after closing of Magnet, while she was on her way home she would call, if necessary.

'*Haan Ma, bolo*?' Pallavi enquired.

'*Munia beti, tera doosra mobile band kyon hai?* Is everything alright?' Madhuri Ma enquired.

'*Arre* Baba, I have put it for charging. The battery died on me. Anyway, tell me quickly, what is so urgent that you have to call me at this time in office?'

'Sukumar Shah called. I could not say no to the poor fellow and break his heart. He is not getting through to you. He is in town and wants to meet you after your office. He said he might even drop by your office later at night.'

'Ma! I am very busy today. I cannot meet him. By the way, what will he do in Magnet? He gets into fights with all my customers. He is not the only moneyed man I know. Rajababa is coming tonight too ... *usko thappar milega* if he misbehaves. Tell him, sorry, not tonight. He has misused my goodness long enough. I was young and innocent and he did a lot of damage only because you took money from him. For years he misused me as my pagadwala. Not anymore. He is history.'

Madhuri softly replied, 'He is one of the best patrons you ever had. Please don't disappoint him baby, *meri khateer.*'

'*Uff*, Ma! ... No! That man is a bastard. He made my life miserable. I don't want to deal with him anymore.'

'Come on baby! At least talk to him. Take his call. Speak to him for a couple of minutes. Do this for me. Look, I don't like Raja, yet you keep in touch. Have I ever said anything? You do this for me. Switch on your other mobile,' said Madhuri a bit sternly.

'*Uff* ! But remember this is the last time I am going to do this. I have done enough for you, Dadua, and our biradari. Now I need to live my life. Let me be. I will be going onto the floor now and I don't want to fight with you.' She disconnected the line.

Pallavi was a bit unmindful when her other mobile rang. While reaching for the mobile she realised that Namita was looking at her in a peculiar way through the mirror sitting across her on the opposite table.

'Hello Sukumarji. How are you?'

'*Jaan.* My love. My darling. My Pallavi. I missed you so much,' began Sukumar Divakar Shah, in an attempt to start wooing the young woman.

Pallavi brought the mobile very close to her lips and said very softly in her liltingly husky voice, 'Do you know that I was thinking of you for some days now? How was your trip?'

'The Europe tour was fantastic. Both business as well as pleasure, it would have been great had you been there,' said Shah.

'Really? You mean it?'

'Yes. I do mean it, my love.'

'You are such an accomplished liar Shah saab! You almost made me believe it, even after knowing you for so many years,' she said in a cutting tone. 'How is your daughter? Did she have a boy or a girl?'

'A boy.'

'You are a proud grandfather now, Sukumarji. What good news. Your wife must be very happy? Isn't it time to settle down?' Pallavi rubbed it in.

'Yes, I am very happy. In fact, I was worried whether my daughter will ever have a child. I am so relieved now,' confided Shah in an unconcerned manner, even if he could understand the drift of Pallavi's speech.

'So, you are in a mood for celebration? Right? And you want to meet me? What will I get from you on this happy occasion?'

'You only need to ask, *meri jaan.*'

'Really? You wouldn't backtrack later? Like you often do?' she chided him playfully. 'But I am so sorry, tonight I am not well, you know, not advisable to meet. Remember the last time we met?' said she in her trademark husky voice and broke into a practised coquettish giggle.

Sexagenarian Shah's heart was beating at a faster pace now and he could feel that a huge amount of his blood rushed southwards to a particular destination in his body. He experienced such a taut feeling after a very long time. He was smiling faintly by the time the conversation was over.

Pallavi disconnected the call, albeit unhurriedly, shut off the mobile once again, and began doing her make-up. In her heart of hearts she abused the likes of Sukumar Shah and muttered to herself, '*Bastards, just because they have money, they feel that they can own anybody. Fuck them.*' All of a sudden she recalled that Ajay Mittal, the metal monarch, had also called her while she was on her way to Magnet. She called Madhuri back, 'Oh! Ma, I forgot to tell you that Ajay had called on my mobile sometime ago. He will be in town tonight. Tell him also that I am sick and cannot make it.'

'Hmm.' Madhuri Ma sounded alarmed at Pallavi's behaviour. 'What happened? What is the matter with you? Why are you cancelling all your appointments? These are all very rich and good patrons. You will lose them, if you behave in such a fashion. Did Raja advise you to do these?' She did not hide her displeasure. '*Saala, gaandu, chutiya, harami*! A good for nothing *matherchod!* He will ruin us. I have told you repeatedly not to pay heed to him.'

Pallavi sternly told off Madhuri over the phone, '*Gaali bakna band karo ... yeh Congress House ya Faras Road nahin hain.* Don't get carried away with your abuses. And, let's not start the topic again, Ma. ... I've already told you that I am done with you guys. 15th August and I am not getting into the dance bar or mujra business anymore. I am also getting my independence.'

'*Toh main kya karu*? Watch a swine exploit you?' lamented Madhuri trying emotional tactics.

'Nobody can exploit me without my wishes anymore. Nobody. Not even you. It took a long and hard journey for me to be where I am today. So stop your histrionics,' Pallavi very quietly said.

'Bless me my Matarani! There is still time ... make this girl realise once again the nuances of this business. Let her understand that there is no place for emotion here. Whatever wealth she has accumulated, one day some monster will definitely take all of it away because this girl is so sentimental. *Apne dhande pe sab rondana hain.* Keeping control over your men is a must ... *Oh meri Matarani!*' Madhuri went on and on with her soliloquy.

This time Pallavi reacted very sharply, '*Ma gaali mat bako.* I am shutting off both my mobiles.'

Suddenly she heard Namita uttering from the other side of the make-up table, '*Bahut charbi chad gayi hai tujhe, Munia.*

Das log kya tere pichhe pare, tu aaj sabko aankhen dikhane pe tuli huie hai. Don't be overconfident because you have some good patrons, the looks, and the money. A majority of us will have no place to go after the dance bars shut down. Bloody fuck, possibly we have to barter our bodies to survive. Fucking diva ... because of your looks and *nakhras,* you have been scoring over us. Since childhood, Madhuri Ma has looked after you and today you misbehave with her. You don't even care for me, your childhood friend. All that you care for is that bastard Raja.' Namita was visibly upset and angry.

Pallavi gave Namita a cold, steady stare for a few seconds and then said flatly, 'Nami, you were never my friend. You tried to compete with me always and were deriding me but you could do no harm to me so far. If you like Madhuri Ma so much, why don't you stay with her and take on her responsibilities. And, by God, I will not sell myself, anymore. You go and get fucked by your Suraj Mithaiwala from Delhi and enjoy the life of a keep! Whatever had happened before had happened because we were powerless and too young to understand. It is time to make our own choices now ... *achcha chal pichhese meri choli ki dori laga de* ... bloody hell it is almost time for my duet ... where is Raima? *Arre koi uski to puchho*!'

Before Roy could ring the doorbell, Bahadur, the caretaker, had opened the door for him. He greeted Roy with his customary boyish smile. Possibly he was standing on the balcony watching the Saturday evening weekend traffic pass by the busy road, and must have seen Roy enter the building. It inevitably meant that Alok Singh, Roy's landlord, was yet to return from his evening walk. Roy felt a bit relieved that he could very gently sneak into his room and be by himself. He was not in a mood for any small talk just then.

'Saab, good evening!' Bahadur said.

Roy nodded his head in acknowledgement and said, 'I am very tired. I will sleep for a while. Don't prepare any dinner for me ... I had it in the office.' He was hoping against hope that Bahadur would pick up the nuances of this subtle hint and in the process discourage Alok Singh from disturbing him upon his return from the evening walk.

Generally speaking, Alok Singh was not an intrusive person nor had he an over-solicitous nature. So far, he had allowed Roy the space and freedom. He was a widower and stayed alone in his four-bedroom spacious apartment, as his sons were settled in the US. So, eventually, he decided to keep a paying guest for some additional income and also to have some kind of a company. Roy came in as a paying guest, about a month ago through the reference of Mohan Joshi, The India Post's chief accountant, who knew Singh. Initially, Alok Singh was a bit stiff and formal. However, during the past fortnight after interacting with Roy he had increasingly started assuming the role of a local guardian. What he liked about Roy was the young man's mature behaviour, cool temperament and genteel disposition. For a lifelong services man and a retired Brigadier, he had always considered strong character and commitment as hallmarks of a good human being. He felt that Roy possessed those traits.

No sooner did Roy finish his conversation with Bahadur the doorbell chimed.

'Hello, Roy! Good evening, son. How are you doing?' enquired Alok Singh.

'Saab very tired, not feeling well,' interjected Bahadur in his boyish enthusiasm before Roy could reply.

'What happened?' The senior citizen sounded concerned. 'Did you check your temperature? What kind of symptoms do you have? Do you have any body pain?'

'It's nothing sir ... probably lack of sleep. I didn't have a good sleep last night. I'll take a nap. I'm sure I'll feel better afterwards. Please don't get anxious.' Roy tried pacifying Alok Singh.

Undeterred, Singh forced Roy to check the temperature and only after it was seen to be normal did he let Roy go and catch up some sleep.

Roy was sleeping peacefully when his mobile started beeping. It was quarter to eleven in the evening. Chirag Shah was confirming the appointment and requested Roy to meet him beneath the Kemp's Corner flyover in half an hour's time.

It was drizzling. Waiting under the cover of the Kemp's Corner flyover, Roy was in a contemplative mood. He was remembering the untimely death of his father in a car accident, under tragic circumstances, last year. He was also thinking of his mother retreating into the Himalayas in search of solace after the tragic death of her husband. As the haze over the uncertain string of thoughts was culminating into some sort of a realistic comprehension, Chirag's black S-class Mercedes swung noiselessly by his side with effortless ease.

'Hello, buddy! Sorry.' Epitome of politeness, the chubby Chirag Shah lowered the windowpane and uttered his excuse as smoothly as his S-class vehicle, though his arrogant body language did not support the statement. 'Come on. Hop in,' he said in his Yankee accent.

'I was wondering if I am bothering you by any chance. In that case we can abort it.' Roy was a bit stiff and just wanted to reconfirm that he was not intruding upon Chirag's time. He wanted to be absolutely sure that this visit did not turn into a favour given and taken issue, 'Look, I just want a connection inside the dance bar and that will be a big help. I do not wish to participate in the entertainment.'

'Relax! Don't you think it's a bit too late to abort?' Chirag commented in a lighter vein. 'No problem. Actually, it is a welcome change,' Chirag reassured him. 'I would have gone out in any case. Oh, I have asked one of my friends from the stock market to join us. He is a big dad in Magnet. They know me of course, but his presence will open all the doors and other openings much wider, you know what I mean?' Chirag winked, looking at Roy fleetingly he started warming up to the role of a classic tour guide. 'Actually I had told Sanjay to book us in. He is a big customer of Magnet. And, you will see the difference tonight. Hello, hey ...' Chirag called out to a bouncer passing by, 'Did you see Sanjay?'

'*Kaun Sanjay, saab? Mota Sanjay? Nata Sanjay? Khota Sanjay? Lamboo Sanjay*?' pat came the smart-ass reply. Then with a grinning face the same man replied, '*Arre haan ... Chirag saab, aap toh chikna Sanjay ke dost ho ... woh toh abhi abhi gaya.*'

'*Chutiya* ...! Come to me for a tip. I will not even piss on you. Fooling around with me, are you!' Chirag too grinned at the bouncer and tipped him. 'Come Roy. Let's go upstairs,' he uttered, and continued his monologue, 'It's simply heaven my dear sir. I am sure Sanjay would have waited for us but for some urgent work. You never know, he might even return. Come on, what you are waiting for?' Chirag goaded Roy as he was warming up without realising that another bouncer had blocked his way.

'Sorry, Chirag sir. *Upar ka* hall *khachakhach* full,' stated the bouncer with a deadpan face.

In an instant, Chirag lost his phony Yankee accent, the polite facade and became aggressive and brash, a typical dance bar patron, and raised his voice, 'What the fuck are you talking, Shyamsundar? You know who I am. Right? Stop this *nautanki*! No fucking around.' Then possibly as an afterthought, to strengthen his argument, he pointed to Roy and said, 'Do you know who my guest is?' and looked aggressively towards the bouncer.

With this sudden reference to himself, Roy got a bit cagey and lightly nudged Chirag with his elbow. Customers waiting in the ground floor lounge as well as in the first-floor foyer looked at them in idle curiosity. The dancers swashing around in their fineries arched their symmetrical eyebrows and shrugged their nubile shoulders to show irreverence to this unnecessary outburst. Liveried waiters paused for a moment in between their services to comprehend the uncalled for tension.

Without responding, the bouncer simply stared at both Chirag and Roy. A firm voice from behind called out exactly at that point of time, 'Shyamsundar, Chirag sir *aur unoko guest ko upar anneko do*. Please sir, come up.'

Roy was startled.

The bouncer was a seasoned one and did not show any sign of remorse or petulance and made way.

Roy looked up at the direction from where the instruction came to the bouncer and saw Manjunath looking at him intently. Roy's steady gaze met Manjunath's; within a fraction of a second Roy could sense a flicker of recognition in Manju's eyes. Within no time, Manjunath transformed himself to the genial steward that Roy could remember from the previous day and gave his guest a reassuring smile.

'Welcome to Magnet,' said Manjunath and shook hands with Chirag and Roy at the top of the stairs. Chirag could still not digest his rejection and very haughtily asked, 'Manjunath, have you seen Sanjay?'

Wily Manjunath was too smart to get into the trap and replied in a very even tone, 'I will try to look him up, Chirag sir. He must be somewhere. Very crowded today.' Then he turned to Roy and said, 'Sorry for bad reception. We generally are not rude persons. Tonight is very busy and bad night. You please excuse us. Where will you like to sit? Mujra or Disco?'

'Wherever you suggest,' replied Roy.

When Roy and Chirag had settled themselves on the couches of the mujra hall, Chirag asked Roy sheepishly, 'Do you think the guy remembers you from last night?'

'Who? Me? I don't know. Possible, but,' answered Roy and continued evenly, 'on second thoughts, maybe because you were showing me off like a trophy possession, the steward must have thought that I am a big shot. A very good tactic.' Roy nodded his head showing appreciation.

Chirag's ravaged ego received its balm and he too started nodding his head in agreement. In an effort to show off his importance within the confines of this dance hall and to further salvage his ravaged ego, he took out a wad of hundred-rupee currency notes from his wallet and started waving it to catch the attention of the dancers on the floor. The smart, tall girl with a shapely figure – whom Roy remembered seeing in a black and gold midriff-showing ghaghra choli last night dancing along with Pallavi – came and stood before Chirag. She was wearing a skimpy little black choli holding her firm bosom in such a manner that there was nothing left to imagination. Her flowing silken black ghaghra was tied so below her firm belly button that there were definite chances of a catastrophe occurring if it slipped even a millimetre downwards.

Chirag looked at the girl blankly; holding the wad of currency notes in his left palm, he beckoned the girl to come further close by crooking his right index finger. The girl very slowly yet surely inched closer to Chirag, fixing her gaze steadily on him. Her lips parted slightly, forming a seductive smile and she hissed, 'Hi, Chirag baby! Wanna have a good time?'

It was surprising – the diction and the accent. Roy was perplexed. So perfect pronunciation. Only someone who had had a very good schooling with English as the medium of instruction would have such diction and accent.

While the girl was picking the currency notes calmly one after the other from Chirag's palm, he extended his right hand to encircle her hips and tried pulling her closer to him. Without flinching and without missing the rhythm of picking the currency notes, in a very soft playful tone, the girl rebuked him, 'Don't do that Chirag baby, not in here.'

'If you don't allow touching, then how am I suppose to have fun, Raima *jaan*?'

'Watch me dance. Tonight I will dance only for you. And come and dance with me.' She picked up the last currency note, and with a single fluid motion took a few steps backwards.

'Sure, you would dance for me. Agreed. But you have to come for the midnight buffet at the Sea-Plaza hotel tonight, with me and my friend Roy. Oh, by the way, Roy ... this is Raima and Raima that's Roy. Raima featured in a number of music videos as background dancer and she wants to open up a dancing fitness centre once the bar closes. Sorry guys ... forgot to introduce you. ... Fucking this dress of yours Raima. Why don't you dance naked instead?' Chirag started laughing at his own joke. Roy was scandalised hearing this conversation and feverishly hoping not to be a part of such conversations any further.

Raima shrugged her shoulders, stepped away from Chirag, picked up the rhythm of the music and started dancing in front of them.

It was almost midnight. Queen's Necklace near Marine Drive promenade would close in a short while. The waiters were serving the last orders. Unlike other days, on weekends, Rajkumar kept the restaurant open till midnight because of popular demand. Precisely at that moment his mobile rang; it was Pallavi. 'Hmm ... *bolo*?' he said.

'Baba ... he is here. Just hurry. He is in the mujra hall. I am off to the floor now.' Pallavi was all excited.

Rajkumar mostly preferred walking to Magnet to meet Pallavi. He always liked roaming the streets of Mumbai at night. It gave him a sense of tranquillity. He had discovered that for him the best place to find solitude was the midnight streets of Mumbai and not the banks of the Arabian Sea at Marine Drive's promenade. Whenever he could manage time, he walked leisurely through the streets, lanes, and by-lanes of this metropolis. However, the current weather in the city was not conducive at all for any kind of leisurely walking. With heavy rains and wind, walking was not a viable option to reach Magnet, more so, because of the urgency of tonight's business. He asked one of his waiters to get a taxi for him.

'Namaste, Raja saab.' The bouncer at the gate greeted Rajkumar.

'Thank you, Manoj. *Bibi kaysi hai*? How is the family doing?' He greeted the burly attendant with affection.

'*Ji* sir. *Sab kutch badia*. All *fit-faat* okay, saab. No tension,' replied Manoj in an affirmative, and in one swift motion held the main door to Magnet open in deference.

'Hello, Raja! How are you doing mate?' Adil Powvala, the white kurta pyjamas clad fair, tall, large, wily, glib Parsi, Magnet's owner, greeted him with friendly warmth at the ground floor main lobby. Adil was walking towards his office behind the main ground floor lounge, after his hourly rounds of inspections of each of the cash counters of the five dance halls in Magnet. This was a part of his daily ritual at Magnet. '*Saala chutiya,*' he whispered to Rajkumar softly, putting an arm across his shoulder, 'I knew you would be visiting us tonight, *gaandu,*' he quipped displaying an easy relationship with Rajkumar. 'Rashid, *Raja saab ko* mujra *hall me leke jana.*' Adil smiled fondly at Rajkumar after giving instructions to his main usher, Rashid. 'Raja, I am sure that your friend must be waiting there. *Saala, gaandu.* You need to leave that girl.'

'Don't glorify yourself with these patented abuses, Adil. Sure, I would keep your advice in mind. But, before that, because I met you, I would like to have a quick chat with you privately. In fact, I had called you on your mobile in the afternoon and it was switched off. Don't you get missed-call messages?' He asked in a sombre voice and looked at him squarely in the eye.

'Why would I need such facilities? *Abe saale dancebarwala hoon* .... In my business, I prefer talking face-to-face. You know that. Come along mate,' replied Adil jovially and took Rajkumar by the arm towards his office and waived Rashid away.

'Today I received Ayesha's reply to my proposal. She wants me to meet Mr Mistri in the US. I believe he has started throwing tantrums like last year to return to Mumbai permanently. What do you think?' asked Rajkumar even before they were seated in the small spartan office room. The question exposed Rajkumar's slightly disturbed state of mind. In fact, Rajkumar himself had observed that he became stressed whenever he needed to address issues related to Ayesha or her father. He could not identify if it was his guilt or the feeling of loneliness that was pressurising him of late.

'Well, what do you think?' Adil counter-queried.

'Look buddy. I am an outsider in your community and strictly speaking in your family also, currently,' Rajkumar stated in a somewhat non-committal manner.

'It's not fair, *chutiya,*' Adil countered, though his body language was not aggressive at all.

Rajkumar leaned towards Adil, who was seated across him, 'I respect, adore, behold ... whatever adjective you may want to use to describe my feelings towards Mr Mistri, for the benevolence and tolerance he has shown towards me. He has always treated me like his son. Took me into his family and allowed me to help him run his business. I am deeply indebted to Ayesha too. But somehow ... I am no longer feeling comfortable with the situation,' he flatly admitted.

'Why not?' asked Adil, not ready to let Rajkumar off the hook so easily. 'We know you for over a decade now. Right?' Adil looked at him quizzically. 'You have been running my uncle's business independently, for the last so many years. In fact, *Damadraja*, you have done a miracle. You bloody rejuvenated the business with a masterstroke ... that master chef of yours, brilliant idea man! I told Ayesha about it a couple of days ago over phone. All said and done you are still my uncle's son-in-law ... you are still married to Ayesha. And, Ayesha wrote a mail to you. Try and understand that she has not cut off the umbilical cord. You have not annulled your marriage officially. Yes, you guys don't stay together. *Abbe bol chutiya,* your point of view,' Adil nodded his head disapprovingly. 'Your misbehaviour towards Ayesha was bloody fucking ridiculous, though. What the fuck did you see in Pallavi, man? You never courted her; neither did you run her family by providing for her expenses. Whatever outsiders might say ... I know that she is not your keep. Then why the fuck did you let your wife go? Ayesha had every reason to be hurt and unhappy. You fucker never even tried to hold her back. Never tried reasoning with her.' Adil widely gesticulated, as was usual whenever he was frustrated.

With his arms interlocked and held close to his chest, Rajkumar replied in a matter-of-fact tone, 'Well, I do run your uncle's business. But for how long am I going to be the custodian of his restaurant? I have been running the restaurant for nearly a decade. For the last so many years, Mr Mistri and Ayesha have not even visited Mumbai. Under such circumstances, I also need to let it go,' he sighed. 'The restaurant is the main reason I am stuck to this city. I had been a nomad all my life. You know that I had no one as a family.' He stood up from his seat and started pacing the small room. Then he went closer to Adil, placed his left hand on Adil's shoulder, and said, 'About Pallavi ... you never understood my sentiment. My emotions towards her are not necessarily a fallout of my carnal desire, unlike most of the people visiting your bar. Don't measure relationships ... for that matter any relationship, be it between a man and a woman, a man and a man, or a woman and a woman ... only in the shades of black or white. All relationships are in the shades of grey. The tint, the tone, and the hue differ; it is very difficult to standardise. I identify with Pallavi at so many levels. Only because she is a dancer in your bar, you feel that she could not be my friend? Is it because she is a woman that I have to have a physical relationship with her? You have such bloody ridiculous and naive attitudes, Adil. I had not expected these, at least from you.' He turned around to go back to his seat and shook his head, 'Earlier you had shown an interest in taking over this restaurant business. You even fought so bitterly with your uncle and cousin over it. Why don't you consider it once more? Here I am, in a fix, virtually begging you to run the restaurant.'

'I have heard about the seven-year itch, but ten years? That's a bit too much buddy. You are behaving very oddly tonight.' Adil laughed off Rajkumar's somewhat sentimental remorse. 'On a serious note, I think, you need to discuss this with Ayesha, and not with me. Moreover, my business priorities have also changed. I think you need to take a trip to Philadelphia to meet them and talk it out. And in any case, you need those legal issues sorted out.' He paused. After a few seconds, he said ruefully, 'The problem is that you and Ayesha hardly talk anymore. Possibly the fault lies with me. I should have warned Ayesha about your affinity towards Pallavi in the early years when you started visiting my bar regularly; else, I should have thrown you out. I mean it. Then your marriage would not have broken. You have hurt Ayesha so much. Bloody hell, I was also upset with her at that point of time, else I would have gone after you.' Adil looked at Rajkumar piercingly and threw his large arms widely in the air.

Rajkumar looked at the large portly figure before him and wondered how Adil could transform himself from a smart dance bar owner to a friend and a family man with genuine concerns. He thought it was such a pity that the outside world would hardly ever get to know the real Adil. To the world outside, Adil would always be the cunning, immoral, and most successful dance bar owner in town.

Adil continued, 'I think there is still time for reconciliation. Now that you are repentant, you should really try to win Ayesha as a friend, at the least, with utmost sincerity. I think she still cares about you. Else, she would not have remained single still, and would have taken a divorce.'

'Point taken. But do you really think you would have been able to stop me from interacting with Pallavi? Don't you know me enough? Didn't you understand my reason enough?' Rajkumar uttered softly, looking straight into Adil Powvala's eyes.

'Don't ... you're such a pighead,' muttered Adil and disengaged himself from the strong gaze that almost mesmerised him.

Adil smiled to himself. He was becoming soft. For a fraction of an instant, he closed his eyes to drive away the nostalgia. Currently, he needed to focus on the problem at hand. He then looked up and said fondly to Rajkumar, 'Anyway, you sleep on it buddy, and think through about what I said.' He paused slightly, and as an afterthought, said in an even softer voice, 'But you need to sort out your association with Pallavi too. Let go of her now. Enough of it! Tell me what exactly you expect out of this relationship with her anymore? Let her live her own life. You are a very dear friend. It is my request. Don't get wasted.'

Taciturn Rajkumar nodded his head in vague agreement and sitting very still in his chair replied, 'Adil, within a few weeks or so from now, you have to close down your bar. I thought that possibly it would be an ideal timing for you to run your uncle's restaurant. You will have an additional stream of income and I will get my freedom. Though you don't really require any more income but ...'

'Do you think they are serious about the ban?' asked Adil. Although his appearance did not show it, his voice betrayed him. Rajkumar could trace an underlying current of nervousness in his friend's voice.

'I think the government is serious this time. I feel the minister has led the government to the point of no return. It is a politics of coalition. One of the partners in the ministry got a fabulous opportunity to showcase the public sentiment manoeuvring skill. Why should they let the opportunity go?'

'Yes. I agree.' Adil had to accept Rajkumar's logic. He gave a friendly squeeze to Rajkumar's hand and released it. 'I doubt that the ban would be very effective. Maharashtra might ban. Some other state might welcome. Never mind, we will discuss this issue once again when a clearer picture emerges. Some of us, those who operate the bars with all relevant government licenses, are still trying to find a resolution. In fact, I have a Owners Association meeting tomorrow ... we will discuss about it there.' Adil appeared distracted and restive. When someone's livelihood was threatened, there was a genuine reason for it.

'Sure Adil. I hope things work out,' said Rajkumar with all earnestness. They stared at each other, shook hands, and parted.

Rashid was waiting outside to escort Rajkumar to the mujra hall, the exclusive and privileged dance hall of Magnet.

When Roy had entered the mujra hall along with Chirag it was fully occupied by customers. A few dancers were standing in the middle of the hall huddled together and were discussing something and having a laugh. A few were entertaining their regular clientele by dancing in front of them. The waiters and stewards were moving hurriedly serving drinks. And then, there was Chirag's lovey-dovey behaviour with Raima. Roy did not feel comfortable at all. He just wanted to explore his options, as he started feeling slightly at home inside this Mumbai dance bar. He moved towards the disco dancing hall. As he was about to enter the disco hall, the door suddenly opened and he saw Manjunath rushing out of the hall.

He saw Roy. 'Good to have you back, Roy sir.' He extended his right hand.

'Hey, Manju. How do you do?' Roy replied and shook Manjunath's hand.

Manjunath held the door back for Roy to enter the disco hall. He offered Roy a seat at the couch facing the centre of the hall and asked, 'What happened? You leave Chirag sir alone?'

Roy nodded, 'Let him have his fun'. Then he politely declined the offer to sit at the couch, instead requested Manjunath if he could have a tall cocktail chair near the bar counter placed for him. He said that he would be comfortable that way because of the leg space he required. Manju nodded his head and went out of the hall to arrange for it personally. Roy slowly started walking towards the bar counter. Suddenly he felt a light tap on his shoulder. Perplexed, he turned around because he never expected anyone to tap his shoulder in here. And, there she was, radiating her thousand watt smile – the girl with the diamond dazzles in her eyes.

'Hello, Roy. *Kayse aana hua* ... oh, sorry, sorry. You speak in English only.' Pallavi laughed. 'How come you are here? Have you lost your way, mister?' Her eyes were twinkling.

Did he blush? He was not very sure. He was thrilled but. He was hoping to meet her. 'Hey, Pallavi! What a pleasant surprise,' he replied, displaying delight.

'Hellooo. Sorry. This is my office. I come here every day. No surprise.' Pallavi narrowed her eyes and in a spirit of a mock fight took her stance and continued, 'Your coming to this place again is a surprise. Don't you have a family? How come you have started visiting Magnet practically every night?'

The seasoned journalist in Roy marvelled at how smoothly she tried extracting information. How intelligently she was trying to appraise him with a clever stance and casual interrogation.

He gave in willingly because he needed to build a rapport with her, 'Ma'am. No family. Just alone.' He copied Pallavi's style of speaking.

'*E Allah! Arre meri Matarani! Aap kisko Ma bole?* Who is your *mam*? ... I am not *Ma*, you Baba.' She made a face.

'Ma'am! Mother? I didn't call you mother.' Roy was slightly disoriented and then realised that Pallavi might not have been exposed to his way of expressions and pronunciations. He politely clarified without being condescending, 'Ma'am is a British way of pronunciation, Madam, it sounds more like *mam ... ma.*'

'*Uui amma*!' She exclaimed.

'Thank you! You too speak English well. Do you practise Islam?' Roy politely asked Pallavi.

'What?' Pallavi was bewildered.

'You said Allah ...'

'My dear English saab that's our way of speaking. Like your Ma'am. I hope you understand. I am a Hindu, I said Matarani too. We respect every religion,' She shifted her weight from left to right foot, rearranged her bangles, raised her eyebrows, and asked very innocently, '*Achcha ek baat bolo* ... why are you praising me so much? I know my English is not good. I am just learning. *Aap ka matlab kya hai?* Will you keep on talking or do you want me to dance for you?'

'Why don't we talk? I have no money to give. Manjunath said the other day that nobody will dance for me if I don't throw money.'

'*Arre Manju ko maro goli.* Who the hell is Manjunath? If I want to dance for you, I will dance for you. Tell me which song do you prefer? Let me dance on that,' said Pallavi nonchalantly.

'What is the perfume you are wearing, *Issey Miyake*? Right? Yesterday it was ECHO.' Roy tried to change the topic.

'*Achcha!* You know so much about perfumes? How many girlfriends do you have, mister?' She tilted her head to a side and gave a knowing smile.

'Why? I don't have any girlfriend, and how does it matter?' Roy replied with a very straight face.

'Why are you telling lies?' Pallavi retorted. 'Such a handsome man and no girlfriend ... all lies.' Pallavi started laughing.

'A girlfriend is serious business. Honestly, I have no girlfriend. Don't have so much time to invest. I just enjoyed speaking to you, that's all. Love is a more serious matter and cannot be professed so easily,' Roy replied earnestly.

Pallavi looked at him intently holding an enigmatic Mona Lisa smile on her face and after a pause uttered, 'Thank you for being so straightforward. At least you spoke the truth. Every other customer talks about how he has fallen in love with me.'

Both of them were speaking so intensely that they did not notice that Manjunath had quietly placed a high cocktail chair for Roy to sit. After a while, Manju gestured to Pallavi to request Roy to occupy the seat. Pallavi said, 'Mister, your throne is ready. Why don't you occupy it?'

Roy replied genuinely, 'I can't just sit; when we are talking and you are standing. You are a lady. It is discourteous.'

'You are a customer. It is your privilege. I have to stand. I am a dancer. I work here.'

'Well, I know. Thank you, but I am comfortable this way, at the moment.' Without finishing his reply he surveyed the hall and continued, 'Anyway, today you have a good crowd for providing you with collections. Sorry, if I am keeping you away from your work.'

'Wow. I mentioned collection only once and you have understood. You are sharp,' Pallavi laughed and clapped her hands.

'Really? You remembered that. I think that you are smart rather,' Roy replied, and casually volleyed his next question. 'Where are you from?'

'I don't invite customers home.' She replied with a deadpan face.

'My question is where is your native place? *Gaon kahan hai*? You know what I mean. I will go there to find a suitable bride. I am sure all the girls will be as smart and as beautiful as you are.' Roy waited for her answer with bated breath.

She answered with honesty, 'Why? What is wrong with me? Anyway, you have asked the question before as well. *Chalo* I will give you the answer. I am from Chambal Ghati. Have you heard the name? The Chambal Valley. Dangerous place. And, I am a dangerous girl. You can propose to me. You won't get any other girl there waiting for your marriage proposal. Everyone else is gone. I am the only one left.' She nodded her head and rolled her eyes mockingly.

'Really? Everyone else married? To whom? The dacoits of Chambal? Why didn't you marry one of the bandits too?' Roy took a deep breath and replied.

'I am a Rajput. Why should I marry a *Baghee* Tomar?' She answered with an inherent pride.

'You are a Rajput? And you are dancing in front of inebriated men? I don't believe you.' Roy uttered incredulously. 'A Rajput woman wouldn't do that.'

'Oh really! And how do you know that Sirji?'

'I was born and brought up in Delhi. I have a lot of Rajput acquaintances.' He shared a little bit of himself to gain her confidence further.

And then a staccato baritone voice raised a question close at hand, 'What happened to the Rajputs of Delhi? Why are we inviting them to big bad *Aamchi Mumbai*?'

Pallavi pirouetted, clapped her hands in joy, and uttered, 'Rajababa. You are *pucca* on time.'

'Why? What happened?' Rajkumar asked smilingly.

'Oh! We are having a debate on Rajputs and *Baghee* Tomars,' replied Pallavi.

'What is that dispute?' Rajkumar expressed his curiosity.

'*Arre* Rajababa, he does not believe that I am a Rajput,' Pallavi informed him and very slyly winked at Rajkumar, 'More so, he feels I should marry a dacoit as I am from Chambal valley.'

'Well, I was only discussing a probability,' replied Roy in his no-nonsense style.

Rajkumar quickly assessed the drift and stated, 'I'm sure you were,' and looked very steadily at Roy.

Roy felt like he was being scrutinised by this man. It was one thing fooling around with Pallavi, but with this person around, it would be a tough game, and he was not yet ready to compromise his cover or reveal his true identity. He looked at the man – average height, tanned skin, very lean body, longish hair pulled into a small ponytail and bound by a black hair band, and a pair of very large and piercing eyes. The charcoal black eyes would see through anybody in a matter of moments. He had also noticed that the man had a very steady gaze. Wearing a pair of washed slim-fit blue denims and a pale yellow polo-neck T-shirt, in his patent leather boots, this man portrayed a sense of physical and mental toughness which exuded caged power within, which he kept in control with a very philosophical yet nonchalant attitude. And, yes he was wearing the manly smell of that well-known perfume Roy loved most.

As Roy was deciding on the next move, the man referred to as Rajababa by Pallavi extended his right hand and introduced himself, 'Raja Mallik – a friend of Pallavi.'

'Roy.' Though he shook Rajkumar's proferred hand, Roy's reply was cryptic.

Rajkumar acknowledged Roy's gaze by faintly nodding his head. He then smiled at Roy and asked very politely, 'So, this is your first time in Magnet?'

Roy was slightly uncomfortable and edgy, 'What do you mean by first time, Mr Mallik?'

'I mean you are a newcomer to Magnet.' Rajkumar made a flat statement.

Roy was curious. He asked, 'Why do you say so?'

'Oh! Slight observation, part intuition, and a little bit of background information.' Rajkumar replied.

'Background information? Well, I am surprised. From where did you get the information about me?' Roy was not only surprised but also curious and returned the steady gaze of the man.

'At Magnet, in the first-floor halls, such as the Mujra and Disco halls, the patrons are regulars, high-rollers, known to each other or rather, know of each other. Rest of the crowd comes through references or with friends, who are regular patrons. So, any newcomer can be identified easily. Secondly, my dear friend Manjunath told me that you have been accompanied by Chirag Shah of the brokerage firm "Prabhudas Shah Equities" tonight, and yesterday was your first day in Magnet. I have never seen you here before either, else I'd have remembered,' Rajkumar smiled magnificently once again.

Roy was amazed. The man was so confidently accurate in his understanding and analysis.

Rajkumar came slightly closer towards Roy with his eyes twinkling and in a slightly hushed tone in the din of the noise said, 'Believe me, I was hesitant to ask for your introduction as most of the audience here suffer from social phobia because of the taboo and prejudice attached to the Mumbai dance bars. And so, inevitably they try to hide their identities. Introductions among strangers are just one short cryptic first name; Ajay, Vijay, Ram, Rahim, Robert, or even Roy, for that matter. Anonymity, which is what we all seek here, so, I completely understand your discomfort and reluctance to answer my questions. I have no issues. I am making the enquiries because Pallavi is a very old friend of mine. She is like family. So, I thought I should ask you a few questions by way of introduction.' He displayed his most disarming smile to Roy and continued, 'Take your seat please. Have you seen Pallavi dancing? She dances so well.'

Pallavi immediately jumped in, and in her lilting voice complained, 'Dekho *na* Rajababa, I am asking him since when to let me know his favourite song and he is continuously refusing. *Arre kal bhi puchhi thi*, he said women were not commodities. I don't want you to dance in front of me. Does any of the logic hold water in a dance bar, tell me Baba?'

Roy smiled and kept quiet. He had already put up his guard and wanted to know why Raja Mallik was curious about him.

Pallavi smiled and continued her dialogue with Roy, 'I told you yesterday. I repeat once again. 'I have to dance. No work, no income. You don't know this business but ask Rajababa. It is not like your office. This office is very simple. If I make no collection from customers, Adil seth gives me nothing.'

Precisely at that point of time, with a very cordial smile, Rajkumar half-turned towards Roy, as if he could read Roy's mind and made an astounding observation to Pallavi, 'Mark my words, Munia, our new-found friend, Roy, is no ordinary man. This extremely handsome young man has an intense personality. His looks exude honesty and sincerity. It is possible that he has tons of money, but he will never blow it in a place like Magnet. So, either he is a jilted fool in search of the substitute of that elusive emotion called love or, better still, he is a seasoned journalist hunting for a human-interest story under the current circumstances. Do one thing, go and ask about him to Chirag and you will get to know things about Mr Roy. I now have a feeling that *apna* Mr Roy should be from the media, maybe foreign media, because Chirag Shah is a media darling and is always giving his *gyan* through television or newspaper interviews about stock markets.'

Rajkumar then faced Roy squarely and uttered in *pucca* English, 'Roy, this is Miss Pallavi Singh, Magnet's principal dancer, a wonderful girl, a dear friend of mine, and I can vouch for her to be a nice human being. Whatever is your intention, please don't hurt her.'

Roy with a momentary decision, said to both his audiences, 'Why are you saying all this? Why should I hurt her feelings? What do I gain by hurting her? I hardly know her Mr Mallik. You have made certain assumptions and you are putting forward your views based on such assumptions; now if you will kindly excuse me, I need to go round the corner.' He knew that through this ploy he could get out of the confines of the hall.

Pallavi replied very explicitly by raising her eyebrows and shaking her head, 'Corner *pe kya hai? Corner pe kutch nahin hai*. Don't speak in complicated English. I told you I have just started learning the language.'

Rajkumar intervened, 'He wants to go to the washroom.'

'Say that then, *na,* why say – round the corner, –' she made a face, and continued, 'Don't complicate things. Your *Round the Corner* is actually straight out of the door. It is in the lobby,' she replied confidently and pointed to the entrance to the hall.

Roy smiled at both of them, nodded his head, thanked Pallavi for the directions, and went out of the disco hall.

Roy was relieved that Manjunath did not show over solicitousness once he came out of the toilet. He silently admired the judgement of this middle-aged man. He could also see the pressure of the crowd this evening.

'Hello, Manjunath.'

'Hello, sir.'

'You have decorated your hall so beautifully. I didn't notice it yesterday.'

'Chameli and Rupa, two of our dancers, are celebrating their birthdays tonight.'

'What about some birthday cakes then?'

'You missed cake-cutting. It happened already, sometime ago, sir. Cakes and candles and "Happy Birthday singing," compulsory, this for all our artists. Our boss, Adil seth pay.' Manjunath with his twinkling eyes provided Roy with the details.

'Am I surprised?' Roy rhetorically asked. 'Yes, I am surprised by your system, Manjunath. I am surprised to see that your owner practises modern management techniques of team-building, bonding, and employee relations in a place such as this dance bar.'

Roy looked at Manjunath to see if the middle-aged steward could comprehend his communication. He thought he could detect none. Hence, he tried re-phrasing the statement in a more simplistic manner to make it comprehensible to Manjunath. Roy was midway through his effort when Manjunath interrupted him politely by placing a hand on his forearm and said, 'Sir, I know what you say. Thank you for liking our efforts. I think you miss the real picture. Celebrating birthdays' is a very good business sense. Customers shower a huge amount of money on their favourite dancers. Good for our collection.'

Roy was dumbstruck. Elementary native business sense prevailed over modern management techniques. Eureka! He was jubilant. He could pinpoint his discomfort, finally. It was the 'cash'! He could hardly see the incredible amount of cash-splurge expected on a Saturday night, especially with the twin birthdays. Something must have surely gone wrong somewhere.

He immediately shared his observation with Manjunath. The moment he did so, he could literally feel a sense of palpable tension within Manjunath. After a momentary hesitation, the senior steward took him aside and carefully whispered, 'Please do not stay now. Some raid expected. We know nothing, but indication is there. You are a nice person. I like you not to get involved in it, though no one creates problem for the customers. But still, please leave and come back tomorrow, if we are open.'

Roy grabbed the slim opportunity to try and further his association. 'But how will I know if you are open?'

'Knowing our *seth*, we will be open. He does not like losing revenue. No right-thinking businessman does. You follow what I say? Take my mobile number and give me a call at 4 o'clock tomorrow afternoon. I will let you know the exact position,' he looked at Roy knowingly, and then in a brisk manner said, 'Please, you go now and take Chirag sir with you.'

Who said that the labyrinth of Mumbai's underbelly was devoid of compassion?

Duet Partner

Chirag was grumpy. Drinking made him even more intolerable. In addition, he was mortified that he could be arrested. It took Roy a considerable amount of counselling to calm him down. Simultaneously, Roy did some quick thinking whether to reveal his identity to the officials and to try and establish a contact. But, he discarded the idea as he felt that by doing so his gain would be narrow and he would lose on his long-term perspective.

After the dancers, the staff, and other personnel of Magnet were safely quarantined, cashier points secured, all exits as well as entry points manned by the police, the customers were allowed to leave Magnet.

Roy politely declined Chirag's offer of a lift and instead decided to take a black and yellow. In the meantime he saw Shiva along with a group of photographers, waiting at the opposite pavement of Magnet. He took out his press accreditation card, showed it to the policeman who was holding the photographers back and went over to his staff photographer, 'Hello, Shiva. Did you get some interesting shots?'

'Hi! Not much, chief. I suppose when they bring out the girls and the money, those would be interesting.'

'Yes, I suppose so,' commented Roy. 'But how did you come to know about it, if I may ask.'

'Balu spoke to me around ten in the evening. I thought it would be a police raid. I was least expecting an income tax raid. In fact, all over the city a number of raids have been conducted tonight by the Police. Everyone wants to score a brownie point with the minister by raiding and discrediting the bars,' replied Shiva, and at the same time he looked at Roy and asked, 'Hey, how come you are here at this hour, sir? Oh, the feature.'

'Yes. I just came to have some first-hand inputs. And, look at this mess. Man, you have spoilt it by organising this raid,' Roy bantered and started walking away from the photographer.

'Tonight is bad, man. Just go home and chill, okay?' Shiva looked at him knowingly.

'Thanks for your advice mate,' Roy replied and waved at Shiva.

Shiva nodded, lit up a cigarette, in a smooth practised motion, started his motorbike, and roared through the late night damp streets.

All the shops in the vicinity were closed. A few taxis were parked some hundred metres away with the hope of being hired by an odd customer who could still be inside the bar, while some of them were waiting for the dancers who were their regular customers. The road was almost deserted, but for the few police constables, those two photographers, and some solitary inebriated customers still coming out of Magnet.

Roy knew that any more waiting on the pavement under the heavy rain was futile. He hailed one of the cabs waiting nearby to take him home. He made a mental note to speak to both Kumudini and Balu about the raid. It was absurd, how nasty office politics could be. Look at Balu's behaviour, just to spike his research, he conveniently lied about his contacts, when Roy asked him in the afternoon for some introduction. He also decided to try and touch base with one of his old contacts from the Finance Ministry in Delhi to take a chance and have a lead into the Income Tax Department.

His mind was immersed in his thoughts; suddenly the taxi driver asked him, 'Sahib, when do you think the madams will come out?'

Roy was slightly perplexed by the question, 'Madams? Which madams? From where?'

'Sahib, as you were inside the bar, I just wanted to know when you think the girls will come out from Magnet.'

Roy asked the cabbie, 'Why do you want to know?'

'I have a dancer as my fixed customer. I drop her home each night, after the bar closes.'

'Since when have you been dropping the girl off home?'

'Nearly six years now, since I have purchased this car.'

'Really? Good. Very good. How many taxis do you own?'

'This is my second taxi. My two sons drive the other car on shift basis. I drive this car only at night. After dropping madam I go to the airport and pick up passengers from the early morning arrivals.'

'Where do you stay?'

'Sir, I stay at Jogeshwari.'

'And your madam?'

'Pallavi madam? She stays at Andheri, Osiwara-Lokhandwala.'

'Pallavi madam?' Roy's curiosity heightened. 'Pallavi uses your cab?'

'Yes, sir,' said the taxi driver very proudly. 'Do you know Pallavi madam?'

'Yes.' Roy was cryptic.

'Nice girl. Last year during my younger son's wedding, she personally attended the marriage ceremony and gave his wife a gold bangle,' the cabbie shared proudly.

'So, why did you leave the bar now?' asked Roy curiously. 'Who will take her home?'

'Sir, watchman Manoj bhai said that it will be some time before madam can come out. Tax department problem. It may continue until morning. So, I thought you want to go nearby – a short trip to Pedder Road. I can do that and earn some money. In any case, once madam is ready to leave, she will call me on my mobile before coming out of the gate.'

Roy could see the opportunity and very casually asked the driver's name. His idea was to get friendly and to try to get a feel about Pallavi.

'My name is Kalidas, sir.'

'Where are you from?'

'I am from Jaunpur, Uttar Pradesh. I came to this city about twenty years ago.'

'My father was born in Allahabad, Uttar Pradesh, though we lived mostly in Delhi,' interjected Roy just to breed familiarity, and then continued, 'So you are in this city for twenty years? It's a very long time.'

'Ji sahib. But you don't look like us. You look like a *firang*.'

'Really! But I am speaking your language ... the way any Indian would speak. I am not a *firang*. So, tell me Kalidas how is your madam?'

'Good girl. Nice girl.'

'Of course, you will say that. She is your customer.' Roy tried picking up a mock argument.

'Why?' retorted Kalidas mildly. 'You said you know Pallavi madam. Then why are you making a judgement, sahib? It is only because she dances in a bar you take her to be a *badnam aurat*,' he spoke passionately.

Before Kalidas could finish his impassioned speech, the taxi reached its destination. Roy paid off his fare, said 'Thank you' and waved a goodnight to Kalidas, without getting into any further discussion.

Lying in his bed before dozing off to sleep, Roy was wondering about what could be the uniqueness in her character that Pallavi could instil such a passionate loyalty in a seasoned cynic; a Mumbai taxi driver.

There was complete chaos and cacophony in the first-floor make-up room of Magnet, where the income tax officials quarantined a section of the dancers. The girls were tense. Some of them wanted to use their mobile phones to inform their families or friends about what had happened in Magnet. The stern lady police constable warned them against using the phones. In fact, she informed her superiors, who came and confiscated all the mobile phones from everyone around.

Chameli and Rupa were very angry. They lost an opportunity to earn good money because of the stupid raid, as both Gautam and Chunilal did not show up, despite promising over the phone that they would attend the birthday celebrations.

The dancers who generally used the first-floor make-up room had their lockers handy. They changed into their regular clothes. They were clustered in groups. Some were chatting among themselves in hushed tones. Pallavi was also there. She was sitting very quietly in a corner of the make-up room with knees pulled towards her chest and chin resting on them. She had faced similar situations before, but of course police raids were different. The first time it was at White-Night dance bar, which she had joined more than a decade ago as an understudy dancer to Mukti didi. The police had raided the bar in search of underage dancers and she was interrogated at length considering she had just entered the permissible age for dancing in a bar. The next time she faced police interrogation was when Babubhai, her erstwhile neighbour in Byculla, was found dead inside his room. The police had questioned all the neighbours including Pallavi, and Madhuri Ma. This happened immediately after they had shifted out of the compound to a two-bedroom flat in Guruji Chawl when Niyati was about a year old and Mukti Didi was very sick.

There was a knock at the door. A young income tax officer peeped in and requested a volunteer from among the dancers. He said that his seniors wanted to speak to one of the dancers. All the girls avoided making any eye contact with him. No volunteer was forthcoming. The officer was rushed. Time was running out. In an officious manner, he zeroed in on a nervous-looking Namita, who was very close to the door, and ordered her to accompany him. Namita started fidgeting out of fear and tears rolled down her face.

Quietly Pallavi stood up from the corner of the room and asked the young officer, 'You want a volunteer? Right? Any one of us?' After receiving an affirmation, she said, 'I will come and meet your officer. Please don't force Nami if she does not want to go. But I have a request. I want to make a phone call to my home. I will do it in your presence. I just need to inform home that I will be late ... I have some guests waiting for me and my family will be worried. I will not say anything about your raid.'

The young officer said that he had to take permission from his seniors.

To that, Pallavi replied very graciously, 'Let's go. I don't need to take permission from anyone. I am my own boss.'

Namita was watching all this and said very meekly to no one in particular, 'I would have gone, but I am not feeling well.'

Pallavi merely shrugged her shoulders and left without further acknowledging Namita's comment.

In the meantime, Raima Khan – the smart, tall girl with shapely figure, who mostly paired with Pallavi for the opening dance sequence on weekend evenings at prime time – came out of the washroom after taking her bath. She had changed from her costume into a pair of imported *Salsa* jeans and a *Dolce & Gabbana* T-shirt. She was watching the drama being played out in the room silently. Generally, she avoided interacting with other girls in Magnet and kept to herself, not even pretending any acquaintance with them. It was not that Raima disliked the girls per se, but she was very sure that they were not of her class. However, out of sheer camaraderie and respect for Pallavi's courage, she decided willingly to pair with Pallavi once again to meet the tax officials and show solidarity.

The moment Anupam Dixit, the Assistant Commissioner, saw Pallavi and Raima enter Adil Powvala's office, which for the time being he had appropriated as his workstation, he became very haughty. *These girls, these whores, have exquisite beauty and use it for ruining all men. They must be taught a lesson, he thought.*

He kept them deliberately waiting in the middle of the room.

After waiting for about five minutes Pallavi could not take it any longer. She spoke to Anupam Dixit, 'Saab, do you require us or shall we leave?'

Anupam Dixit was not expecting the challenging question from the dancer. He ignored the question for the simple reason of ego and also to put a bit of a mental pressure on these whores.

Raima too was getting edgy. Still, she kept her composure and repeated the question in her upper-middle-class English accent, 'Sir, do you require us here?'

Anupam Dixit looked up startled by the out-of-place accent and was forced to reply, 'You have to wait. I am busy.'

With her honed intuition and quick-wit Pallavi immediately understood the ploy of the tax officer to put them under psychological pressure, by keeping them waiting and so immediately answered back, 'Okay, we will wait in the make-up room since you are busy. Call us when you are free.'

Anupam Dixit got very angry and felt predictably challenged. 'No, you will wait here,' he retorted.

'No, saab. We will wait in the make-up room. And, please do not raise your voice. Do not treat us as if we are your servants,' said Pallavi without displaying an iota of nervousness. She started walking out of the room.

Raima followed suit.

The entire room became silent, very silent. The few officials present inside the room were not expecting such spirited rebuke.

'You are not my servants, but you work in a place that is under investigation and we need to ask you some questions,' said Anupam Dixit, trying to maintain authority.

Pallavi stopped in her tracks, turned around, and said, 'I have no problem if you ask me questions. However, you are treating us as if we are criminals and testing our endurance. You kept Raima and me waiting. Please don't test our patience. Why are you treating us like garbage? What is our crime?'

For the first time during the evening, Anupam Dixit felt unsure.

Pallavi fixed her stare on Anupam Dixit's face and continued, 'My working in a dance bar does not make me a criminal. Therefore, you need to treat me with respect. Would you have done the same thing if I'd been working anywhere else, say in a bank or a college?'

Pallavi kept on looking evenly at Anupam Dixit.

To break the impasse, a young officer intervened, 'We need to know your name, please?'

'Pallavi Singh.'

'Raima Khan.'

'For how long have you been working here?'

'Me? For a very long time. Raima ... maybe one year.'

'Please understand that if need be, we may call you as witnesses at a later date.'

'Are we not supposed to call for our lawyers now?' asked Raima, pointedly.

'No, it is an informal discussion. Please tell us how you get your earnings?' asked Anupam Dixit regaining composure.

'Why? Why should I tell you?' Pallavi replied.

'Do you file income tax returns?' asked the young officer smilingly. 'I am sure you do not. Yet you earn. It will be helpful for you to cooperate with us. Not paying income tax is a crime.'

Pallavi said calmly, 'How did you presume that I don't pay tax? Well, I don't blame you or anyone here. It is a very common perception. But I do file my returns and a friend of mine handles it for me. You want to speak to him?' She answered in a very dignified manner. No answer was forthcoming from her audience. She continued in an even tone, 'In terms of our earnings, we, the senior artists, split our earnings fifty-fifty with our owner. Newcomers and juniors do it thirty-seventy or forty-sixty. Majority share goes to the owner.'

'What are your average daily earnings?'

'It varies.'

'Yes, that's why I said "average"'... explained the young officer.

'Anywhere between ten to fifteen thousand rupees.'

'Are you sure that is the real figure?' the young officer asked, with a smile on his face.

'I think so,' Pallavi replied, without a blink, keeping a poker face, devoid of any expression.

'How many dancers are there in Magnet?'

'About sixty.'

'So, even on a lower scale, your owner earns about one hundred fifty thousand rupees on an average per night as commissions from the dancers on top of his earnings from the food and beverages? Right?' asked Anupam very softly.

'I don't know.' Pallavi was uncomfortable for the first time. She added, 'Please, you need to ask this question to our owner. I am not the right person.'

'Do you have a daily collection target?' the young officer interjected politely again.

'Saab, I don't understand what you are asking. We are dancers ... we dance, take our "pack", I mean payment, and leave. After that we do not have any connection with all this. ... I need to go to the toilet. I request you to ask Adil seth, our owner, about all this.' She tried evading further questioning.

'Of course, we will ask him. We wanted to have an idea,' said Anupam Dixit. 'By the way,' he slightly hesitated before taking on a fatherly tone, 'I am happy that you file your returns. Please remember that it is your duty. You need to give it to the nation. That money is used for our national work. Bank officers and college teachers file tax returns. That could be one of the reasons why they are respected.' Anupam had his say, but at the back of his mind, he appreciated the spirit displayed by these girls. Maybe all hopes of rehabilitation of such girls by integrating them within the mainstream society were not lost. He dismissed Pallavi and Raima with a wave of his hand, without looking at them.

Anupam Dixit, in spite of his initial stoic behaviour, touched a chord within Pallavi with his concluding remarks on respect and honour. Something, that she craved all her life. She wanted to live life with her head held high.

Unknown to her, that night Pallavi had one more admirer in Raima, albeit a silent one. For the first time in her tenure at Magnet, Raima felt like making an acquaintance with her duet partner. She wanted to invite this gutsy girl soon for a cup of hot chocolate at her apartment in Lokhandwala. In fact, she thought that if Pallavi was interested, both of them could perhaps dance together in the music video she had received the offer to choreograph a week ago.

Rigours of Life

The weather was indolent with a very dull-grey dawn. It had been raining continuously last night. Warnings had been issued for people to stay indoors. However, for Rajkumar it was a different story altogether. Even on such a sluggish morning, he was out of bed for his daily run. It was the rigours of life which had taught him the necessity of starting his day very early. Although at this stage of life he was under no compulsion to continue with such rigour anymore, he enjoyed maintaining the regime. He also enjoyed the smell of rain. Moreover, he could not sleep last night. He was worried about Pallavi. He was concerned about Roy too.

When Manjunath came in suddenly last night to the Disco hall and requested him to come and meet Adil at once, Rajkumar should have smelled something fishy. But, he cursed himself, for not reading the early signal. When Adil took him out through the back door of Magnet and put him into a taxi, the seriousness of the situation dawned on him but it was too late to argue with Adil at that point of time about Pallavi. He felt so gutless.

On finishing his morning ritual, he immediately tried calling Pallavi on her residential landline number, knowing fully well that it was too early for that household to be functional.

The moment the phone in the living room rang, Madhuri felt irritated. She had repeatedly instructed Basanti, a poor distant relative, who worked as their full-time housekeeper, that the phone should be kept disconnected throughout the day, today, and not be connected at all, otherwise incessant calls would disrupt the work and rhythm of the house, and more importantly, Pallavi's sleep would get disturbed. Yet Basanti forgot to disconnect the phone after using it to order milk and eggs from the nearby grocer's about ten minutes ago.

Last night was a nightmare. It was only in the early hours of dawn that Pallavi returned home. Her mobiles were switched off throughout the night. Sukumar Shah kept calling on Madhuri's mobile, kept enquiring incessantly about Pallavi and increasingly became abusive in his behaviour. Unavailability of Pallavi's as well as Namita's mobiles, coupled with Sukumar repeatedly calling her, forced Madhuri to return early from Namita's mother's flat a few streets away, where she had gone for her regular tête-à-tête. Until an angry and exhausted Pallavi walked in through the front door at five, Madhuri was mortally afraid, thinking of all kinds of calamities and horrors.

The phone was still ringing.

Any intelligent housekeeper would understand the situation and act accordingly. Basanti was a *kaamchor* and behaved irresponsibly. She should be chucked out immediately. What was the use of keeping people of your own biradari as your housekeeper if they fail to understand the nuances of the business? In fact, the system of appointing housekeepers from within the biradari was considered just because they would be more attuned to the requirements of the household and would maintain the secrecy. Else, in this city you would get thousands of very efficient housekeepers, Madhuri thought and prayed that the phone would stop ringing of its own. But it was still trilling and she had to reach for it.

'Hullooo,' responded Madhuri in her belligerent mood.

'Hello Madhuriji. Raja. Good morning.' Rajkumar spoke in his staccato style.

'*Boliye ji,*' Madhuri did not bother even remotely to hide her irritation.

'Can I speak to Munia please?' Rajkumar ignored Madhuri's temperamental reply.

'She is sleeping,' Madhuri made a flat statement.

'I know Madhuriji that she must be sleeping now. She must have also come late last night because of the income tax raid, but ...' Rajkumar tried responding politely.

Even before he could finish, Madhuri cut him off, 'Raja saab, I think you should stop bothering her. She has her own life and we are running a house. We respect you a lot, but you cannot always interfere in our lives.'

'Sure. I will stop bothering you, if Munia feels so. Let me speak to her now.'

'Why?' asked Madhuri forcefully.

'I am requesting you; that's why! Please.'

'Let me check. Hold on.' Madhuri switched on the cordless and headed towards Pallavi's bedroom, loudly cursing the maid for her callousness.

Madhuri even contemplated lying to Rajkumar by saying that Munia had requested not to be disturbed. Alas, it was only wishful thinking. She knew that Munia would surely take Raja's call at any point of time and any hour of the day.

'Munia wake up. Raja's phone.'

'Uh ... um ... Phone?' Pallavi asked, her eyes barely open, and extended her hand. Madhuri placed the cordless in her hand.

'Hello, Rajababa,' Pallavi said, softly.

'Hello, Munia. Sorry to wake you up. Are you all right? Why did you not call me?'

'I am okay. I got home only at five.'

'You could have still called me.'

'I know that, Rajababa. But I was so tired and angry. That income tax officer, he was behaving as if we were *kachra*. He was so rude.' Pallavi could let out her frustration and anguish without any pretensions to this man and continued, 'Why is it that people always behave as if all of us are dirty? That we bring in evil. That anyone can coerce us into compromising ourselves easily ... I felt so dirty last night ... Oh God!' She started sobbing very softly.

'Please don't cry. Who said you are dirty and evil? How well do they know you? I know it is difficult, but at this point of time just ignore it. You have a long way to go, and one day everyone will realise your true value.' Rajkumar counselled the young woman gently. 'I will call you in the evening. Please rest. Believe me you are the best human being I have ever come across. I am sorry that I woke you up, but I was simply worried.'

'Thank you, Rajababa.' Pallavi was about to hang up when she remembered something from last night, 'Hello ... hello ... are you there Rajababa?'

'Yes Munia ... tell me.'

'You know I told the officers that I pay income tax. They could not believe it. But they did not harass me after that. Thank you for educating, helping and motivating me to pay tax and file returns.' She felt peaceful after sharing her thoughts.

'You are welcome, Munia. I am very happy and proud of you.'

'*Achcha*, Rajababa, did you meet Roy later last night? Where did he disappear?'

'Munia, take rest. This is not the time to think of someone whom you remotely know. I am sure he had his reasons for disappearing. Maybe because of the raid he left early and could not say bye to you. Wait. Give him sometime before judging him.'

Pallavi felt satisfied and returned to her sleep. It was unfortunate that there was no one around at that point of time to witness the serenity she radiated.

Roy had scanned all the newspapers that Sunday morning. Most of the newspapers had carried the report of the police raid. Only The Times Express carried the income tax raid on Magnet on its front page. Roy knew that he needed immediate expert guidance and a macro-perspective on the Mumbai dance bars, as well as the trafficking scenario. He should be able to look at and understand the big picture and should not stray into discussing sporadic and specific raids, political statements, and counter statements in his article.

He rang up one of his old contacts, a senior officer in the Finance Ministry in Delhi at his residence, as his mobile was coming switched off. He was told that the gentleman had gone out to visit his relatives and would return later that evening. Roy left his name and mobile number with the servant, with a request for the gentleman to return his call.

His next call was to his mother. It came unreachable. It was a perpetual problem at Hrishikesh Ashram, bad connectivity. Last Sunday too he couldn't connect with her. Once more Roy dialled his mother's mobile number. Once again, he had the same recorded female voice informing him that the mobile was unreachable. This was his sixth attempt since early morning. He became slightly worried; he decided to call the ashram landline number.

'Namaskar! Swami Chinmayananda from Atmatdaya Ashram speaking.' A very faint voice responded from the other end.

'Hello. Namaskar. I am Roy. I am Mrs Martha Kashyap's son. I want to speak to her please.'

'You want to speak to Mrs Martha Kashyap? You said you are her son?' Swami Chinmayananda repeated at the other end.

'Yes, please,' Roy responded patiently.

'Where are you calling from?'

'I am calling from Mumbai. Can I speak to my mother please? Is it possible? Else, can I speak to Swami Amritanandaji? He knows me well,' Roy replied with a hint of impatience.

'Sir,' Chinmayananda's voice came alive very faintly on the phone over some static, 'Marthaji has accompanied Guruji Maharaj and a group of devotees from England on a visit to the Valley of Flowers a couple of days ago. They should be returning to the ashram soon ... maybe in the next few days. I will keep a note for her saying that you called. '

'The Valley of Flowers in July? During monsoon?' Roy was a bit disturbed.

'Yes sir. You can ask Guruji about the timing later on. Namaskar, once again.'

Roy messaged his mother on her mobile, 'Tried calling you ... not getting through. Please call me when you can. Love.'

The Sunday Lunch

Lunch on Sundays was a ritual in Alok Singh's house. He and three of his childhood friends would have lunch together at his place every Sunday and play contract bridge until late evening, come hell or high water. Afterwards, in the evening, they would share a drink and disperse. Since last week Alok Singh had included his erudite and handsome paying guest Roy in the invitee list for the lunch. This Sunday too, was no exception.

While having lunch, Alok Singh enquired, 'How is your health, Roy? I believe you went out last evening and returned very late again in this adverse weather?' He was concerned. 'You shouldn't have gone out last night,' he commented with a fatherly concern.

Just to assuage the sentiments of his worried landlord, Roy explained that he had no option but to go out as he was trying to gather some data for one of his assignments. Singh was mildly curious. What could be the assignment for which he had to work on a Saturday night when he was not keeping well, even if he was a journalist?

With a slight hesitation, Roy explained, 'I have to write an editorial feature on the dance bars. My usual contacts and sources are no good for this story. I am also unable to make much headway because of lack of contacts in the city circuit. I am trying to get some contacts and information for the last couple of days. I know that as a journalist I should not have said these words but …' He stopped midway on seeing Alok Singh and his friends exchanging knowing glances.

Mahinbhai, one of Singh's friends, a plump and dignified man with a head full of neatly trimmed grey hair and equally thick and long grey sideburns asked, 'Why do you want to write an editorial on these bars? What's so great about them?' This was the first time he had ever spoken to Roy directly.

Roy answered honestly, 'My editor feels that it is an important social, socio-economic as well as socio-political issue for this city, which needs to be commented upon considering the current situation.'

Kamal Lulla, the frail and humorous dentist friend of Alok Singh, quipped in between taking a bite of the mutton chop, 'What about you, Roy? What do you feel? And, by the way, did you get caught in last night's raid? Was that the reason for your reaching home so very late at night?'

Roy nodded.

Zafar Khan, the lanky sculptor, the youngest of the lot among Alok Singh's friends, with his mystic smile exclaimed, 'What did you feel when you were inside a dance bar? I mean … I have visited a few, but always got nervous every time I had visited one … more of a question of moral turpitude.'

Roy felt slightly perplexed, engulfed by such divergent remarks from this distinguished group. Remembering the exchange of knowing looks among the assembled gentlemen he, however, was certain that there was more to come. He took a deep breath and pushed aside his plate. The rich spicy food combined with lack of sleep was making him lethargic. He looked around the dining table and replied with complete candour, 'To start with, I am yet to comprehend the full socio-economic impact of the dance bars on our society. I hardly know the genesis of this genre, other than published reports in the popular press, which I do not consider to be complete. I have observed a definite trend among magazines and weekend supplements to gloss over the so-called glamour and physical part of it. I have also seen electronic media exploiting the visuals of dances and dancers. All of them have stories pegged on soft interviews of the dancers, followed by comments from the representatives of non-governmental bodies, either for or against the issue, as well as some comments from the authorities and Dance Bar Association's representatives. Mainline English newspapers have taken a pro dance bar stance, in line with their readership profile, while language publications, I mean Indian language publications, have taken a critical view of these bars, which is again understandable, considering the segment they cater to. I have seen non-governmental organisations predictably polarised on the issue, which may be based on their funding and ideological impulses. I do not think much credence be given to the web media because of the fact that most of the opinions expressed are either very personal, or bizarre, or comical, in my opinion. The funniest part is the authorities, the politicians, and the bureaucrats, who instead of informed governance took refuge in moralistic subterfuge, possibly to create and enlarge constituencies.'

At the end of his monologue, he realised that the others too had stopped eating and were staring at him intently. For a moment, Roy felt that possibly he had misjudged the host's concern and these seasoned bridge enthusiasts could guess that he did not hold much tricks. Alok Singh was the first to break the silence, 'Roy, for how long have you been working on the assignment?'

'Three days, sir.'

'Three days? Are you kidding?'

'Actually, two and a half days to be precise.' Roy corrected himself, considering that Alok Singh was a stickler for perfection.

Mahinbhai, spoke next, 'How much time do you have for your knowledge gathering?'

'Not much. I have to submit the story latest by Thursday for its publication in the Independence Day issue on Monday, when these bars would be banned.'

'So, in effect, you have very little time left. Right?'

'Yes, sir,' Roy replied with a bit of hesitation. As a journalist his ego was getting hurt, he could not accept or communicate the fact that he had hit a dead end.

Mahinbhai interjected, 'The subject of dance bar does not begin and end with dance bars Roy. It is centred on prejudice. In case you have some time tomorrow, you can drop by my office and I might have something to share. Just give me a call in case you are coming. Alok has my number.'

Roy nodded in agreement and said, 'I will definitely like to understand in detail how you are placing prejudice in the context. But if I may say so, I am curious to know how you know about this business.'

Mahinbhai replied flatly, 'I am a lawyer and my firm does some pro bono work for the bar dancers in this area.'

'Oh. *Mahin bhai*! I mean, are you Mr Mahendra Goradia of Goradia, Bengzon and Lall by any chance?' Elated, Roy connected the dots and wanted to double-check.

'Yes, I am.'

'By Jove! What a coincidence. I have an appointment with you through the recommendation of the ED of Commerce Bank tomorrow morning.'

The Untold Tale

Roy reached the office of Goradia, Bengzon and Lall, Attorneys & Counsellors-at-Law on the ninth floor of the Tower Chambers at Nariman Point at the appointed time. When he announced his name to the receptionist at the front desk of this elegantly furnished law firm, a smartly dressed office boy escorted him to an elderly secretary, who in turn walked him through to the corner office of Mahendra Goradia.

The room offered a panoramic view of the vast expanse of the Arabian Sea. Sitting across Mahendra Goradia, Roy could see the Governor's bungalow dotted with trees at the tip of Walkeshwar Road, with the not so tranquil Arabian Sea in the foreground, as the morning weather was unusually bleak with a not-so-clear sky carrying the hangover of the stormy weather of the past week. Despite that, Mumbai from this vantage point camouflaged her wounds well, and to any observer she would still look ravishing, contemplated Roy.

'Isn't the view nice?' observed Goradia, to this young and handsome journalist as if he could read Roy's mind.

'Indeed. It is.'

'At night, it's even more heavenly, especially with a clear sky,' the senior attorney stated.

'I guess it would.'

'Life too plays tricks like this on us ... same as this view. What you witness from a distance may not always be the same once you go nearer or vice versa,' said Goradia with a wistful look in his eyes.

'It's a question of perspective, sir. If you allow me to say so.'

'I couldn't agree with you more, my dear young man,' Goradia seconded Roy's observation. 'By the way, what would you like to have? Coffee? Or, tea?'

'Coffee would be fine, sir.'

'Sylvia, can you organise some coffee in the library please. We should be reaching there soon. Kindly inform Mrs Rao that we will be visiting her domain.' Goradia spoke on the intercom to his secretary unhurriedly, in a very soft voice. He then turned to Roy and said, 'Mrs Rao is our librarian, a very competent lady. Come Roy, let's go to the library.'

Amidst the receipts of venerated utterances of 'Good Morning Sir' – the customary morning salutation offered by everyone working in this prestigious and well-known law firm – Mahendra Goradia walked Roy through its spacious well-appointed offices to the library a floor above. En route to the library, he said, by way of introducing his law firm to Roy, 'We occupy three floors. This one is for the seniors. Library and bigger formal conference rooms are on the tenth. We have paralegals and juniors on the eighth. We mainly do Corporate Law including M&A and Cross-Border, Commercial, Capital Markets, Dispute Resolution, Patents, so on and so forth. And, we have a very large pro bono portfolio as well. We take our pro bono work very seriously and pursue it judiciously. We broadly work on the areas of injustice against "disadvantaged women" and "underprivileged children."'

The library was really impressive, covering half of the tenth floor. Roy could see at least half-a-dozen lawyers using the library.

Goradia took him to one corner of the room. Roy saw before him a floor-to-ceiling massive bookshelf indexed with titles such as Dance Bar, Permit Room, Mujra, De-notified Tribes of India, Criminal Tribes of India, Para-Prostitution in India, Thugees, History of the East India Company in India, Adult Entertainment, Trafficking, Customs and Rituals of the Tribes, and so on and so forth. The bookshelf contained numerous old and new books, magazines, folder files probably containing clippings of various newspapers and magazines of India and abroad, travelogues and memoirs. Roy even saw a few videotapes and DVDs of documentary films. When he looked at the collection closely, he was in fact amazed to see that one of the DVDs, *The Courtesans of Bombay,* was produced by Merchant Ivory Productions. As his eyes hurriedly scanned the titles of books and magazines, he knew that he had found a treasure-trove.

While coffee was being served, Goradia indicated Roy to a secluded cosy seating arrangement for two near a large window overlooking the Arabian Sea and also close to that particular bookshelf.

Once both of them had settled down, Mahendra Goradia took a sip of his black coffee and excused the bearer. He then turned around and asked Roy, 'Young man, I know you are eager to start your research but in case you have a bit of time for me, I would like to narrate a story that might help you in your research. Do you think you have some time for that?'

'Kindly go ahead, sir. And oh! Also permit me to use your library as long as I can for today and tomorrow. This, I have a feeling, will be very helpful.'

Goradia nodded and promised that he would keep Mrs Rao informed of Roy's request once his narration was over. He then said, 'The story I am going to narrate took place about three decades ago in this city. It was around the Christmas vacation of that particular year. Inder Kumar Gajanan Singh – the young, handsome, and dashing heir of one of India's erstwhile princely families, well-known for their association with heritage hotels and love for the game of polo – came to Bombay en route to England while returning to his university. He had planned for a couple of days' break in the city to relax and then visit one of his aunts staying in Goa before proceeding to England. Bombay, at that point of time, to this young man and many more of his generation, was an epitome of permissiveness. On that particular night, Inder Kumar wanted to witness the nightlife of Bombay that he had heard so much about.'

'Interesting!' Roy interjected.

'This city has had a long history of adult entertainment, such as cabaret shows since pre-independence days. Some of the finest cabaret shows were held at a now defunct classy top-floor restaurant in the Eros Cinema building near Churchgate Railway Station. Ritz Hotel as well as Ambassador Hotel had regular cabaret shows even two decades after our independence. The original Blue Nile Club, at New Marine Lines, would host a bevy of striptease artists; notable among them was an Anglo-Burmese dancer, Tamiko. As it was still the period when strict rules of prohibition were enacted, the customers at Blue Nile would watch her cabaret sipping either tea or coffee, which was considered to be the embodiment of sophistication. It would be very erroneous to believe that Bombay or Mumbai, whichever name we call this city by, was a pristine city before the dance bars invaded it.'

Roy nodded his head thoughtfully and asked, 'Do you think references of such performances would be available with you in some newspaper or magazine clips or books in your archive?'

Goradia said, 'They should be.'

Roy took out his notepad, made a note and requested Goradia to continue with his story and said, 'Hope you will not mind sir if sometimes I interrupt and ask questions or take notes. I might like to record you even for my ready reference.'

Goradia nodded and continued with his story, 'By the last quarter of 1970s, a copycat venue of the Blue Nile came up in the Colaba Market area. However, it was absolutely and completely downmarket, in comparison to the original one and the patrons were of a different breed altogether. They lacked taste and refinement and demanded more skin. Sometime later, to the best of my knowledge, Fishermen's Wharf, the first discotheque-cum-night club in Worli was established and was confirmed to be bankrolled by Iqbal Mirchi. If my memory serves me right, Caesar's Palace and Sonia Mahal were the two very popular permit room-cum-beer bars in Bombay at that time. These were the precursors to the modern day dance bars, which came into being in their current avatar around early to mid 1980s.'

Roy interjected, 'What do you think sparked it all off?'

'The creation of dance bars had roots in the Maharashtra government's liquor license policy as well as in latent support by the then government to increase the consumption of liquor after the so-called abolition of the prohibition. After the province of Maharashtra was formed by dividing the earlier Bombay Presidency, the state modified its liquor policy and the word *prohibition* was replaced by *permit*. Certain chosen places, such as selected hotels or restaurants, were given *permits* and could serve only beer, and were called *permit rooms* or *beer bars*. Individual adults having licenses or permits could visit these permit rooms or beer bars to drink beer. However, soon the expression *permit room* lost its relevance, as in its eagerness to increase sales ...'

Roy conjectured, 'I would imagine that indiscriminate licences were given to hotels and restaurants to serve liquor by the authorities and thereby to try and enhance revenue for the state?'

Goradia nodded in agreement and continued with his story, 'Yes, you are absolutely correct. You can refer to certain interviews and briefs we have preserved in our library ... most of these are authored by noted legal luminaries and their dedicated teams who made huge contributions to the movement of preservation of the rights of dancers of Mumbai's dance bars. What we did as a firm was different but their contribution was terrific. Anyway, to come back to the point we were discussing, it was during this period that some of the permit rooms started adopting sales promotion techniques to attract more and more customers. The government did not stop them, or I would say, turned a blind eye to such efforts for reasons best known to them. Because increased liquor sales translated in increased excise revenue for the state. The permit rooms very quickly introduced live orchestra. Then they added mimicry performances to their repertoire. And lastly, when they tested no resistance from the authorities, they brought in service waitresses.'

Roy raised his left hand index finger, 'So, this is how the nomenclature of a permit room transitioned from permit room to beer bar to ladies bar ... I understand.'

Goradia nodded, 'Over time, these sales promotion innovations too lost their sheen. The permit room owners then introduced live dance performances with recorded music. Profits soared. At the same time, the Hindi movie industry was also going through its transformations. They started introducing raunchy songs and dances termed as *item numbers*. The permit rooms or beer bars or ladies bars started copying those song and dance routines. Sales skyrocketed. The profit margin encouraged the owners of various Irani Cafes, Udipi Restaurants, and Punjabi Dhabas in the city to hurriedly convert their restaurants to permit rooms and subsequently to dance bars.'

Roy asked, 'What about the licences?'

Goradia replied, 'The licences to hold performances under Bombay Police Act 1951 in such permit rooms were issued under, "Rules for Licensing and Controlling Places of Public Amusements (other than cinemas) and Performances for Public Amusement including Melas and Tamashas, (1960)" by the police. Moreover, I think on the last count, the total number of licenses required by a dance bar from various authorities to legally conduct its business was eighteen. I have to check the exact number from the team handling it though.'

'How many permit rooms converted themselves into dance bars at that point of time?'

'Initially, there were about twenty to thirty odd dance bars till about three quarters of 1980s. However, within the next decade, the number increased tenfold to more than two hundred.'

'What would be the current numbers?'

'Currently, there are around thirteen hundred dance bars in the state of Maharashtra. I think Magnet, Dark Horse, Red Rose, and a few others were the early birds and well-known ones in the dance bar circuit.'

Roy was mildly surprised, 'In slightly over twenty years, the number of dance bars went up from thirty to thirteen hundred? What a phenomenal growth! And, you want me to believe that authorities woke up only now?'

'Yes. You are right. I will come to that. Now, listen carefully. As opposed to mushrooming of permit rooms and conversion of traditional eating joints to permit rooms and subsequently to dance bars, there was another aspect to this scenario.'

'And what would that be?' Roy asked. He could feel that a greater dimension would be revealing itself soon.

Goradia replied, 'Even before the permit rooms started operating in Bombay, Noor Mohammad-Beig Mohammad Compound, in short NB Compound, or simply Compound, or at times referred to as Banarasi Chawl, opposite the "Congress House" near Kennedy Bridge close to Opera House, in South Bombay, used to cater to the mujra lovers. This was the hot spot. Another hot spot was a few select pockets of Foras Road near Bombay Central. Of course, as usual, there were some downmarket varieties available in the city's red-light areas as well.'

Roy piped in excitedly, 'By Jove, our office photographer told me that I should visit Congress House to get my story.'

Goradia stared at Roy. He then said, 'I will come to it. Mujrawalis or Agrawalis, as these performers were generally known, were from Uttar Pradesh, Madhya Pradesh, and Rajasthan, the central Indian provinces and their bordering areas. All such dancers and singers occupied the tenements at the Compound or Banarasi Chawl, near Opera House close to Kennedy Bridge and also stayed at Bachchu Bhai ki Wadi, Banaras ki Gali, at Foras Road, near Mumbai Central.'

'So, you mean to say we have Banarasi Chawl or Compound and Banaras ki Gali ... two different entities. Interesting.'

Goradia nodded and continued, 'Since very early twentieth century, the cotton barons of Bombay had patronised mujra. Moreover, the film stars, movie producers and financiers, diamond merchants, share brokers, builders, and the underworld, all of them had taken to mujra-mehfil*s* like fish to water. Bombay was steadily emerging as the epicentre of the sub-continental entertainment world. Movie industry was flourishing. Bombay was also positioning itself as the financial capital of our country. All these factors attracted a section of traditional entertainers from the central Indian provinces of Madhya Pradesh, Uttar Pradesh, and Rajasthan, like any other professionals, to venture into the city for new business opportunities. Some of the prominent traditional performing communities that started migrating to Bombay were Kanjar, Banchra, Kabootam, Bedia, Nat and Rajnat who mostly followed Hinduism, and Deradar who followed Islam. These entertainers mainly migrated to Bombay's Compound and Foras Road and Calcutta's Sonagachhi and Boubazar areas.'

Roy was bewildered, 'But I've never heard of them!'

'Don't get worried. Most of us are not aware of the vastness and complexities of our country. But these are real people we are talking about. And, just hold on to your thoughts. You will find the answers to all of them.' He then pointed to the bookshelf and said emphatically, 'Once my monologue is over, please go through the books and magazines here ... you will have the necessary corroborations.'

Roy smiled, 'Such monologues are highly illuminative and very welcome. Please don't even think of discontinuing.'

Goradia continued, 'The NB Compound used to rock after sunset; mellifluous tunes, staccato rhythms of percussion, and the tinkling sound of *ghunghroos,* heady mix. Interestingly, a very large section of young mujra dancers, to cater to the new demand, sought jobs in the dance bar circuit later on. Keep that in mind for further reference.'

Goradia paused and then went on. 'And, let me correct a generally held misconception. In media, whenever I see either mujra or bar dancers being reported or discussed about, I come across the name Congress House, which is near Kennedy Bridge, as their bastion. This is utterly incorrect. As far as I can remember, neither mujra performers nor any other dancers ever stayed at Congress House. It is the NB Compound where they used to reside and some of them reside there even today. NB Compound is situated in the same lane but opposite to Congress House.'

Roy interjected, 'Since the time I heard about it, I was wondering about the issue. Incongruous, isn't it?'

'Correct. Actually, what must have happened, I think, is that over the years for ease of locating the area, the dancers as well as the connoisseurs of mujra, possibly used to direct their chauffeurs or taxi drivers to take them near Congress House. That was how possibly the misconception took root. It is high time that is corrected. It is a shame that no one from our vigilant media ever really looked into it. A revered institution such as Congress House, associated with the genesis of the venerated Indian National Congress is somewhat maligned, unnecessarily. One of our staff, who stays in that area, once said, and I quote, "Congress House has nothing to do with mujra. There are about seven buildings in Congress House Compound and they are occupied by respectable families. No hanky-panky." It is the same aversion to exploring the details, as well as not doing first-hand fact-finding, that we term all mujra performers as well as bar dancers as harlots in one single stroke. It is so easy to act as Goebbels and malign by twisting facts to suit your purpose.'

Roy said, 'I couldn't have found a better source for this untold story, I think I know now where I must start digging. But, sir, what happened to that prince?'

Goradia, 'Ah, yes! We had left him on his way to a bar, so we need to cut the long story short but before that would you like to order lunch or want to have a cup of coffee?'

'Coffee would be fine.'

'Okay, eventually the hero of our current story, Prince Inder Kumar Gajanan Singh, reached NB Compound sometime around midnight via the usual cabaret and nightclub routes. The dashing young man graced the mehfil at Sushila Bai's room on the third floor of the building. This was where he met Munni. Munni, exquisitely beautiful, and gregarious, God's gift to earth; Inder Kumar, handsome, debonair, gallant and courteous Rajput. The atmosphere inside the mehfil became a cracker of an evening. The inevitable happened. Cupid released all his arrows. Prince Inder Kumar and Munni fell in love. They thought of marriage. Inder Kumar never reached either Goa or London. After about a fortnight, a worried Gajanan Singh senior landed in Bombay in search of his eldest son ... I recess my story here. You tell me what would have happened next?' Goradia asked, his eyes twinkling.

'Who? Me?' Roy was caught off-guard. 'Well, how could I? It's so speculative. It could have various permutations.' Roy tried evading the question though it had stimulated his brain.

'Indulge me, son. Let me see how your thought process works. In the meantime, let's have the coffee served,' Goradia coaxed Roy.

Goradia walked to the librarian. Roy puzzled over what he thought would have happened. When the senior lawyer came back, Roy was still frowning. 'They eloped and got married?' Roy answered tentatively.

'A possibility, but what else?' Goradia was non-committal.

'Father objected. Money came into play,' Roy was less tentative this time.

'A plot for a pot-boiler of a Hindi movie?' Mahendra Goradia raised his eyebrows.

'You don't agree?' Roy questioned. 'It is but natural. How could such a marriage be approved in an erstwhile princely family so many years ago, counting the prejudice and social stigma attached to the girl being a mujrawali?' Roy became even more confident and stated passionately.

'Predictable reply, good try, I suppose. Considering that even the modern day social scientists as well as policy makers, mostly, are not careful about these understandings, I am not at all disappointed with your reply. It has confirmed my belief even more ...' Goradia paused. Roy looked puzzled. A peon walked in with the coffee tray, the aroma permeating the library corner. After the coffee was served, Goradia continued, 'Roy, we should not be presumptuous. Mostly, the current administration displayed assumptive behaviour on the topic of dance bar and thereby they have made mistakes. They are socially myopic. They do not reflect enough maturity in their thoughts as well as in their actions to nurture a nation and handle its social issues like dance bars.'

Roy looked intently at Mahendra Goradia.

Goradia continued, 'The strong and forceful opposition to the marriage came actually from Munni's family.'

'What? Why?' asked Roy, his curiosity peaked. 'The girl would have been fortunate enough to be associated with a respectable family with high social standing,' he commented with disbelief.

'As we have already discussed, Inder Kumar never wanted to have Munni as his keep but wanted to marry her. However, the tradition from the girl's side prohibits marriage. If Inder Kumar wished to have her as a keep, her family would have agreed; but not on marriage. Moreover, Munni was madly in love with Inder Kumar and was eager for marriage, which was considered an unpardonable sin in her community,' replied Goradia matter-of-factly.

'Are you serious? Tradition prohibits marriage! What nonsense are we talking sir, with due respect? Okay, I have heard about the *Devadasi* system, but that was practised in the temples of southern India years ago. I have never heard of such a thing in my life, and that too in modern independent India. It's insane. In modern times and social structure, how could the inhumane tradition be in force?' Roy became impatient. After a slight pause, he provoked Goradia with his ultimate question, 'And even if it does, how is it relevant to the dance bars?'

Mahendra Goradia looked at his watch, and then looked up and saw a very determined face eager to learn and resolve issues. 'Roy! Your question has two parts; the first being the communities rejecting the institution of marriage. Let me tell you that even in today's India it is true ... especially among Bedia, Nat, Kabootam, and their sub castes from Madhya Pradesh, Uttar Pradesh and Rajasthan; marriage for girls is not at all acceptable. Their girls would rather be someone's keep. The keepers of the girls are called pagadwala*s* and the system is known as *Baithana*. Pagadwala is someone who pays a monthly salary, pagad, for the girl to be monogamous with the person. *Baithana* means to keep. These girls very carefully catch such men who are usually good looking, rich and married. They feel married men are easy prey and more stable than young and un-married men, who are volatile and fickle. Looks are important too, because the progeny then has that much more chance of being good looking. In these communities, a girl's birth is highly rejoiced and a baby boy is frowned upon. For your information, these girls do not part with their children. The *pagadwala* never really has control over the children. It is the mother, the girl, who keeps the offspring'.

Roy was getting incrementally fascinated listening to what Mahendra Goradia had to say.

Goradia again looked at his watch, took a pause, thought for a moment, and then said, 'Roy, I have a pre-confirmed conference call, so if you allow me some time and meanwhile you browse through the books to familiarise yourself, I shall be back in a jiffy. I shall also ask for working lunch to be served here.'

Goradia went out of the library.

Roy was mulling over Goradia's last statement and thought, why on earth would tradition forbid marriage and that too in today's India. Where did dance bar fit in? What nonsense was that? He started walking towards the bookshelf to browse through the books.

'Do not be in a hurry,' cautioned Goradia while they were having their lunch. 'It is a very serious and complicated social issue. The root cause of the problem very surely and easily is the devilish British Imperial Act: *The Criminal Tribes Act, 1871* and its successive amendments. This is the Act that broke the backbone of over one hundred and twenty-five Indian communities, castes, and tribes nearly one hundred and thirty odd years ago. Go through the Act. It is on the third row of the bookshelf.' Goradia gestured with his thumb towards the bookshelf and took a sip of his soup.

'This Act branded people from these groups as hereditary criminals or in simple words as "born criminals." These people were disallowed to pursue any gainful employment as well as any business by the British administration. They were kept under constant police watch by the British. Local zamindars were made responsible for their good conduct, or else were severely penalised by the British administration. At the time of our independence in 1947, there were over thirteen million people in this category. You are a member of the media of modern India ... please go back and re-study your history now,' said Goradia very politely yet pointedly. Then he chided Roy for ignoring his food, 'Come on son. Have your food. You would not solve this deep-rooted problem by foregoing your lunch.'

Roy took a deep breath and said, 'Yes.'

Goradia continued, 'Though very limited in number, but in certain scholarly studies you would find references of special settlements that had been created by the British in various parts of India to segregate and house these communities away from the mainstream Indian life. Adolf Hitler was not the first to create and use the concept of ghetto. Queen's England had created ghettos in Meerut, Jabalpur, Hubli, Sholapur, Bijapur, Ahmadabad, and in many other places to purify the souls of these so-called *born criminals* with the help of the Salvation Army, long before the Second World War.'

Roy hurriedly finished the remaining of his sandwich and started scribbling notes and said, 'I am an Indian. By birth, I am part British. My mother is British. I am feeling horrible now. I had no idea about all these.'

Goradia smiled and patted Roy's hand. 'I know that Roy. Don't you worry! Listen to the untold tale ... Just imagine, these communities were kept completely quarantined from the mainline Indian society for over seven decades by the force of British Law under the surveillance of the Salvation Army and zamindars. The British kept this as one of their many secrets. It is a pity that Indian history books published after we attained Independence do not even talk about the issue, forget understanding the total socio-political and socio-economic ramifications that ensued.'

Roy nodded and scribbled in his notepad that he needed to research this aspect thoroughly.

Goradia continued calmly yet passionately, 'Roy, when you are given the responsibility of writing a story, a story such as this, you must dig. Dig deep. You will be surprised with what the catalyst was and who set off such a chain of events that our society has permanently been affected. Read the reference books, I have them all in the library ... and in case you get tired listening to my monologue, as I said earlier, please let me know ...'

Roy immediately objected and said, 'Tired? Me? No. Are you feeling tired, sir? In that case, we should stop.'

'Okay!' responded the senior luminary. 'To put the matter further into perspective, as an aftermath of the Sepoy Mutiny of 1857, which we can safely term as India's first war of independence, the British administration was determined in suppressing all remaining free-spirited Indians. Secondly, the British wanted a settled village society under the control of the conservative and pro-British zamindars, the permanent settlement. They knew that it would make the governing of this huge continent less cumbersome and less tedious. They further planned to club a number of villages to form a district and by clubbing a few districts to form a province. They also decided to hold a census in the Indian sub-continent to have a firm grip over the Indian population. Through the census, they actually wanted to map the entire socio-economic and socio-cultural practices prevalent in India during that point of time so that they could adjust their strategy for dominating this country accordingly. The work on the first Indian census began immediately after the Sepoy Mutiny around 1860 and concluded in 1871. The results of the first Indian census were published in 1872.

'As you know, a census is the process of obtaining information about every member of a population including his or her vocation. Hence, during the conclusion of the first Indian census and the introduction of the Criminal Tribes Act in 1871, jurist James Fitzjames Stephen – uncle of Virginia Woolf, the renowned writer – who formulated the Indian Evidence Act, 1872, and also wrote the book, *Liberty, Equality, Fraternity* made a startling comment. You can refer to the books on the shelf. He observed that *if there is caste-based work destiny, such as a carpenter's son will be a carpenter, a cultivator's son will be a cultivator, an ironsmith will hereditarily pass on his trade, by the same logic, crime as a trade in India will be hereditary. Criminals are born to it and must commit it;* which if one cares to analyse is such a horrendous observation.

'However, as a result of it, simultaneous to the first Indian census, the British promulgated the Criminal Tribes Act, 1871. The Act was directed at those sections of the population of India which the British Administration was not comfortable with and expunged these people from life for good, branding them as born criminals. These Indian communities, castes, and tribes were, simply put, forcefully socially excluded by the British. In those times, whoever opposed the British colonial expansion or was not fitting into the British administration's conception of a model citizen was perceived as a potential criminal.'

Roy made a sharp comment, 'How come in modern India we never discuss such history?'

Goradia smiled and said, 'Listen to the whole story and you be the catalyst for propagating it. ... Many of the wandering minstrels, fakirs, petty traders, rustic transporters, village charmers, musicians, dancers, and even disbanded groups of soldiers of defeated Indian kingdoms, camp-followers, were included in the list of the Criminal Tribes Act, 1871, and in its later amendments. The Act was initially promulgated in the then

Central Indian Province, consisting of the current Uttar Pradesh, Madhya Pradesh and Rajasthan, and was slowly extended to whole of the then India. The fiercely independent "North West Frontier Men" too were declared criminals.'

The senior counsel leaned closer towards Roy and said, 'Please concentrate and listen very carefully ... due to social exclusion forced by the Criminal Tribes Act, men of these communities were either unable to find employment on account of political bias or were historically prevented from getting into gainful employment or business because of social prejudices. Now since the men were unable to earn, the responsibilities mainly rested with the women. For nearly seven decades, women from a handful of communities of performers, who were also a part of over one hundred and twenty-five socially excluded communities, had to please the rapacious zamindars and the gentries during British rule to earn a living for their families. These women were defenceless and were forced to become harlots and concubines. They were the bread earners.'

Pallavi's comment about who would run her house if she did not earn flashed in Roy's mind. The reference points were connecting, he thought.

Goradia continued, 'Socio-economic and socio-political pressures forced these women to live as concubines or harlots because without the zamindars' permission these communities could do nothing, not even move out of their ghetto-like settlements with the Salvation Army controlling their movements. In fact, this socio-political reason was the biggest deterrent in the lives of these simple people who were simply trying to live.

'Hence, those handful of communities, as I have mentioned earlier, which had some latent tendencies of concubinage and harlotry took the easy way out and started degenerating socially.

The British administration knew about it but did nothing, as it suited their purpose of governing a foreign land. Slowly, the Khaps, the caste panchayats, along with the influential and unscrupulous male members of these communities and tribes, took advantage of the situation and a sort of a verbal decree was promulgated that the girls should not get married and would only be allowed to pursue their traditional community practice of concubinage. The caste panchayats and the male members saw their economic prosperity in the process. That they were debarred from working for nearly seventy years under British had made them totally lazy, while their women earned for them. And, I know such practices do happen today as well.'

Goradia continued, 'Let me take you down the pages of history a little more before we come to the present century. Apart from branding the free-spirited and rustic Indians as criminals for self-benefit, the British imperialistic administration had also deliberately overlooked the atrocities within the communities of the castes and tribes because the British regime was involved in, what people would term today as institutionalised trafficking, from these communities, in all likelihood.

'After India's first war of Independence in 1857, the British were out to get us. Elaborate schemes to de-humanise the Indian society were made, so that it would become easy for them to dominate the country. They formalised a process through which all British and other European soldiers in India were permitted and encouraged to hold and possess young Indian girls as concubines or even as prostitutes for their own carnal pleasure. The administration created an official system under the Contagious Diseases Act, throughout the 1860s, in conjunction with Cantonment Regulations, and a specified number of Indian girls were placed with each army regiment in India for providing carnal pleasures to the British officers. These women were kept in such appointed houses called *chaklas*. These women were allowed to consort with British soldiers only, and were registered by the Cantonment Magistrate, and tickets of licence were given to them. Besides the *chakla*, the brothel, there was in each and every Cantonment a prison-like hospital called *Lock Hospital*, in which the patients, generally these girls, were confined against their will for check-up and treatment of sexually transmitted diseases. These women were obliged to go regularly to these Lock Hospitals, for examination, due to the prevalence of veneral diseases among the British troops. Invariably, such unfortunate women were from rural areas and mostly from marginalised and poor communities. These women were placed under a lady brothel-keeper, called the *mahaldarni,* whom the villagers used to refer to as *Chaklc ki Choudurayen.* One of her duties, among others, comprised procuring more such women as and when required for the *chakla*.

'Promulgation of indigenous communities as criminal tribes and allowing their degeneration made it easy for the British to procure women as prostitutes for their solders from such communities as well.'

Mahendra Goradia looked at Roy, who was listening attentively drinking in every word. Taking a deep breath, he said, 'Coming back to the atrocities committed even in 21st century India within such communities, we had documented a case study of a girl called Neelam. I would like to narrate it to you as it will help you understand the ramifications better.'

Neelam's Story

Neelam had an oval face with a high forehead. Her cute and small nose had given a character to her face. Her skin had the hue of bronze. Her hair had turned reddish brown at the edges without proper care, as she was unable to oil her hair ever since she was brought at the *panchganga* venue.

Just to break her resolve, she was not given food for the last few days. Yet, her glands had oozed sufficient juices that had kept her going. Despite her servitude, she was a deliciously attractive woman. She would have made a very alluring concubine and could have made a lot of money for herself, for her family, as well as for the community. Yet, she rebelled, and the biradari had to punish her for being a rebel.

With her veil lowered, she was forced to balance a huge stone on her head under the dry, hot afternoon sun and was made to stand still. She was not given even a morsel of food, while everybody else around her feasted. Had she failed to keep the rock balanced properly on her head till the community feast was over, she would have been publicly lashed.

The Khap was in progress.

Neelam had to pay the price for marrying, being faithful to her husband and for refusing to become a harlot.

Neelam had declared to her friends that she was happy in her marriage. She advised them to get married, instead of obeying the community rule of joining harlotry and becoming a sexually profligate woman. How could the Khap tolerate such propaganda? The *panchganga* had to react, or else its hold over the entire community would be shaken.

Community members from all the nearby villages were invited to gather and to take part in the feast along with the members of the Khap. Families who were reluctant to join the feast, even though they were marginal in numbers, were issued an order akin to warrants and some Khap members were sent to fetch them, specially the women, if necessary, by force.

Neelam was the worst sufferer. She did not want to leave her husband who belonged to a different community. She loved him. He was a caring and loving man. After listening to her 'case' the Khap fined her family for allowing her to marry. The family had no option left but to auction its cows and goats as well as the very small patch of land that had been bought recently with savings from its meagre income of selling milk, and thereby pay a part of the fine imposed. Else, the family would have been excommunicated, thrown out of the village, and their property would have been confiscated. After the family paid the fine, it was asked to leave the venue of the *panchganga,* the council of community leaders.

And then Neelam was put on sale to recover the balance amount of the fine.

She was made to stand in an open field under the sun. Her veil had already been taken off. Elderly women from the community came forward and lowered her sari suggestively as far below her navel as possible to display her smooth and flat belly with no stretch marks, indicating no pregnancy. Men, from her community, intending to take part in the auction came forward and groped her butt and felt her thighs for their firmness. Throughout the auction, she was leered at. Her womanhood was flaunted and exposed in the worst possible manner through vulgar public display so that she could fetch the highest possible price at the auction.

The bidding process started with the auctioneer shouting prices, 'Rupees five thousand ... going ... six thousand ... going ... seven thousand ... going ... eight thousand ... gone.' Bangilal, the man who bought Neelam by paying eight thousand rupees, immediately took her to Delhi and sold her off to a brothel keeper for triple the amount.

Little was known about Neelam's fate thereafter. At least the Khap was no longer interested in her. They wanted to make a power statement and made it. Some said that Neelam's husband fought tooth and nail through legal processes and got reunited with his wife after some years and they were residing on the outskirts of Delhi. Some said she died of evil diseases. *Any which way who the hell cared,* was the attitude displayed by the whole biradari.

The then state administrative machinery had behaved predictably: mute and gutless. It was an anachronism. In independent India, on the one hand the community people were harassed on the silliest of pretexts by being stigmatised as born criminals by the police with its traditional mindset, and on the other, gross social misadventures were overlooked by the same police and administration in the name of not intruding upon community traditions. The fact remained that the social ambivalence to deal with such kind of malefic activities required political will, which, simply put, was tremendously lacking because it needed a strong resolve on the part of the opinion leaders to continuously provide educational, economic, social, and infrastructural reforms for the oppressed.

Roy appeared shocked at Goradia's narration.

The veteran lawyer continued, 'Son not just this example, we uncovered more inhuman and barbaric punishments meted out by the Khaps on the pretext of justice and fair play. The Khap had various devious ways of punishing the rebels and extracting its pounds of flesh, such as *tel–kadhahi* oath, *khunita* oath, and so on. *Sanch ko aanch nahi*, they would say that is, Truth is without blemish. Take the oath and prove it.'

'In *tel-kadhahi* oath, a large quantity of mustard oil was poured into a big cauldron and heated until it boiled furiously. Depending on the Khap's relationship with the accused, this form of testing the innocence was used. The accused was made to take *tel-kadhahi* oath when the Khap wanted to prove the former guilty. A very small copper coin was dropped into the cauldron of boiling mustard oil. After getting the defendant bathed, he or she was asked to trace and to retrieve the small coin out of the cauldron. While retrieving the coin, if the accused uttered a single murmur or if the accused's hand got burnt, which generally was the case, the person was pronounced guilty as charged.

Khunita, or *belcha*, or shovel, is an iron tool generally weighing about two and a half to three kilograms. For the oath-taking procedure, it was first heated in fire. As usual the accused was bathed, and then five fig leaves were tied on his or her right palm and the person was asked to walk seven steps holding the red hot shovel on the right palm. The trick here was to tie bigger and thicker leaves on the defendant's palm and heat the shovel a little less, if you wanted to prove the person innocent. Otherwise, very small and thin fig leaves were tied so that the red hot iron shovel burned the leaves as well as the palm of the accused. Predictably, in the process, the person was proclaimed guilty by the Khap.

'Essentially, through all these methods, Khap members had terrorised the community,' Goradia paused for breath. The young journalist in front of him was soaking it all up and Goradia thought he should lay the whole picture clearly before this eager listener. What Goradia did not know was that his listener was also rationalising for the girls in the dance bar continuing there; that the memory of one particular girl was intruding his thoughts. He was amazed how the dancing girls endured the societal degeneration and had not revolted en masse. How the administrative machinery in 21st century India kept mum. Roy's admiration for Pallavi grew further.

The Impression

Goradia continued, 'As I said, the British saw an easy opportunity to degenerate the morality, which helped them rule our country easily. More unfortunate was the fact that after gaining Independence, we did nothing to correct the situation. So, this was the precious reason of practising a degenerated community tradition for over a century till now, that prohibited Munni to marry Inder Kumar.' Goradia looked at the contemplative figure of Roy.

By now, the lunch was over. Leaning back in his chair, Goradia said, 'The Criminal Tribes Act, 1871, and all its subsequent amendments were repealed after we became independent. The Habitual Offenders Act replaced it, which, except the premise that an entire community can be born criminal, is more or less same as the Criminal Tribes Act. With the abolition of the Criminal Tribes Act, these communities today are called 'De-Notified Tribes' or DNTs or *Vimuktya Jati* in the bureaucratic circles. Independence of our country and denotification of these communities has not ended their misery. The biased attitude towards them continues even today within our society. One does know for sure that the Criminal Tribes Act, 1871, and its amendments are part of the syllabus leading to discussion of crime watch in police training academies. The trickle-down effect being that every time there is a crime in the vicinity, the DNTs become the first suspect. The communities are still vulnerable, even today, in independent India. The British had confiscated the land possessed by them and these communities were forced to live in the ghetto-like so-called correctional technical schools under the supervision of the Salvation Army for nearly seven decades. So these people have mostly lost the habit of cultivation.

'The links between my story and the ban on dance bars are manifold and at multiple levels. That's why I made the earlier comment regarding our policy makers being presumptuous and ill-informed. The first and foremost fact is that in the Mumbai dance bars we have majority of the dancers from these DNT communities and tribes emerging out of Madhya Pradesh, Uttar Pradesh, and Rajasthan. From a situation of concubinage, harlotry, and prostitution, working as a dancer in a dance bar is a much safer option for these women, as they are not forced to deal with the demand for retailing physical favours and dancing in a bar is financially more rewarding.'

Roy had formed an impression by now. He was now looking for a conclusion. He felt restless. This was more than what he had bargained for. He knew that Kumudini would feel vindicated. He leaned forward and asked urgently, 'What more, Sir?'

Goradia obliged, 'To start with, show me a comprehensive list of bar dancers or performers and prove that the majority of them are foreign nationals as allegedly claimed at one point of time by politicians and bureaucrats as a reason for banning the dance bars. Where is the record? Don't show me sporadic instances. Moreover, if foreign nationals have managed to come into the Mumbai dance bars, the first and foremost failure is of immigration services and security forces and not a fault of dance bars. The control mechanism has failed. On the contrary, I am sure, the majority of the dancers, currently performing in the bars, would belong to certain castes, tribes, and communities we have discussed before and they would hail from that particular geographic region of India, especially the central provinces of India, and are mostly DNTs. The root cause of their exploitation lies at that originating point, in their communities, in their provinces, and in their torturous past; not surely in the dance bars. The need is to rehabilitate the DNTs honourably. Make a change in social attitude. Dance bar is only a manifestation. It is the end of the supply chain. If you stop the dance bars, some new genre of such entertainment will evolve because the communities have to survive, or else the girls will possibly be forced into hardcore flesh trade. It would be like jumping from the frying pan into the fire. From a somewhat barricaded and protective situation of a dance bar, you are pushing the girl to unknown situations with hardly any control mechanism working. I don't think wise and mature policy makers should do that. I am not advocating promotion of dance bar business; but closing them is not a solution as long as the anomalies and atrocities in the communities are not sorted out. These people need livelihood; they need our active participation to include them in our lives.'

Nodding his head, Roy wrote the point down. Goradia's tone changed, his sentences were more urgent, the bright spark in his eyes made Roy wonder how his opponents could bear his gaze in the courtroom.

'Secondly,' Goradia continued, 'please produce a list of total number of dance bars in existence in Mumbai as well as in Maharashtra currently. How many of them have all the valid licences? Whose fault is that? In any case, the dance bars in Mumbai and Maharashtra came into existence only because of a definite impetus for promoting liquor sales in the province by the government itself and not because of the dancers.

'Third is the question of prostitution in dance bars. How conclusive is the proof? Maligning is very easy. If we are to stop dance bars because of those being the dens of flesh trade, what are we doing about nefarious activities in Mumbai's red light areas? And what about the various massage and beauty parlours and escort services, which are being advertised with impunity in the national newspapers?'

Roy smiled and inwardly agreed to this very valuable argument.

'Dance bars being the den of criminals? Same question? How conclusive is the proof? Why would the criminals not use pubs, or country liquor bars, or coffee shops of five-star hotels? Why would they use only the dance bars as their meeting point or rendezvous spot? Kindly enlighten me?' Goradia questioned.

'The policy makers have raised the bogey of exploitation of women. How are dance bars exploiting the women? The argument that is being propagated is that the girls are forced into dancing in the bars. By whom? The exploitation is within their communities and in their originating states and is in existence for over centuries. These girls are very sensitive as well as secretive in revealing their caste identities because of the long history of debased practices in their communities and also because of fear of oppression at the community level. The moment they step out of their villages, they change their names, their identities. They adopt new names. They don't disclose their real identities most of the time. What have the local governments done sincerely about rehabilitation of these girls and addressing the social issue? The operative word being "sincerely." Policy makers are possibly wilfully shying away from tackling the problem at the community level – at the beginning of the supply chain,' remarked Mahendra Goradia.

Roy asked, 'Is there any textbook solution to this problem?'

'See, if we look around at Netherlands, Hungary, Germany, Switzerland, Czech Republic, there are ample models available to discuss and adopt as control mechanisms for the Mumbai dance bars. The way the United States controls running of "strip clubs" is also a model. Instead, someone thought of making it a political propagandist issue without providing any solution. Hence, the problem will always remain open ended.' Mahendra Goradia shook his head vigorously and concluded.

Roy looked at Mahendra Goradia and hesitated, but eventually he decided to ask the question that was nagging him all through their discussion. He thought for a while, weighed the pros and the cons, and then asked, 'Sir, your briefing is very effective. However, I have a question and am wondering if you will answer it without taking it personally. I mean no disrespect to you but I need to ask the question, if you don't mind? Can I sir?'

'Sure. Please go ahead,' replied Mahendra Goradia with a smile, gentle and cordial.

'How can you so authoritatively comment on dance bars and social exclusion, if I may ask?'

'I had expected this question at the beginning of our discussion Roy. Then, I thought, possibly Alok had briefed you about me. Therefore, I remained silent. Else, I would have clarified it long ago.'

Mahendra Goradia paused.

'To start with, our firm does pro bono work in some areas related to servitude and trafficking, and as a natural corollary, we have closely researched and examined the Mumbai dance bar issue. We are representing a portion of bar dancers through our pro bono work. We know of a lot of aspects on a first-hand basis. Second and most importantly, Prince Inder Kumar Gajanan Singh was a friend.

He still is a friend. He was in school with me in Dehradun, though a few years junior to me as well as Alok. In fact, he was in the same class as my younger brother. But, we picked up friendship. We had gone for shikar together ... did camping together. Inder's uncle was Alok's senior in the army. I also read a lot on the subject because of these reasons. There have been some pathbreaking studies done in India on social exclusion and DNTs; very importantly, seminal works of noted writers and social activists are available aplenty. I wish our policy makers read them seriously. Even a book on the strip clubs of the United States is a highly recommended study for you too. You can look them up on the shelf.'

'While you mentioned the US strip clubs, I recently heard from a source of mine from the central ministry that the ban on dance bars is also happening allegedly because the US Government is putting pressure on us to improve our rating on their watch list of "Trafficking in Persons." How will you react to this piece of information? My source from Delhi told me that the US State Department has linked certain release or restriction of aid with improvement of our ranking from the Tier 2 watch list. That would mean that the US would withhold non-humanitarian, non-trade-related foreign aid if we do not improve our records,' said Roy.

'Though I do not have first-hand knowledge, come to think of it, that could be a possibility. More so, when a dance bar is a highly visible issue and we can divert attention from the real grass-root causes by creating controversies around it for the time being, presumably. I suppose, you know that child labour and bonded labour also form part of trafficking. So are dowry for marriage, forced child marriage, children being subjected to involuntary servitude and children being held in debt bondage. We should understand that trafficking does not mean commercial sex work alone.'

'One last question sir, I know I have taken a lot of your time, but ...' Roy hesitated.

'Roy, I am happy to help. Go ahead, please.' Mahendra Goradia smiled indulgently.

'In my summation, can I take a parallel between the heinous Criminal Tribes Act, 1871, used by the British on millions of innocent Indians to subjugate their spirit to that of the recent amendment of the Bombay Police Act, 2005, with reference to dance bars of Mumbai in independent India? I think if we analyse these in perspective both the Acts truncated human dignity as well as infringed upon human rights very strongly.'

'Hmm...' Goradia thought for a moment. 'Yes, such a parallel is possible. However, you need to get to the details and put them in perspective.'

Roy closed his notebook, smiled earnestly, and shook Mahendra Goradia's hand while thanking him profusely for the marathon briefing. He took Goradia's permission to return to the library the next day for his study as well as reference checks.

As he was about to leave, Mahendra Goradia said very softly, 'Roy, I have only one request. If you use Inder and Munni's story, please don't name names or use very specific descriptions. I don't want to make a private grief public. You will agree that was not my intention.'

Roy nodded. 'Now that you've mentioned, names and specific identities will be strictly off the record, sir.'

The sun was about to set. As it was raining, Roy took a cab to his office. He was wondering whether he would be able to incorporate all the necessary inputs in one story. He thought, considering the magnitude of the issue, only a series could possibly do justice. He had to discuss it with Kumudini.

Redeeming the Future

Rajkumar Mallik rarely succumbed to stress. Yet he felt agitated. He did not have a viable solution to the problem at hand and neither could he see a solution evolving in the near future. He never liked to be a part of any problem. He always wanted to be a part of its solution. After a week, in all probability, Pallavi would lose her current job. Dance bars would close down. She had asked Rajkumar to suggest a possible solution. He did not have an answer yet and was feeling agitated.

'Munia, why don't you return to your village for some more time and relax?' asked Rajkumar during their evening telephone conversation.

'How could you say that Rajababa?' Pallavi asked in an incredulous voice. She paused for a while, expecting a reply. When there was none, she resumed, 'Rajababa, you know I recently visited the village. What will I do there now? I have done whatever I had to do there. I bought a jeep during the trip, which can ferry passengers to Gwalior, Agra, Mathura, Faridabad ... rented it out to a travelling agency. This would fetch some steady income for Mangiram Mama and Kamala Mami. Construction of the second floor of the house is complete. I have refurbished the complete house. Mama and Mami are comfortable in the ground floor. I have also purchased some milch cows for them. Those will fetch some more income. If Niyati ever comes to the village, she will have the entire second floor to herself. I will use the first floor. I have nothing else to do in the village. I have told you all this Rajababa, then why are you forcing me to repeat it.'

'So what do you propose?' Rajkumar asked.

'I need to earn more now as you told me earlier. I need to build up resources. Else, who will feed me? I have used most of my savings to buy this flat at Gulmohur Apartment. It is a very nice apartment. I have three properties now, one in Mumbai, one in Mirpura, and one in Bhopal. But I do not have enough savings to run my family after one year. How will I take care of Niyati's education? I promised Mukti Didi on her death bed that I would take care of her daughter and adopt her as my own. And I did. You know the facts. Niyati is my daughter now. She is my responsibility. I need to secure our future. I will not go to Pushkar Gupta begging for help ... he had declined to recognise his own daughter after Mukti Didi's untimely death. I don't want to see that imbecile's face ever.'

'Ask Madhuriji to start spending money for family expenses. Why can't she do it?' Rajkumar started getting upset.

Pallavi hesitated for a few moments but after all Rajababa being her selfless friend she had no other option but to reopen her wounds, '*Aapko malum hain, phir bhi.* As per our biradari traditions, she is not supposed to spend any money. Rajababa, she has bought me ... the panchayat, Dadua, sold me to her. I have to run the family expenses. I have to hand over a fixed portion of my income to her as long as I am in the profession. What she does with her money is her business. You know that Niyati is actually her granddaughter but I took on the responsibility. Rajababa, please don't remind me of all this just because I did not listen to your advice and bought this expensive house and went to the village when I should have concentrated otherwise. I am so sorry, Rajababa.' Pallavi started crying.

Rajkumar made only a grunting sound. He was getting angry with himself for not being able to offer any suggestion to Pallavi for an effective alternate income channel. He still felt that she should not have bought such an expensive apartment last year in Mumbai and exhaust all her savings. But who knew then that dancing in bars would be banned and her secure livelihood would face such a dire threat so soon!

'We are bar dancers, Rajababa ... I am a mujrawali. You know how much our society respects us. They think we are filthy. They cannot even imagine that we are dignified in our personal lives. I need the money power to fight it out. I want to take a further tuition in spoken English. The earlier tuition I had from Mrs Braganza made me confident and comfortable in conversing in English. Now I want to improve my conversation skills further. Can you request Mrs Braganza to start quickly?' requested Pallavi quite passionately, 'You know, from my childhood I wanted to learn English.'

'Surely I will,' replied Rajkumar. 'Oh, I was wondering. Why don't you visit Niyati in her school? You will have a change of scenario and she too would be happy meeting you. You have never visited her school. You always send Madhuriji.'

'What to do? I cannot interact with other parents or teachers. Though legally I am her mother, but what other introduction can I give? People around, other parents, will ask me questions about my family, about Niyati's father. I cannot say that I am a mujrawali. Can I? Do you think our society will be able to accept it? I don't want to lie and pose as a housewife and concoct a story about Niyati's father as well. If I do that Niyati will come to know, eventually. I don't want to lie to her. In a few years when she is older and more mature I'll tell her everything.'

'I understand. You are doing the right thing,' Rajkumar replied.

'So, isn't it better that Madhuri Ma visits the school on exits and on parent-teacher days? She is the grandmother and an elegant elderly lady. No one has any reservations about her. She gets away with just saying that she is the grandmother and can converse in Hindi only.' Pallavi sighed. She had discussed all this with Rajkumar before.

Suddenly Rajkumar's voice came alive, 'I have an idea. Why don't you take up a course, either in hairstyling or beauty and make-up? You already know a lot since you've been doing your own hairstyling and make-up. Just formalise the knowledge. You can start your own hairstyling and beauty treatment salon.' He felt charged up, 'First go and visit Niyati. On return, start English and beauty training classes. In the meantime, we will find a suitable place in Lokhandwala or in Bandra for an upmarket salon. Do the interiors. Appoint some expert beauticians, hair cutters and stylists. Inaugurate around Christmas and New Year. What do you say? I'm ready to put in a one-time investment, which you can pay me off later. I know you have a head for business and are an expert in maintaining relationships. The business will work. You need to plan and redeem your future. You need to take charge to make the change. You be the change.'

Pallavi liked the suggestion and she said so to Rajkumar and took his leave to get ready to go to work saying, 'Will discuss with you tomorrow Rajababa ... now let me rush for office, though for a couple of days more only. Oh, will you visit my office tonight?'

Bedni

Roy reached his bachelor's pad quite late that evening. The discussion with Kumudini took over an hour, and afterwards he had to key in a few discussion points and certain references on his laptop for the morrow's research.

When he entered his Pedder Road apartment, Alok Singh was sitting on his favourite couch in the living room and watching news on television, enjoying his daily quota of brandy. He greeted Roy with a very warm smile. 'I heard you made Mahinbhai work nonstop for over seven hours?'

Roy replied with a smile, 'That's because you recommended me, sir. Thank you so very much.'

Alok Singh said graciously, 'You are doing a great job. We should all help. By the way, in his position, he charges an hourly rate of a hundred-thousand rupees for consultation. So, it is over seven hundred-thousand rupees of revenue foregone.'

Roy replied in a lighter vein, 'His firm also does pro bono. I suppose it should go to the pro bono time-sheet and account.'

Alok Singh as usual enjoyed the quick wit and invited him for dinner. After an initial hesitation, Roy accepted. He wanted to use this opportunity to know more from Alok Singh about Inder Kumar Gajanan Singh.

They agreed to meet at the dinner table after Roy had taken a shower and freshened up.

'What is your impression about Inder Kumar Gajanan Singh, sir?' asked Roy at the dinner table.

'What exactly do you mean by impression, Roy? If you could clarify?' asked back the stickler for perfection.

'Sir, I did a Google search on Prince Inder Kumar once I returned to office after my discussion with Mr Goradia. He is a very handsome man. I have inputs about his family hotel business and the polo clubs, and his patronising various charities. I also read about his brother, Sunder Kumar, an accomplished shooter, who represented the country in Commonwealth Games. But I need to know from you on a first-hand basis: how was he as a friend, as a person, what was his reaction when he could not marry that lady ... what was her name?'

'Munni Bai,' replied Alok Singh softly.

'Yes, Munni.'

'Inder was one of our best friends. We are occasionally in touch. Very honourable man. Whenever I am in Delhi, I am forced to stay with him at his bungalow or his Mehrauli farmhouse. He is a thoroughbred, of princely blood: courteous, upright, transparent. If you are curious to know, he does not discuss Munni with us at all. That is his personal issue. One more thing, he had never visited Mumbai again.'

'You mean to say that he never tried to connect with Munni again?' Roy was curious.

'Yes, during the initial period he tried his level best, but Munni's family in all probability by then had transported her out of Bombay. Pity, she could never be traced. All her family members also vanished from their tenement near Congress House. Since that world was, is and possibly always will be shrouded in mystery and in Italian mafia like *Omerta*, non-disclosure and silence, no neighbour ever parted with any kind of information about Munni to Inder Kumar.'

Roy, so very subtly and softly took the chance of asking Alok Singh the inevitable, based on the knowledge he had gathered so far, 'Sir, was she a Kanjar or Banchra?'

Alok Singh reacted very sharply, dropped his fork and knife on the plate, and then realised that Roy indeed had had a very intense session with Mahendra Goradia. Being a very competent journalist, it was but natural that he would ask such questions. He took a deep breath and said, 'No, she was a *Bedni* ... a Bedia girl,' and resumed his dinner.

During the rest of the dinner both were silent and in a contemplative mood. Once the dinner was over, Roy once again thanked Alok Singh for all the help which Singh acknowledged with a nod. Before leaving the dinner table, Alok Singh very softly said, 'Be very careful Roy, you have stepped into a world of intrigue, deception and debauched glamour. Don't lose your perspective.'

Silence is Golden

The countdown had started. The closure of dance bars was a certainty. Only a couple of days were left. Dusk had set in. Pallavi was getting ready to leave for office. Her mobile rang. It was an unknown number. She frowned, hesitated, but curiosity overrode prudence. She took the call.

'Hello ... Pallavi?' enquired a female voice.

'Yes. *Aap kaun*?'

'Hi, Pallavi. I am Renuka.'

'Who?' Pallavi couldn't place the caller instantly.

'Renuka. I was in Magnet about a year ago. Remember me?'

'Oh, yes! Renuka from Delhi, *na*? What happened to the movie you were acting in?'

'Oh! So, you remember me ... it's still being made. *Saala* my producer is bankrupt, rascal. Whatever! I had my share of fun. Now the bastard is setting up a DB across the Arabian Sea!'

'*Achcha*? You seem to like your producer very much. You are not at all unhappy that the film is not being made? What happened?' Pallavi was curious.

'It's okay, babes! He is a good businessman. He has made it up to me. I made my share. He is also okay with me being friends with others. It's cool, doll,' crooned Renuka.

'Where did you get my number from?'

'Well, there are ways, baby doll. Oh! You don't mind me calling you baby doll, *na*? You are so gorgeous. I liked you so much in the Magnet. Actually, I always wanted to cuddle you. That's why I told that bastard Sameer that for his overseas DB he should consider you as the lead dancer. We will do items together, baby. It would be fun. What say?'

Pallavi ignored the pass. She thought that she might be imagining things that did not exist. Might be the impending financial insecurity had made her hypersensitive. She asked, 'What overseas DB?'

'Sameer and I are opening up a dance bar in Dubai next month. We will take you as the lead dancer. We will pay you a fixed salary and a commission in dollars. Once you settle in, we can discuss Mumbai style payment at fifty-fifty. We will provide you with a one-bedroom furnished flat too. Our local partner knows you. He has seen you in Magnet. He says that your body is soft like butter. Are you game? By air, Mumbai will hardly be of any distance. When can I meet you? I am at the *Marriott*. Come and meet me tonight if you are free. We will have a good time baby and talk.'

'Let me think Renuka. Thank you for calling me. I will call you maybe tomorrow or the day after. I have to go now, have some work in the kitchen.'

'Kitchen? Oh my God! What are you doing in the kitchen? Don't you have a maid? I am sure you can afford one. Your butter-like figure will melt baby ... what will you do then!' Renuka sounded amused.

Pallavi felt the barb, yet maintained her cool. Rajababa said never to lose one's cool unnecessarily. The moment you lose it, you lose control over the situation. 'I enjoy cooking. It relaxes me. And, I have a big modern kitchen. Okay? Bye.' Pallavi disconnected the phone.

She immediately called Namita.

'Nami, can you explain why you shared my mobile number with Renuka without even asking me?' she pounced sans preamble.

'I didn't give it? Did she tell you I gave it to her?' Namita was aggressive.

'If you didn't, why are you getting angry?' asked Pallavi.

'Simply because you are accusing me without any basis, that's why.'

'No, I have solid proof. I changed my number only two days ago, as I do not want customers to disturb me once Magnet is closed. This number is only with you, Madhuri Ma and Rajababa. Both Ma and Rajababa do not know Renuka,' Pallavi said in a matter-of-fact tone.

'No, it's not me. You have to believe me!' Namita's tone turned defensive and conciliatory. 'Pallavi, *sorry re.* Vicky gave Renuka your number. Sorry *yaar.* I came to know about it sometime ago, but was afraid to tell you.'

'How does your latest boyfriend know my private mobile number?' Pallavi had never felt so upset with Namita before.

'I didn't give it!' Namita uttered so softly. 'He always fiddles with my phone, you know that. Maybe he copied your number. I have beaten him up, lots! But I am sorry.' Namita was barely audible.

'But why did he do that? Where the hell did he meet that girl? Nami, she is evil. You need to speak to Vicky seriously about not interacting with such people.'

'Oh, Vicky met her in the *Marriott* yesterday. He had gone for dinner with a foreign merchandising agent from Paris, who wants to source a huge amount of women's tops made of

Murshidabad silk. Renuka spotted him in the lobby along with this French woman and latched on to them. Vicky even told me that Renuka had the guts to make a pass at the French woman.'

'Oh my God! Don't tell me. I thought I was imagining! That girl is not straight.' Pallavi said.

'Oh really !' Namita felt comparatively relaxed, as she was no longer haunted by any guilt. In fact, she was quite glad that Vicky had gotten in touch with Renuka. If Pallavi agreed to go there, she might be able to latch on and go abroad too.

Namita knew that she was not even half as beautiful as Pallavi. She was also older than her. But, more importantly, this being the glamour business once you lost your grace, you either retire or would get forced, at times, to trade yourself, both of which she was not ready for, presently at least. She had no option but, under the current scenario, to hitch up with Pallavi.

She thought of trying her luck directly. 'Why don't we go abroad together Pallavi?' she asked with apparent innocence, 'Lots of girls are going. Once the dance is over in Mumbai bars, what will we do? How will we run our families? Such huge financial responsibilities ... how will we meet them?'

'What is the guarantee that the income will be adequate abroad? What is the guarantee that they will not sell us off further? You know the kind of things that happen abroad? Mumbai is my city and I am not going to leave it. In any case, I might start some business and am planning for it. Rajababa has advised me not to rush into anything.'

'You and your Rajababa – that ill-tempered arrogant man. What can he offer, Pallavi? He is a middle-class man. I do not think he has enough money. You might feel he is smart but he is not handsome at all. He is at least double your age. Are you going to stay with him, permanently, you fool? Madhuri Ma will kill you!'

'Frankly speaking, I would have loved staying with him all my life, Namita. I am like a daughter to him. I'm very dear to him like a family member. Namita, of all people, you should know that he is the only person who has never treated me like just another body. Have you ever looked into his eyes? So clear ... so pure. Moreover, there are other facts you don't know about. So, please don't criticise him. He did you no wrong. And, he did a lot of good things for me. I know you don't like him but that is not either his or my problem. It is because of your nature. And, stop commenting on my personal matters.' She waited for a few moments, firmed up her mind and said further, 'Nami, you are jealous. You were always jealous.' Pallavi continued her statement in a flat and unemotional voice, 'I know Madhuri Ma just tolerates him because of me. She is afraid of losing me and my money in her old age. Rajababa has sacrificed a lot for me. He is my best friend,' Finally, she confided to Namita, 'I want to leave the profession, Nami. And I would, by God. I just want to have a normal, peaceful life. I want to get married and have a family of my own.'

Namita was pained to hear that Rajkumar was Pallavi's best friend and not she. She kept her feelings in check and said, 'Okay, let me then do one thing Munia. Let me give an advertisement in the matrimonial columns of The Times Express. We will say, – *Wanted top executive or businessman groom. Bride: very fair and beautiful religious Hindu girl. Height 5 feet 4 inches. Weight 53 kg. Age 29 years. Self-employed. Can dance and sing very well. Loves cooking. Can converse in Hindi and English. Apply along with horoscope, photograph and bank statement.* – A lot of applications will come and we will select a groom for you.' Namita started giggling over the phone.

Pallavi did not even smile. She was sombre and replied thoughtfully, 'I am sure that lots of replies will come if you put out the advertisement exactly as you have narrated. But, you forgot to mention something,' Pallavi paused, took a deep breath and uttered softly, 'you need to write ... "*self-employed as a bar dancer*", instead of self-employed, and see the difference in the responses.'

Namita did not answer.

Pallavi got even more irritated with Namita's silence and went in for the kill, 'I am not very sure if you still remember our journey, Nami. Maybe you are indifferent. Maybe you want to forget it. But how can I? It is my past that has made my present and will definitely impact my future. I have not forgotten my past. I don't want to. I want to learn from it and improve my life. I know life is tough. But, I also know who I am. I will make a good wife and a mother. I need to find the man who has the character and the mental strength to be my partner.'

Namita remained quiet. She proved that silence is golden.

BOOK 3

- Inclusion -

21st Century: The 59th
Independence Day and After

No More Dancing ...

Past midnight, when India celebrated her 59th Independence Day on 15 August 2005, the dance bars of Mumbai became mute; bars that were once spectators to glittering and opulent nightlife. Over hundred thousand dancers and nearly another hundred thousand support staff lost the chance to earn their living and were made redundant. The DJ consoles became quiet. The spotlights diminished and faded out. Rightly or wrongly, the euphoria surrounding a unique yet controversial element of Mumbai's nightlife evaporated. No more dancing. The dancing stopped. But what would happen to those thousands of dancers? What would their future be? And, what was their fault? What made us exclude them from our lives? Was it only because they were a disadvantaged lot of women dancing in the bars? Who would hear their stories and take corrective action? Provide them with solutions? Remedy the century old degeneration forced upon their communities? Unanswered questions; questions defying answers ... ...

The Quest

On his way to Hrishikesh, at both Mumbai and Delhi airports, Roy saw copies of the current edition of The India Post with his cover story on display at the book stalls. He had a sudden impulse to pick-up a copy but resisted it. He was fighting within himself a battle of letting go the memories of the last couple of weeks, memories of a dazzling smile that was continuously haunting him in his sleep and recurrently visiting him in his dreams. He had never been enamoured by a person so much. He shook his head literally, in an effort to drive away the thought physically. He took a deep breath and forced himself to focus on the present.

He knew that his story was just the beginning of exploration; the debate would continue. He knew that he was not going to let the subject move away from his radar and would definitely be following it up periodically in future. However, now that he had complied with his Executive Editor's request, he wanted to devote his time and attention to a very important and urgent personal matter. He was on his way to Atmatdaya Ashram in Hrishikesh to meet his mother, who was keeping an indifferent health post her trip from the Valley of Flowers, whom he had not met for quite some time and whom he was missing.

Roy remembered his mother as a God-fearing person. She had introduced him to the concept of God by constantly prompting during his childhood, 'Be good, God is watching you,' a refrain that still echoed in his ears. It was dusk now; the world around him was steadily slowing down. In the semi-darkness of this hour, while travelling towards Hrishikesh, he prayed to that God, delving into his heart, his subconscious and his soul, for his mother's speedy recovery.

Surrounded by mighty mountains on three sides, with its peaceful ambience, Hrishikesh is at an altitude of nearly fourteen hundred feet and is considered to be the gateway to heaven, literally. Martha Chandrabhanu Kashyap Fishbone, née Martha Fishbone, Roy's mother, was recuperating here at Atmatdaya Ashram. After the hustle and bustle of Mumbai, the glamour of her dance bars and rigours of a journalistic life, visiting his mother in Hrishikesh was a welcome change for Roy; therapeutic and a quest towards self-discovery.

After the tragic death of her husband, Professor Chandrabhanu Kashyap, just over a year ago, Martha had devoted herself completely to social work. She was, in any case, attached to the destitute children's home of Atmatdaya Ashram in Delhi since its beginning some ten years ago. For the last one year, she chose to work as a full-time volunteer of the Ashram.

Roy understood his mother's loneliness. In a sense, he felt relieved that she had immersed herself in social work to keep herself busy and deal with the loss of her partner. What he could not bring himself to face was the fact that his father had a clandestine affair at the age of sixty-two, with a lady colleague who was practically half his age. In fact, the lady died in the car accident along with his father. The police investigation had revealed that they were closeted together in a hotel room in

Agra for about a week, while his father had given an impression of being away for an international conference. For Roy, it was painful. He had worshiped his father as his only hero all his life and could not believe that his father was actually capable of deceit. He thought that his father had enough boldness and honesty to be open about his feelings, even if it be a relationship outside marriage. At least, he taught Roy to think, speak, and perform accordingly. However, Roy had enough maturity to rationalise that possibly Chandrabhanu might have missed some sparkle in life and had taken a mis-step only once. Roy did not condone his behaviour, yet he was not ready to write him off from his own memory completely. But it hurt him to see his mother trying to boldly face the social scandal and the whispering campaign surrounding them. On rebound, she totally eradicated the existence of his father from their lives; therefore, she left Delhi and immersed herself in the social work of Atmatdaya Ashram in Hrishikesh. Roy too changed his job from the newspaper in Delhi, where he had worked for nearly seven years, to The India Post magazine in Mumbai so that he could seek relative anonymity, apart from a change of scene. He had to leave the city that was laden with family memories. Yet, how could he forget his father? He also remembered the stories of his childhood, narrated by his mother of how enthusiastic his father was to find a name of right connotation for him. Roy was born in the month of May, and that particular day in that year according to a certain Indian almanac, was 25th of *Baishak*, the birthday of the great Indian poet and Nobel Laureate Rabindranath Tagore. Young Chandrabhanu did not require even a moment to think, and named his son after the great poet, philosopher, and patriot. Martin Fishbone, Roy's maternal grandfather, with his traits of ancient history, suggested the middle name 'Royce', the King, for his grandson. Eventually, Rabindranath Royce Chandrabhanu Kashyap became 'Roy' to everyone. He even used 'Roy' as his pen name for his by-lines. Only his father and some select family friends addressed him as 'Rabindranath.'

During the last month or so, Kumudini's infrequent remarks, as well as his own continuous thinking about his goal in life and his loneliness, led him to resolve to bring back peace and happiness into his mother's life. He knew if he could achieve that, he too would be blessed with immense happiness. So, when he received a call from Swami Chinmayananda that his mother had fallen ill, Roy rushed to meet his mother at Hrishikesh, though he was assured that his mother's medical condition was not very serious.

He reached the Ashram when the evening prayer was almost over. As the prayer was in progress, he sat down on the steps leading to the spacious prayer hall, overlooking the mighty Himalayas, his rucksack besides him. The Ashram inmates and devotees were singing melodious songs in praise of God. He could hear devotional songs, evening prayers, and tolling of the bells from the surrounding ashrams too. The entire atmosphere exuded serenity. He felt very humble and blissful.

Someone tapped lightly on his shoulder and he woke up. He could see a young monk looking at him smilingly, 'Namaskar, I am Swami Chinmayananda, Guruji's secretary. You must be Marthaji's son?'

Roy was perplexed, it took him a while to focus and remember his surroundings and then he replied hurriedly, 'Yes. Yes. Namaskar. How did you recognise me?'

The young monk clarified, 'Swamiji pointed you out to me. He is waiting for you in the office.'

'I felt so peaceful sitting here. The prayer had completely relaxed me. I am so sorry that I dozed off.' Roy tried to hide his embarrassment and stood up. 'Since how long the prayer's been over?' he asked.

'About fifteen minutes,' Chinmayananda replied without any trace of rancour. 'Actually, while leaving after the prayer, some devotees saw you sleeping here and informed us. You must be exhausted from your tedious journey? Let's go to the office. Let me carry the bag.' The young monk extended his hand for the rucksack.

'Thank you very much. I can manage it,' said Roy and picked up his luggage. 'Please tell me how is my mother? Can I meet her now?' Roy pleaded.

'Of course you can meet Marthaji. Swamiji will take you to her. That's why we need to rush.'

'What is the doctor saying?'

'She will have to have her medication for some time and will have to take rest. She suffered exhaustion during the recent trip. She needs to relax and take a break,' Chinmayananda assured Roy while they were walking towards the inner courtyard of the Ashram.

'I am so very obliged and indebted to the Ashram for taking care of her. Do you think it will be all right if I want to take her with me to Mumbai?' enquired Roy.

'Please do not thank us. We are only performing our duty. She has been serving selflessly for the cause, that is very dear to our hearts. She is one of us. As far as the question of taking her to Mumbai is concerned, I would rather request you speak to the doctor, but if I were you, I would wait for some more time to allow her system to settle down,' replied the articulate monk very sincerely, while gesturing to Roy to enter a large brightly-lit room on his right a couple of flights up.

Swami Amritanandaji looked at Roy with his kind smiling eyes. He was sitting behind a large wooden table, with neatly piled newspapers and some religious and other magazines on one side and an old telephone handset on the other. With his clean-shaven head, lean and tall figure wrapped in a simple saffron-ochre cloth, a Rudraksha mala adorning his neck, he stood up to welcome Roy. 'Hello Rabindranath. How are you?' he uttered so fondly.

'Pranam Swamiji, I am alright,' Roy bowed his head and replied very politely.

Amritananda held him by his shoulders and replied after looking at him, 'You have lost weight. Is everything all right in Mumbai? How is the city treating you?'

'I am alright; just finished a gruelling schedule. Didn't sleep properly for about a week,' Roy replied.

'That city can be very cruel, if you are lacking in the fighting spirit. I can tell you that as an expert,' Amritananda commented, as if he had some insider information on the city.

'Really? How can you do that residing at Hrishikesh?' Roy expressed curiosity.

'I have an invisible, emotional, umbilical cord attached to that city. A part of my soul resides there, you may say,' Amritananda smiled as he said so.

'You look great as usual, Uncle Amrit. Rather smashing, if I may take the liberty of saying so?' said Roy with his usual candour. As he finished making his comment, he suddenly realised that young Chinmayananda was still around, and was trying his level best to dissolve into the background, as quietly as possible, amidst their conversation. Roy felt embarrassed at his indiscretion. He fleetingly looked at the receding figure of Chinmayananda and then back at Amritananda and said, 'I am so sorry. Please excuse me.' In fact, memories related to his father had flooded his mind and numbed his senses by meeting one of his father's beloved erstwhile colleagues as well as a friend, after nearly five years. He had become nostalgic. Apart from his father, it was Mr Amrit Banerjia, the erstwhile young Associate Professor of Economics, currently known as Swami Amritananda, who had always insisted on addressing him by his formal first name – Rabindranath, instead of his abbreviated middle name 'Roy' for 'Royce'. Roy's association with him continued and the relationship grew even after Mr Amrit Banerjia became Swami Amritanandaji, after renouncing worldly pleasures.

However, the uncle in the Swami did understand the emotional turmoil Roy was going through. He could feel the numerous unresolved conflicts that weighed on Roy's soul. Very fondly he said to Roy, 'Come, let's go and meet your mother, Rabindranath.'

Martha was in her room. She too was waiting eagerly to meet her son. She knew, and Swamiji had repeatedly counselled, that Roy needed healing too. He told Martha that in her grief she could not afford to overlook and exclude her responsibility towards her son and be selfish to find her own solace.

Roy could see from a distance that his mother was looking tired. With her silver locks knotted into a bun, her spectacles perched on the bridge of her aquiline nose, crossing one leg over the other, part-sitting and part reclining on a couch-chair, she was reading a book.

Swamiji knocked lightly on the open door. 'May we come in, Martha?'

Keeping the book away unhurriedly on the small table next to her couch, Martha stood up. Her face looked exhausted, but dressed in a saffron robe, her tallish figure looked elegant.

Roy dropped his rucksack, rushed into the room, and hugged his mother, 'Oh Ma! I missed you.'

Amritananda looked on indulgently.

Martha held on tightly to her son. She kissed his forehead. 'How are you, Sunny? It looks like I have not seen you for ages. Are you eating right? I think you have lost weight.' She held him at arm's length, adjusted her bifocals, and started inspecting him critically. 'You definitely look thin. I can feel it in your hug.' She rubbed the open palms of her hands on her son's forearms and sealed her conclusion.

'I thought so as well.' Amritananda added.

Roy smiled at Amritananda, then turned around to his mother and took both her hands in his and enquired, 'First answer me Ma ... are you going to be with me in Mumbai this time, once you are okay, or not?'

'But how could you lose weight? I think you are not eating right. Are you taking sufficient rest?' Martha was undeterred in her query and held on to her son's hands.

'Martha ... let it be,' Swami Amritananda intervened. 'He has travelled a long way; let him freshen up and have dinner.'

'Okay, okay! Well, my dear lady and gentleman, let me have the last word, please,' Roy said, shaking his head, 'I am not thin, I am slim. It's in vogue in the first city of India. I think you guys are out of touch with the real world outside the Himalayas.' Roy grinned and successfully diffused the tension that was building up within the room. He felt peaceful after ages.

That night Roy had blissful sleep. Even the otherwise ruthlessly disciplined Amritananda gave Roy the leeway to sleep and had issued instructions to all inmates to not disturb Roy, who was housed in the guest wing, which was in the outer courtyard of the Ashram.

Just a while ago, Martha practically had to countermand Swamiji's order and force Chinmayananda to wake up Roy so that he could freshen up and meet her.

Resting his head on his mother's lap, Roy was busy discussing the events that kept him busy during the past three months, in the balcony adjacent to Martha's room. Shortly, dusk would set in.

'So you like Kumudini? How old is she?' enquired Martha holding her son's hand and looking intently into his eyes.

'I like her Ma but only as a friend, as a colleague, as a professional. She is not my girl friend. And, how does her age matter, Ma?'

'Roy, you are already thirty years old. Don't you want to start your family, Sunny?' Martha asked.

'You are my family.' Roy held on to his mother's hand. 'I will think about marriage later on, Ma. Right now, I am not really thinking about it. You need to get back to shape first. I am really sorry for not being there for you. Not being in touch for the last three months.' Roy was playing with Martha's fingers with his eyes downcast.

'If I go and stay with you in Mumbai, how do you propose I will spend my time?' She asked and continued, 'What are your plans for me?'

Roy was caught off guard but with his natural candour he looked up and replied, 'Ma, frankly speaking, I haven't thought about it. The only thing I know for sure is that I want you to be with me from now on. Balance I will figure out as we go along. We also need to decide what to do with the Delhi apartment as well as the Allahabad house. Both are dead assets, in a sense. They are under lock and key with no real value except the sentimental one.

I suppose, if you agree, we can consider letting them out on rent or dispose them off and think of buying a property in Mumbai. Anyway, it's just a spur-of-the-moment thought. We need to think it through. You need to feel comfortable.'

Martha looked at her son indulgently. 'You know Sunny, I am very proud of you. I don't know if I have ever said so to you.' She smiled at Roy. 'But I am curious to know about the girls in your life. You know why? Because you are lonely in Mumbai and loneliness at times forces us to look for friends or companions, who may or may not be the right choice.'

Roy sat upright. For a moment he felt as if his mother could see and read all his thoughts. However, facing his mother squarely he said, 'That logic is very convoluted, Ma.' Though for a fraction of a second he thought if his mother's intuition was correct and if that could be the reason he was thinking of Pallavi so much. However, he kept his thoughts to himself.

'Really? You think so? Well, all your discussions are revolving only around The India Post, Kumudini, Freny and office politics. You have discussed nothing else. Don't you have any other friends in Mumbai? Are you still as introvert as ever? How do you spend your spare time?'

'I hardly get any time after office work. I lead a team of six. I need to discuss and allot work to them. I have my column to take care of and special features. Moreover, reading, reading, and reading ... where is the time?'

'Your books ... and the library,' Martha looked a little lost in her thoughts. 'We need to bring the books out of the Delhi house,' she concluded, and with a forced smile, resumed her questioning, 'How about your paying guest accommodation? How is your landlord? Are you comfortable there? I know it's a little too late to ask, and I am sorry for that, Sunny.'

'Alok Singh, my landlord, is a nice man. Retired Brigadier. He treats me like a family member. In fact, when I was researching my last feature, I kept very irregular hours and he got worried. Oh, I forgot ... I need to call him and let him know that you are alright. He even gave me the contact details of an eminent cardiologist in Dehradun, his childhood friend, Dr Anand.'

'What was your last feature about? Has it already been published? I remember your feature on the Delhi street urchins ... so insightful,' Martha smiled.

'Oh, that! ... my current article is related to the de-notified tribes; the impact of a long forgotten piece of statute, the Criminal Tribes Act, 1871, on our society ...' he paused for a while, and suddenly pointed his right index figure jokingly at his mother and said, 'You, the British, created havoc in our country's social fabric through this Act.' He paused again, smiled and then thoughtfully added, 'The story is in the context of Mumbai dance bars. It was an experience and learning for me. Ma, you would not believe that most of the dancers of Mumbai's dance bars are from the de-notified tribes. Even today they face horrific traditions within their communities, and yet in the cities, within our government and policy making system we are so blissfully unaware of them. Or, rather we don't want to understand them.'

'Interesting!' Her initial reaction was cryptic. After a brief pause she said, 'I hope you are not hooked on to the habit of visiting dance bars. No good.' Martha looked steadily at Roy.

For a moment, Roy hesitated. On a second thought it was clear to him that he was not hooked onto the habit of frequenting dance bars, but of course Pallavi's memory haunted him. For the time being he felt that it needed to stay in the background because of the recent family tragedy. He replied, 'No Ma, I am not. It was part of my assignment; a good learning experience. I met a couple of interesting people, a senior lawyer specially.' Roy kept a straight face. 'Now can we discuss something else please?' He deliberately avoided sharing the details with his mother about Pallavi, lest she become agitated and concerned about his behaviour and character. He could not afford his mother to have an uncalled for trauma, because after the incident with his father, she had become unnecessarily stoic on certain behavioural issues. So, very casually, he changed the drift of their conversation, 'Oh, I require your permission to travel to Dehradun in a couple of days, maybe day after, to meet Dr Anand. I want him to come and have a look at you.' Roy held his mother's hand lightly.

'Sunny, you need to discuss this with Amrit maharaj. He has been overseeing my treatment and, in all fairness, you need to consult him.'

'Okay. Let me now go and attend the prayer,' and he got up.

'Sunny, I will ask the kitchen to send our dinners in my room. Don't keep me waiting for too long after the prayer.'

'Sure, Ma.'

Innocence and Mind-games

'Niyati, don't cycle so fast. Relax. Slow down,' Pallavi cautioned the young bundle of energy. 'You may hit someone. Slow and easy, just enjoy the ride.'

'I will, Mommy,' the little girl replied, without slowing down even a bit. She was enjoying her freedom.

'Munia! See these two pullovers. Look at the designs? Nice, *na*?' enquired Madhuri.

'Yes. Very nice,' Pallavi replied mechanically.

'Dehradun is so nice. We should visit the place often together,' Madhuri made her comment while searching for her purse inside her big handbag to pay for the pullovers, at the shop.

'Of course, you can visit the place as many times as you want. But how can I? How do you propose I will earn my living?' Pallavi looked at Madhuri. 'Will you be happy if I leave my work and settle down here?' She made a face. 'Niyati, come back,' she called out to her daughter.

'Did I ever suggest that? I was just wondering,' Madhuri said putting the pullovers inside her bag. 'Come on! Let's go to the other side of *ghanta ghar*.'

'*Nani, not ghanta ghar!* Please say clock tower.' Niyati started giggling while cycling past them.

'Don't giggle darling,' Pallavi chided Niyati gently. 'Now, come back. And listen, Nani is old-fashioned, that's why she said *ghanta ghar* in Hindi, instead of clock tower. We need to respect our mother tongue. Okay, darling?'

'Yes, Mommy. I am so sorry; I didn't mean to be rude. It sounds so funny ... *ghanta ghar.'* Once again, she started giggling innocently and stopped her cycle close to Pallavi.

'It's okay, love. Remember to always respect others' sentiments. Now, let's get back to your hostel quickly. Else, we'll be late. Tomorrow, I will come again at the same time after school to fetch you. Let's pray there's no rain tomorrow, also.' Pallavi planted a kiss on the forehead of her daughter.

'Munia! Munia! Have you gone off to sleep?' Madhuri called out softly.

'Trying to ... why?' asked Pallavi.

'How will we run our household if bars are not allowed to hold dances?' Madhuri looked at the ceiling of the hotel room and started imagining what life would be without enough money during her old age. Suddenly, she sat up on the bed and asked, 'Should we start our mehfil again in the Compound?'

'What nonsense are you talking, Ma?' Pallavi got irritated. 'Let me sleep. *Uff,* you are becoming impossible, day by day.'

After sometime, without looking at Madhuri and simply facing the curtained window of the hotel room, Pallavi stated in a very matter-of-fact tone, 'I am planning to admit Niyati in a school in Mumbai next year. I will start a beauty parlour. I have requested Rajababa to find out a suitable place.' Pallavi confided. 'I have decided to settle down to a regular life. I want to marry.'

'It does not happen in our biradari, you know that. Still why do you insist? It's foolish,' Madhuri became angry, spoke hoarsely, and sat up.

'Why? What is foolish in this? Why is it necessary to follow that tradition even today? What could be the compelling logic for it? Ma, there are growing numbers of families in our caste who do not participate in the profession any longer. They also live. Why cannot I?' Pallavi was getting upset with Madhuri.

'No one can change our traditions,' said Madhuri flatly. 'Look at Mallika. She has settled down so well with Aditya Narayan, that Bengali from Siliguri with so many tea gardens, as you used to taunt and mimic him. Aditya was interested in you but you couldn't care less then. Today, Mallika and Aditya are a happy couple. They have kids. What do you have?'

'Aditya has not married her and she stays in Mumbai alone with the kids. Not in Aditya's house in Siliguri. Whenever Aditya is in Mumbai, he is with her. That is not the life I am looking for.' Pallavi couldn't control herself any further. The pent up emotions of so many years, buried deep inside her heaving chest, erupted, 'Why this restriction? What does the biradari have to do with my life? The times are a changing! What did they do to my mother? I know that Shankar Baba had her killed after my birth, when she refused to return as the concubine to the zamindar from whom he had taken money. That bastard Sukumar Shah told me about it. He also said that my father was that bad character zamindar who gave a lot of money to Shankar Baba to be with my mother. He is no more. So is Shankar Baba. I do not hold any bitterness against them. Neither do I want to embarrass our elders. But, henceforth I want to live my life the way I want to. I have compromised enough. I have earned enough too. I also made you rich. Now, I want my own family. I want to lead a normal and regular life.' Angry Pallavi looked for an answer from Madhuri.

The spiteful, humiliated, nervous, and calculative Madhuri couldn't take it any longer. She struck back in a harsh tone, devoid of any civility with wild and vulgar gesticulation of her hands, 'Who will marry you, *saali haramzadi*? You had multiple men in your life. You don't even know who your father is; your mother is dead and still you yearn for her. I stood by you, sheltered you and you are still not bothered about me. I tell you, only some third-rate God-forsaken man with no hope and integrity will marry you and live off your income. Do you think you can be a housewife? You are born to be a concubine. Where will you have that man who will accept you and overlook your past?' Madhuri had started her mind games. She knew that she could possibly keep control over Pallavi only through psychological pressure. 'Go off to sleep. I am feeling sleepy now. *Saali randi*, now you want to become the immaculate virgin ... let me sleep, don't disturb me,' as always, Madhuri turned her back towards Pallavi without taking the conversation to a logical conclusion. She was afraid of losing control over her golden goose in her old age.

'Don't you turn your back on me!' Pallavi shouted at Madhuri and pulled at her shoulders. 'What have you and the elders in the community done for me, except for using me as a tool to fill your coffers? The men came in my life because of you.' She forced Madhuri to turn around and look at her, 'Look at me, you miserable woman. You and Dadua worked as my pimps. You brought the men. I have not slept with anyone of my own free will. It was forced on me as the community decree. You have pandered my body and earned pots of money when I couldn't voice my opinion. You, Dadua, Mai ... all of you lived off my hard-earned money. Did you ever go to the ministers to ask them to change the systems? You wouldn't and why would you? Did you not stand to lose heavily? Why did you not send me to school? Why would the police always raid our homes in villages even when we were not connected remotely to any crime? Why do the powerful, rich men lust for our bodies? Why do we hide our real identities from the society at large? Why do we change our names when we leave our villages? Why do we never mention our real origin? Why do we not make friends outside of our community? Why has everyone failed to create opportunities for us to have a normal life? Now, we can't even dance legitimately. What should we do? Sell our bodies? Go back to the old system of *randigiri* ... the life that we all wanted to give up and forget; do we revive that? Is that what you want? Tell me, that's what you want, isn't it? Of course that's what you want! You did not even spare your own daughter! You made your daughter a harlot. All you wanted was money and more money, and yet more money, you avaricious woman!' At the end of her soliloquy, Pallavi felt humiliated. She got up from the bed. 'But, no. Enough is enough. I will not dance to your tunes anymore. You will now live with me on my terms or you move out. Don't worry, Niyati is my responsibility, I would never trust her with you! Given a choice you will put her up in trade too, your own granddaughter, for money. Noooo ... it ends here and now,' she yelled and went out to the balcony, adjacent to the hotel room. Feeling frustrated, she started weeping uncontrollably. She did not want anyone to know of her weaker moments.

Voice from the Past

'Rabindranathji, Rabindranathji', Roy could feel someone mildly shaking his left shoulder. The sun was about to rise. When he opened his eyes, Roy could see the translucent morning sky radiating with the orange glow of the upcoming sun. He felt slightly disoriented primarily because he was yet not used to being addressed as 'Rabindranath' and secondly the locale – he was yet to adjust to the scenic beauty of Hrishikesh. He turned on his side. The ever smiling countenance of Chinmayananda rose before him.

Roy's first question was, 'Is Ma all right?'

Chinmayananda assured him she was, and then informed him that Martha and Swamiji were at the main eastern terrace and they had sent in a request for Roy to join them at the earliest.

As Roy stepped onto the terrace a slightly familiar staccato baritone assaulted his ears. He had never expected this voice from his recent past to be present at the sanctified terrace of this Ashram, that too at the crack of dawn. He was also bewildered to see Swami Amritanandaji sitting beside the man in a very relaxed manner, as if they were long-lost friends.

By taking a few more steps towards this group, Roy could see that his cover story on the dance bars of Mumbai was on full display. His mother was seriously engrossed in reading it. Raja Mallik was enjoying a mug of hot milk.

Swami Amritananda spotted Roy first. 'Rabindranath! Good morning. Please join your mother for a cup of hot Horlicks. We have already asked for it.'

'Good morning, Swamiji,' he replied, then kissed his mother on her forehead, took a seat beside her, and nodded to Raja Mallik.

All three smilingly welcomed Roy.

Swamiji continued, 'Martha has already informed us that you do not drink tea. It's coffee, milk or fruit juices. If you have changed your drinking habit, you need to update us.' He made the statement with a very straight face.

Rajkumar in his typical baritone played along, 'I think he drank fruit juice, a couple of glasses. That was my inside information. Well, I don't know if it was laced with vodka or anything. But, if necessary, I can find out right now. As you know, the world is nothing but one single global village these days, courtesy mobile phones.' As he was making his comment on Roy's drinking habit, he placed his mug on the table in front of him.

'Nice meeting you again, Roy. I am glad to know that you are Professor Kashyap and Martha's son. I have great respect for your father. His book "Subaltern studies – dynamics of class struggle and racism" is one of the best.'

A curious Roy nodded his head in acknowledgement.

'Aha! By the way, my full name is Rajendra Kumar Mallik, also known as Rajkumar Mallik. In Mumbai I became known as Raja Mallik, an easy offshoot of my name, evidently.'

'Rabindranath Royce Chandrabhanu Kashyap.' He remembered Rajkumar's comment about anonymity in Magnet during their meeting. 'But, how did you locate me? Why?' Roy asked.

'Well, to be honest, I was expecting a far more intelligent question than this one,' Rajkumar commented. He continued, 'You wrote a very controversial report in a national English magazine of repute. You talked about a sin committed and prejudice displayed for over a century by our society. You talked about the long-forgotten Criminal Tribes Act, 1871, unknown to the majority of the present Indians. You talked about British prejudice. You said that we Indians do not know about ourselves.'

'Yes, I did. As a journalist, it is my duty. So what?'

'You traced the roots of the dance bars of Mumbai to this Act and to the provincial Maharashtra government's liquor policy of the past. You compared the heinous Criminal Tribes Act, 1871 used by the British on millions of innocent Indians to subjugate their spirit to that of the Amendment of the current Police Act, in independent India. You have put them in perspective and stated that both the Acts truncated human dignity as well as infringed upon human rights very strongly. You have demanded honourable rehabilitation of the dancing girls and stopping of the age-old custom of their concubinage.'

'Do you feel I have written something wrong?' Roy asked.

'Did I ever say that?' Rajkumar gave a disarming smile.

Martha intervened, 'Mr Mallik, I am sorry to say so but you seem to be unnecessarily badgering my son.'

'No Martha, not really. But if you feel offended, I am truly sorry,' and he bowed his head slightly.

'It's alright. But what do you actually want from Sunny? Why did you take so much pains of going through to Mr Goradia and Roy's landlord, as you were explaining to us, so hurriedly to trace him?' asked a bewildered Martha.

'Yes, you are right. I could have waited. I should have waited, actually. But when I came to know that Roy would be a guest in the Atmatdaya Ashram in Hrishikesh, I couldn't wait any longer. There would be no one in the world except Swami Amritanandaji, my friend for over four decades, who would understand me better than anyone else, myself included. I was very clear that he would be the best person on planet earth to introduce me to Roy, properly, once again. How could I let this opportunity go? Acquaintance with you was a bonus. Moreover, I am leaving for the US in a couple of days and might take a fair amount of time to return. So, I thought it would be nice to get acquainted now,' Rajkumar replied with a very steady gaze.

Roy was still not convinced and was cryptic in his question, 'What do you really want from me?'

'Nothing! I just wanted to know you. I had met you just once in Magnet and that too with so many people around. I was curious. I read your article and liked it very much. I understand now that you were doing your research. Remember my prophecy, when we met, that you could be a journalist? And it came true,' said Rajkumar with his most captivating smile. 'You would not believe that I have not met Amrit for a fairly long time in person. I did not want to miss this opportunity. Now my purpose is served ... time to visit another friend of mine in Dehradun.' He turned around, looked towards Swamiji and continued, 'I am leaving for the US to meet Ayesha and Mr Mistri. I am sure you will wish me luck. And oh! This is for the children. Sorry, I almost forgot.' He took out a sealed white envelope from the side pocket of the short white kurta he was wearing over his trademark jeans and handed it over to him. He then faced Roy once again and spoke very emphatically, 'Please take care of your mother. I am very happy to meet both of you. I believe Martha is also planning to visit Mumbai. Once in Mumbai, if you need anything, any assistance, please give me a call without any hesitation. Here is my business card. My mobile is always available, 24 hours, 365 days, and has an international roaming facility too. Amrit also has all my contact numbers. He is my guru. You cannot miss me.'

Rajendra Kumar Mallik shook hands with Roy and Martha, embraced Amrit and walked out of the Ashram terrace very casually with his head held high, and tears of joy streaming from his eyes. If all went well, Pallavi would be a very lucky girl indeed. Trust her to pick out a gem among men.

At long last, he would have the opportunity to seek absolution from Ayesha, his beloved, whose misunderstandings he had not set to resolve. But things were coming right, probably, for all of them, and joy was probably waiting in the wings ... after so long ...

Chinmayananda came and very politely reminded Swamiji of an appointment. Amritananda nodded his head, handed the white envelope to Chinmayananda and said, 'Donation for the Delhi Children's Home. Send the receipt to Mr Mallik's Mumbai office, you know the address, it's in the file. Send the cheque to the bank today. It should be for ten lakhs rupees.'

Martha asked Swamiji, 'Ten lakhs? Any reason why he gave it now?'

He replied very politely, 'No, why should there be any reason? Rajendra has been sending across the donations every year for the last five years, for the same amount, exactly.' Before leaving, Amritananda said to both of them, 'We need to talk. I have some time free around late afternoon. We could meet then.'

Roy was curious. Martha nodded her consent, she knew Amritananda very well and how his mind worked.

During the late afternoon meeting, Swamiji turned towards Roy and said, 'I am also very curious. Rajendra wants something from you Rabindranath ... I am definite about it.'

'How are you so sure about it Uncle?' Roy asked in a tentative voice.

'Yes. I am.' He stopped pacing the length of the balcony, 'Else he would not have made such an effort to find you out so quickly. I know him for far too long to believe otherwise. Did anything happen when you visited the dance bars during your research?' Swami Amritananda looked at him pointedly.

'Happened? Happened what Uncle?' asked a bewildered Roy.

Martha intervened, 'Sunny, what did you do in the dance bar? Did you misbehave? Got drunk? Do something naughty with the girls?' She was equally puzzled. Then again, she nodded her head in self-denial and spoke out loud, 'But you are not such a person. What could happen then? Anything you can think of, Amrit Maharaj?' She looked up at Swamiji.

'You met Rajendra at Magnet. Right?' asked Amritananda for reconfirmation.

'Yes, of course, Uncle.'

'You went in there for research? To experience its ambience? For inputs? Right?'

'Yes.'

'Do you have any idea who owns Magnet?'

'I think some relative of Mr Mallik as far as my source told me.'

'Correct. You did your research well. Magnet is owned by Adil Powvala, Rajendra's brother-in-law and friend.'

'Oh, oh my God! What did you do, Sunny?'

'Nothing Ma. I did nothing,' replied Roy, trying to pacify his anxious mother.

'Look, son, I am not making any insinuation. I have read your article cursorily ... it is well written and has lots of interesting input. I will read it again. But I need to know whether you cultivated any dancer there?' reiterated Swamiji very calmly and looked at Roy.

'No. I did not. Yes, I spoke to a couple of them. But that was part of my learning process ... I knew nothing about that world.'

'Sure, I understand. But can we have the names, please?' Swamiji asked.

Martha felt that she might be missing something. She asked, 'How is all this relevant Amrit Maharaj.'

'Wait, Martha. Don't get tense. Relax. Have faith,' Amritananda spoke calmly to Martha. 'The names. I am waiting, Rabindranath, the names please?'

'Pallavi, Raima ... Nisha,' Roy replied.

'Pallavi ...? You spoke to Munia you mean?' Amritananda double-checked the answer.

'No. I did not speak to any Munia,' Roy politely debated.

'Okay. You did not speak to Munia, but Pallavi. Pallavi Singh. Right?' Swamiji asked and Roy nodded his head in confirmation. 'Munia is Pallavi. Kind of Rajendra's adopted daughter ... *muh boli beti*, you could say his god-daughter, if you want to stretch the point. Are you familiar with the concept?' Swamiji raised his eyebrows and asked with a hint of mischievousness.

'Really? Oh yes, I remember now, he called her by that name once or maybe twice.' Roy became very quiet and thoughtful. He was not aware that his mother and Swamiji exchanged concerned looks.

'Will he harm Sunny in any way, Amrit Maharaj?' The mother in Martha was concerned.

'Why would he?' Swamiji soothed away her fears, 'He wouldn't have come and met Rabindranath in my presence in that case. No. You be rest assured that Rajendra will never disrespect our friendship. Never.'

'Aren't the bar dancers prostitutes?' Martha reacted very sharply. 'Why would Rajendra Mallik adopt one such girl? What are you hiding, Sunny? Did you learn it from your father? Was I in self-denial about you?' she cried out loudly.

Roy dashed to her side, dropped on his knees, held her face cupped in his palms, and said very softly, 'Don't cry, Ma. Don't cry. I have done nothing that would hurt or dishonour you.' He touched her forehead with his. Tear drops started rolling down his cheeks.

'What was it then? Why did that man take the trouble of travelling all the way from Mumbai to Hrishikesh on his way to the US?' She felt uneasiness building up inside her and said, 'I'm not feeling good ... feeling suffocated. I need to rest, Amrit Maharaj.'

Roy became very concerned. Amritananda too. Both of them carried her inside the room and helped her to lie down on the bed.

Afterwards, Amritananda took Roy aside and said, 'Please be with your mother now. We will talk later. You need to go to Dehradun tomorrow morning and fetch Doctor Anand. I will advise Chinmayananda to allocate the Ashram jeep.'

Swamiji was about to leave but turned around, 'Rajendra said that he got your contact information from your landlord and one Mr Goradia ... did they call you to inform?'

Roy looked up at the tall figure standing near him and made an apologetic face with cheeks stained with tears, ran his fingers through his hair, and said, 'No, they did not. Actually, I switched off my mobile since the time I've been here. Maybe I should call them and find out. Could be they tried and never got through. In any case, I should keep Mr Alok Singh informed about Ma. He is really a nice human being.'

In the Future

Pallavi had felt slightly disoriented, yet so very happy since the time Rajababa visited them unannounced. Though Madhuri Ma was not at all pleased, she could not do much except grumble. Afterwards Rajababa went to Niyati's school along with Pallavi and met the little one. He left immediately after that for Delhi to catch his flight. Rajababa told her that he came over just to see Niyati and her before his urgent trip to America.

He shared one other important information, which was still resonating in her ears, 'Roy is a very good boy. I have checked him out. He is not married and his mother is a very nice yet very strict British lady. If your intentions are honourable and you are serious about leaving your profession and community for good, and you have the strength to get integrated into mainstream society, and in no way knowingly cause any grief to Roy or his mother, only then will I help you. Otherwise, I cannot help. Think through. You have my blessings.'

'But Baba ... how would I contact him? ... I know nothing about him.' Pallavi pleaded.

'I know where to find him. Call me when you are ready. And, for your information, Roy is a very good journalist and his father was a very well-respected professor.' Rajkumar kissed her forehead and gave her an affectionate hug. They bid adieu to each other.

She was oblivious of the fact that this was the last meeting in person between them.

'Niyati! Please don't cycle so rashly. Slowly, baby ... cycle slowly. I told you earlier also. Did you forget Rajababa also told you to be careful in everything you do? Come on, be a good girl and don't harass Mommy anymore,' Pallavi was cautioning her daughter as usual. It was a sun-drenched afternoon in the hilly city, which she would be leaving the next day.

'I am okay, Mommy. Don't worry. I'm fine, see.' said Niyati and looked at her mommy sideways while cycling down the narrow pathway.

The tiny girl wanted to fully enjoy the freedom she had for just a couple of hours more. Her mommy had promised to take her back to Mumbai next year. She was negligent and took her eyes off the road for a few seconds. The cycle skidded on the way, caught between a cleft of ragged stones. She lost control.

An old man, squatting on the edge of the road, was enjoying his smoke. Niyati's tiny frame tumbled on him. With the sudden impact, the old man as well as Niyati rolled together and settled on the edge of the road on the dry gutter in a tangle. The cycle fell on top of them.

Pallavi witnessed the entire episode in a kind of slow motion in disbelief. She froze, paralysed for a moment. Then in one swift motion, she leapt from the sidewalk bench where she was sitting, in front of the small take-away restaurant, and ran towards her daughter.

Roy was accompanying Dr Anand to the jeep parked near the clinic. The commotion nearby attracted his attention. He looked casually towards the source of the commotion and was bewildered to see a very beautiful young woman making a hundred-meter dash towards the other side of the lane to the tangled mess of a tiny kid and an old man. The woman looked somewhat familiar but he could not recognise her immediately. He felt slightly perplexed.

Dr Anand had by then settled inside the jeep and urged him to get in so that they could proceed quickly to Hrishikesh. Roy took his seat. The jeep slowly moved away from the scene of the commotion.

Roy felt as if he had missed something. In his subconscious, he was processing the data of the commotion and suddenly realised that the beautiful woman on the other side of the lane looked so much like Pallavi. 'Yes, it was Pallavi,' he was sure. Roy initially failed to recognise her as she was sans make-up and costume, and was in a different surrounding. She looked so beautiful and serene in her simple pink-on-pink salwar kameez. It then struck him that this could be the reason for Rajendra Kumar Mallik's Dehradun visit. He came to meet her as well. But why was she in Dehradun?

He looked back through the rear of the jeep, craning his neck. However, by now, Dr Anand and he had traversed further and the jeep had already taken a few more turns, so nothing could really be ascertained.

Dr Anand looked at him.

Roy just shook his head and said, 'I thought I saw someone I knew.'

The elderly doctor nodded his head in understanding and said, 'It happens to me too ... more so, if I care and think very deeply about the person.' With a reassuring smile, he concluded, 'Don't worry, I am sure you will meet the person soon. This accidental crossing of paths is definitely an indication of something of greater importance in the future.'

•

Delicious Ambiguity

The doctor found nothing particularly wrong with Martha except high blood pressure. He immediately put Martha on appropriate medication. After a good night's sleep, Martha was feeling very relaxed.

While the three of them, Martha, Roy and Swamiji sat on the terrace, Swamiji broke the silence by reading aloud from one of his old scrapbooks, which he had carried with himself while coming to visit Martha, '... *Now I've learned, the hard way, that some poems don't rhyme, and some stories don't have a clear beginning, middle, and end. Life is about not knowing, having to change, taking the moment, and making the best of it, without knowing what's going to happen next. Delicious ambiguity ...*' He looked up from the scrapbook and said, 'When I read about Gilda Radner, the American comedian, actress, wife of Gene Wilder, I was so easily transported to the world where Rajendra belongs. In fact, about him, I can use another expression from my scrapbook.' He shuffled a few pages and read out... '*In our worldly-wise ways a so-called bad decision makes a good story*'... and then he closed the scrapbook.

'By whichever name you address him, Rajkumar Mallik, Raja Mallik, or Rajendra Kumar Mallik, he is a maverick, super-talented yet totally a nomad. He was a very good student yet because of his political beliefs he allowed his career to go astray. He could have been the best undergraduate student in our college. He was also a very good athlete. In inter-college debates, he was the best debater. It was but natural that he would be recruited to join politics of the time as was the convention in Kolkata those days. We were all in a group of believers and thought of bringing change to our social system for good governance and we were all arrested by the police together. We were also in jail together. All of us broke out of jail together. Well, I am talking so openly because, later on certain amnesty programmes were announced by a subsequent provincial government for the political prisoners and the legal cases against us were withdrawn. After coming out of jail, I decided to complete my studies and to teach, and later on, pursued spirituality to serve the people, as both of you are aware.

'Anisur, one of our other friends, went to London. He runs a chain of food-stores, along with his brother, in London suburbs currently. Mahua, the girl who had recruited Rajendra in our party and later on became a very close friend of his, could not make it. She died in the prison hospital. Soumitra died in Bihar in a police encounter while working with the underground about a decade ago. Tapas works in a Mercantile firm in Kolkata. However, Rajendra possibly did what we all wanted to do; work in the villages at the grass-root level.

'He is an orphan. He was adopted by our school teacher Mr Indubhusan Mallik. After Mr Mallik, his mentor, died of a heart attack when we were inside the jail, Rajendra never returned to Kolkata, as he could not reconcile himself to the fact that he could not do anything to help his mentor as he was inside the jail. I know the guilt haunts him even today. Being an orphan, after the death of Indubhusan Mallik he had no family moors, so he drifted and ultimately reached Banaras.'

'Oh My God! And I had suspected his motive in donating money to our Delhi Children's Home. I am so sorry Amrit Maharaj,' Martha honestly exclaimed.

'It is alright. You did not know him, Martha.' Amritananda softly replied. 'I want both of you to know him well. If I am correct in anticipating why he was here, I think you need to know his story first.'

Martha was bewildered, yet kept quiet to listen to what Amrit Maharaj had to say further. Roy looked at the Himalayas far away in the horizon.

Swamiji continued, 'He had worked in Banaras and its surrounding villages for a very long time teaching children. He also did voluntary work for the adult literacy programme among the Banaras boatmen. He stayed for a long time in Banaras because Aunt Lata, a child-widow, the niece of Indubhusan Mallik, was banished to Banaras by the Mallik family as per the old Hindu custom prevalent then. Rajkumar stayed with her and looked after her because he felt that he owed it to Indubhusan.

'Some eleven or twelve years ago, the younger brother of a mafia leader-cum-politician was found annihilated under mysterious circumstances in Banaras. Media speculated that the incidents were results of gang rivalry. However, I had heard from a very devoted disciple of our Ashram, who was posted in one of the police stations of Banaras during that period, that Rajendra had a hand in it because this mafia-group tried raping a teenage girl on a Dev Deepavali day and he had objected to it. My disciple knew about Rajendra because whenever I had visited Banaras along with my Guruji, he used to come and meet me.

'He left Banaras around that time and settled in Mumbai. Aunt Lata by then had passed away, so relocation was not an issue. A talented Parsi girl Ayesha Mistri, Magnet's owner's cousin, fell in love with Rajendra and they got married. Currently, they are separated. You must have heard him mention the other day that he would be visiting her as well as his father-in-law Farokh Mistri in the US. He runs the family restaurant on their behalf in Mumbai. I know he still loves Ayesha. They had their misunderstandings because of his protective behaviour towards Munia. I understand that for any woman to accept such wild and odd behaviour from her husband is difficult. But my friend is a maverick, I have already mentioned that. And, there is a price attached to being a maverick's wife or friend.

'Rajendra Kumar Mallik is a haunted man. At the most, you could consider him as a guest in your life; you can never ever consider him to be a life-long feature in your existence. He would try to be good to you. He would try to stand by you in your hour of need, most of the time. However, never expect a lifelong commitment from him. For him, there is always a next project, a next cause, waiting. He is always restless, because I feel he is still seeking his roots, seeking himself. Look at his thinking pattern, if I have to explain it very quickly and in a very simplistic manner; he saw an image of a father in Farokh Mistri that somehow he did relate to Indubhusan and surely, he took all their responsibilities unflinchingly upon himself. He identified Munia's tragedy of birth with that of his own. So he moved heaven and earth to bring peace and joy in her life.'

He paused and took a deep breath. 'Rajendra is the part of my soul that I was referring to just the other day, Rabindranath.'

Martha looked very keenly into her son's eyes and then she looked back to Swami for direction, silently.

Roy was engrossed in his own thoughts. After a passage of a brief period of time he raised his finger, 'I have a question?'

'Shoot. Who's stopping you?' answered Swamiji.

'Who was the girl the mafia tried molesting?'

'By now you should have guessed. It was Munia; Pallavi.' Swamiji answered calmly.

'Yes, I thought so too. Just wanted to double-check.'

'So you can understand Rajendra's commitment to that girl. I am sure he might have misunderstood your goodness while dealing with Munia for something else. What he did was to bring it up on the table not so very subtly to judge your inclination. He is my friend too; hence once he heard of your connection with the Ashram, he has brought my friendship into play. Don't get unnecessarily worried. But I would request you to be honest with yourself about what happened and please take your mother and me into confidence.'

For Roy time was at a disadvantage. He initially wanted to discuss his experience at the unique dance bars of Mumbai and its people with his mother. But when he felt that her unhealed wound about her personal tragedy was affecting her behaviour, he stopped short of discussing about Pallavi and that was the mistake he did. However, because of Rajendra Kumar Mallik's over enthusiasm and unusually protective behaviour, people closest to him started suspecting his motive unnecessarily. He looked at Swamiji and his mother and simply said, 'Nothing happened. I am sure people visiting those bars don't usually carry human decency and that's possibly where I scored some marks.' Roy wanted more time to delve into and decipher his own emotions. He decided to sleep on it and speak to his mother and Swamiji later on to clear the air once and for all.

Predicament

Roy's predicament was that he was unable to decipher his own feelings about Pallavi. Was it infatuation? It could be a probable; a distinct possibility. He hardly knew her even a month ago. Even now he knew nothing really worthwhile. Yes, her vivacious presence had attracted him towards her. It was necessary to be vivacious for her to be coveted by the people of the night, to be the queen of Magnet. Was he falling for the cultivated personality she projected because of his loneliness in Mumbai? Of course, she was beautiful but beauty cannot be the only criterion to be in love. How Rajendra Mallik could even harbour the thought and invade the sanctity of the Ashram and obliquely insinuate at his supposed behaviour in Magnet. What was it that provided him with the idea? Yet, he felt good thinking about Pallavi.

On the other hand, his mother had pointed out that Kumudini had intellect and empathy. Kumudini liked him too. He knew that. It could be an easy way out for him to find a solution for his quest for a partner. However, even when he was alone in Mumbai in the last three months or so, it did not occur to him. So, was he imposing his mother's thought onto his own? Was he conforming?

What could love be? Do you rationalise before falling in love?

Sleep provided him the respite from his conflicting thoughts and turmoil.

'Hello! Alok Singh Speaking!'

'Sir, Roy here. Good morning.'

'Roy. Good morning. How is your mother?'

'Much better Sir. Nothing to worry. Only blood pressure is high. Doctor Anand had visited her too.'

'Oh really. That's good.' After a slight pause, Alok Singh asked, 'How are you Roy?'

'I am good Sir.'

'We are very proud of you Roy. You wrote a marvellous article. Especially Mahinbhai, he was so impressed that he immediately called you on your mobile but it was switched off.'

'Sir. Actually I kept it switched off. My apologies. Please convey my regards to Mr Goradia. I will call him very soon.'

'Sure and thank you Roy for calling. Oh, did your uncle contact you?'

'My uncle? Who was that Sir?' Roy was curious.

'Why? Don't you have an uncle, Mr Raja Mallik?'

'Raja Mallik?'

'Yes. He had contacted Mahinbhai's office with a reference from 'Wadia and Joshi,' the solicitor firm. He introduced himself as a distant cousin of your father. He said that he was looking for your contact number after reading your article. As he saw Mahinbhai's quotations in your article, he contacted him, and through him he had reached me. Once I said to him that your mother is sick then he became even more insistent, that I put him in touch with you.'

'And?' Roy was getting very irritated with Rajendra Mallik's behaviour.

'He had a good reference, so, I perforce had to give the Ashram's address; and before I could even conclude he himself gave out the complete address of the Ashram and also other details about the institution. Said he knows all about it. So I was convinced about his bonafides. Is there anything wrong?'

'No. Nothing Sir. Yes, I have spoken to him. Thank you.' He tackled Alok Singh's anxiety. However, Roy was furious with Rajkumar's self-serving importance. He had no option but to call Mahendra Goradia immediately to apologise for this insensitive man's intrusive behaviour, now that he came to know about it.

'Mr Mahendra Goradia please ...'

The woman's voice from the other end asked for his name.

'I am Roy. He knows me.'

'Hello Mr Roy! This is Sylvia. Sir is busy in a meeting. Are you back in Mumbai? No. Oh! How is your mother? Okay. Great. Kindly leave your contact number with me and I will connect him once his meeting is over in an hour or so. Is that all right? Good day.'

The Prince and the Dancing Girl

Ever smiling Man-Friday of Amritananda, Swami Chinmayananda, was back in the act, 'Rabindranathji, would you mind coming to Swamiji's office please? Mr Goradia will call you shortly from Mumbai. He had called earlier but Swamiji was busy with some visitors so we had to request him to call now.'

'What about the phone at the general office?' Roy was not very comfortable speaking to Mahendra Goradia from Amritananda's room.

'It is not working.' Chinmayananda replied.

'I had used it in the morning but ...' Roy was a bit surprised.

'The connections are very unpredictable here. Else, if you want to speak from your mobile, you need to go to the main road, reception will be better there. Calls drop frequently inside our Ashram.' Chinmayananda tried explaining while they were heading up to Swamiji's office.

As they were talking, they reached the office, the room where Roy had met Amritananda the day he first arrived.

'May we come in please? I have Rabindranathji with me.' Chinmayananda uttered in a reverential voice. He indicated Roy to wait for an answer before parting the heavy curtains hanging in front of the door.

'Yes Chinmaya. Please come in.' Swamiji replied, as usual, in his mesmerising energetic voice.

'Good afternoon, Uncle.' Roy said.

'Good afternoon, Rabindranath. You can take the call from the extension kept near the sofa. I need to finish the proof-checking of this article for our magazine. Thank you Chinmaya, you may leave now.' Swamiji nodded at Chinmayananda, turned to Roy and looked quizzically at him, a faint smile lighting up his face.

'I am sorry that I disturbed your work.' Roy said genuinely.

Even before he could finish his statement the phone rang. Swamiji indicated Roy to pick-up the extension, which Roy did.

'Atmatdaya Ashram. How can we be of help please?' Roy said.

'Is it Mr Roy?' Sylvia enquired.

'Yes Sylvia,' Roy replied.

'Hold on for a moment please. I will put Mr Goradia on the line. Oh ... your voice is very feeble; you need to speak a bit more loudly please,' she said.

Roy put his hand over the mouthpiece and informed Swamiji, 'Sorry Uncle. I might have to talk a bit loudly, if necessary. The connection is weak, I hope you don't mind.'

Swamiji nodded, without taking his eyes off the proof-copy he was reading.

'Hello Roy! Where are you hibernating?' Mahendra Goradia's voice echoed through the receiver into Roy's ear.

'Sir. How do you do!' Roy said.

'How do you do! I believe your mother is doing well now. Alok told me. I am happy. Does she know about the lovely article you have written?' Mahendra Goradia stated.

'Ma is doing well. Yes, she did read it. Thank you for your compliments. I am glad that you have liked it. Without your guidance the article would not have been possible,' Roy uttered honestly.

'What nonsense Roy, don't be so self-effacing. It is you who brought out the issue. By the way, the side-bar, the "Box item" as you guys call it, on Inder and Munni, was brilliantly written without naming names.'

'You liked the treatment of that story?' Roy enquired.

'Of course! Look at the appropriate headline "The Prince and the Dancing Girl",' Goradia commented.

'It is not original though, it is inspired by a movie title – *The Prince and The Show Girl*. Made in 1957; I remembered it because it was one of my father's favourites. He used to love watching 1950s and 1960s movies.' Roy laughed genuinely.

Roy's laugh attracted Swamiji's attention. He looked fondly at the profile of this exceptional young man and took a short break from his proof-reading.

'But son, I am also happy, because of the way you treated Inder and Munni's story with dignity,' Goradia said.

'They deserved that respect, Munni Bai and Prince Inder Kumar. They were exceptional personalities. Even three decades ago they had displayed exemplary bias-free thinking. They had the courage to fight prejudice.'

Mahendra Goradia said, 'I couldn't agree with you more.'

'It is sad that the society did not recognise that love. In fact, the way you had started your briefing to me with Inder Kumar and Munni Bai's story, it made my understanding of the subject that much easier.' Roy explained excitedly. 'Can I ask one more question about Prince Inder Kumar? Just for my understanding?'

'Of course Roy.' Goradia replied obligingly.

'Did he marry later on? How about his family? I did a Google search but there was nothing.'

'No. Roy. Inder is still single.'

'Oh! I missed such a brilliant ending. 'Prince in waiting ... I would say... that Munni Bai must have been a terrific lady.'

'Yes, she was,' Goradia replied wistfully.

While Roy was engrossed in discussing the nuances of his article with Mahendra Goradia, what he did not notice was that Amritanandaji by now had pulled out the copy of The India Post containing his article from the neatly piled books and magazines on his large writing table. He flipped through the pages and after locating Roy's article had started reading the 'Box-Item.'

'Thank you, Sir. Thank you for your kind words. I will be in touch with you once I am back in Mumbai.' Roy concluded his talk with Mahendra Goradia.

'Thank you Roy, and wish your mother a very speedy recovery. Good luck.' Mahendra Goradia disconnected the line.

'Thank you, Uncle. Sorry to have intruded on your quiet time.' Very sincerely Roy apologised. However, Amritananda was keenly reading the side-bar of his article and did not answer. He simply indicated to Roy to take a seat in front of him at the table.

Once he finished reading the specific portion of the article, Swami Amritananda looked up. His eyes had a strange, inexplicable look. He stared straight into Roy's eyes, thought for a while and uttered in an exceptionally calm voice, 'Rabindranath, we have a much larger and important issue at hand than what I had initially thought of.'

Roy was bewildered at this statement.

'You are about to enter a social vortex. Do you possess enough skills to come out of it unscathed?' Swamiji rhetorically quizzed Roy.

'Are you trying to scare me? I accept that emotionally I am slightly vulnerable presently because of my father's untimely death and Ma's denial to face the situation. What has happened has happened, but life goes on. Anything you want to let me know further? Am I missing something here?' Roy narrowed his eyes and looked at Swamiji.

'How do you want to tackle Rajendra?' Swamiji looked at Roy, his eyes twinkling.

'That pompous ass!' Roy looked at Swamiji and said very clearly, 'Sorry for my language. But that's what he actually is. He might be your friend but lacks sophistication and social grace. Frankly, he had no understanding of my dealing with Pallavi. I had required certain answers to be corroborated. I had four sources providing inputs to me, and as a journalist, I needed to verify all controversial input from at least two other independent individual sources. That's how I work, and try and keep my stories error-free. If he felt I was head over heels in love with that girl, then he is a complete fool.'

'But the girl might now feel used. Do you have a view on that?' Swamiji asked.

'I never promised anything. In fact, to a very direct question I told her to her face, love does not happen overnight and beauty is not the only criterion for falling in love. To me, purity of heart and emotion are much more important elements in love than a body. Conscience and soul, once they are corrupted, you are lost forever.'

'What did you do, Rabindranath? You rejected her very existence founded on her looks, primarily. Moreover, you created more hunger in her soul to come out of that dungeon. Bravo! Rajendra Kumar Mallik was on the prowl for such a groom for Pallavi,' Swamiji threw up his hands in the air smilingly.

'What nonsense Uncle! Why should I marry Pallavi? I am not in servitude. I have not created any hope in anyone. Neither have I promised anyone, anything. It must be your friend's wishful thinking and presumption.' Roy protested, perhaps a bit too forcefully.

'Did you not like the girl at all? How come you have discussed everything with your mother, barring this girl and your visit to Magnet in detail?' Swamiji asked his question with a poker face.

'You know that it is not that simple, Uncle. I stopped short of discussing with Ma because I felt that possibly she was revisiting her wounds with my narration, and I became scared. As far as Pallavi was concerned, I liked her because I did not expect a personality like her, of her mental calibre, to be present in a dance bar. Maybe it was a flaw in me as I was never exposed to the stark realities, as someone said to me once.' Roy felt that he was providing far too much explanation for his behaviour.

'Have you finished?' Swamiji asked.

'No. Not really. Even I am thinking why I am explaining so much. However, let it be clear once and for all. I respect you and love you. So, I have no issue discussing it with you.' Roy heaved a sigh of relief once he could truly state his position.

'Sure Rabindranath. I understand. Please state your *position.*' Swamiji looked at him fondly and laid emphasis on the word position.

'You may not believe it but I have never spoken to her outside of her workplace. Whatever I did discuss with her was in her place of work with a maddening crowd and a huge amount of noise, and millions of currency notes floating all around us, surrounding us. Though, I could understand that her yearning for a better life is genuine. So could be that of a thousand other girls who are victims of such heinous crimes committed by their biradari and our bloody social insensitivity. Possibly, my fondness towards her came from the fact that despite such disadvantages, she still looked at life so positively.' Roy took a deep breath.

'Okay, how about we invite her to our Ashram for darshan and prasad once?' Swamiji suggested.

'Oh! Uncle, but why would you want to do that?' Roy asked in a surprised voice.

'Why not? You are my godson. I want to see the girl who has impressed you so much. In any case, it would also give me an opportunity to get introduced to Rajendra's *muh-boli-beti*.' Swamiji said in an unusually light voice.

'But that is not fair, Uncle. You cannot change your jersey so quickly!' Roy smiled.

'But before I invite Pallavi, I need to understand something more from you. Who is this Mahendra Goradia?'

'He is one of the best corporate lawyers of Mumbai. He runs a huge law firm.'

'How did you know him?' Swamiji asked.

Roy narrated the story of Alok Singh's customary Sunday lunch, he discussing his assignment, Goradia's briefing.

'Mahendra Goradia never really interacted with you before you started writing the story?' Swamiji asked.

'No. Never.'

'And you knew nothing about Munni Bai and Prince Inder Kumar before he told you about them?'

'No.'

'Did you ever discuss this with either Pallavi or Rajendra?'

'No, Uncle. Why?' Roy was curious. 'No. I do not ever discuss my story before publication with anyone except my editor. For clarifications, if required, I might check some information with my sources, I might conduct interviews with them but I never give away my story. No serious journalist, I suppose, would do that. But why are you asking me all this? What is the connection?' Roy's brain started whirling.

'I wanted to be doubly sure.'

'Sure about what Uncle Amrit?'

'That Rajendra and Munia do not know about it. Goradia and Singh did only speak to Rajendra when he intruded their privacy to find you out.' Swamiji paused, collected his thoughts and after a while he said, 'With your research you might have achieved a marvellous fiat. If my senses are directing me correctly, you might be able to reunite a father and a daughter, who have never met, if they want to. I am sure, each of them is not even aware of the other's existence.' Swamiji laughed in joy. He was genuinely pleased. 'See my Lord's blessings. You are blessed, Roy.'

'Hold on! Hold on! Hold on for a second! Munni Bai, Inder Kumar, Munia…?' Roy asked incredulously.

Swamiji nodded his head in agreement. 'First clue – Mahendra Goradia told you that Prince Inder Kumar and Munni were in love thirty years ago and wanted to marry. This incident happened in Bombay. Thereafter, one couldn't find Munni anymore. Rajendra, on the other hand, had told me long back that Shankar Baba, Munia's great-grandfather and the clan headman had obliterated all clues before he killed Munia's mother Munni after she delivered a girl child because she fell in love and wanted to marry someone in Bombay. This also happened about thirty years ago. And, the marriage did not take place because of community tradition.'

'Great coincidence, of course. Pallavi is from Chambal Valley. Where was Munni Bai from?' Roy questioned.

'Chambal Valley; as far as I remember Rajendra telling me, it was a place called Bhind. But, I will cross-check with Rajendra, once again. Possible second match of clues.' Swamiji said.

'Munni Bai was a Bedni, a Bedia girl. Alok Singh told me. Pallavi says she is a Rajput, but could be a lie, as she had winked at Mr Mallik after that,' Roy informed Swamiji about the incident.

'As Bedias don't marry off their girls traditionally, they follow matrilineal society. That means most of the times they keep the mother's gotra. When they want to hoodwink, they use the illegitimate father's gotra. Bedias and Rajputs have a long history, Rajendra told me that. Inder Kumar is a Rajput, don't forget,' Swamiji said.

'One more input Uncle. Mahendra Goradia told me that Prince and Munni met at the third floor of Compound in Sushila Bai's mehfil.'

'Okay. We will call Rajendra in the US tonight. He might have barely reached there. We need to have confirmations.' Swamiji said.

'And after that?' Roy asked.

'We need to consult Mahendra Goradia and Alok Singh if it would be prudent to contact Prince Inder Kumar. I would request Rajendra not to discuss anything with Munia until we get a positive feedback from Inder Kumar that he might want to establish contact. Till then all this is under wraps, Mr Investigative Journalist. What a mess you have put me into?' Swamiji had a hearty laugh.

Roy said, 'I am thinking aloud. If both of them submit blood for a DNA test, things can be proven conclusively. After all, Pallavi will become Princess Pallavi.'

'So you will marry her, the princess?' Swamiji asked Roy with a faint smile.

'Over my dead body! I always stay away from super riches. Please, I am in enough trouble already, so no more jokes please, Uncle. I beg of you. I don't want Ma to be upset in any way.' Roy folded his hands in a namaskar and displayed his brilliant smile.

The usually taciturn Rajkumar was ecstatic when he received a call from his friend Amrit on his mobile. It was early morning in Philadelphia. In a few hours he would go and visit Farokh Mistri in the old age home. Ayesha had to accompany a group of students of her class to New York on a week's study tour. In fact, she left within a couple of hours of his arrival. They could not even say 'hello' to each other properly. With the pressure of time on her head, he too, did not want to disturb her, except on her way to the airport made her introduce him to the nursing centre, so that he could be with Farokh Mistri during her absence and made her promise that they would meet for dinner immediately on her return; then he checked into a hotel.

Farokh Mistri otherwise lived with his daughter, but as she was travelling for a week they decided on a short-stay at the old-age home for Farokh's comfort because Ayesha did not want her father to stay on in their bungalow alone under the care of two part-time helps. So she decided to close the house, alert the security company and used her contact with the university to arrange for her father's care. Though she was aware of Rajkumar's impending visit, she did not want him to be burdened with her father's care in a foreign land. Moreover, she wanted both him and herself to have some space.

Once Rajkumar informed his friend Amrit of his up-to-date status, only then he realised that Swamiji might have something to say and had called specifically for that.

'Yes Amrit, please tell me how can I help?' Rajkumar's clear and loud voice resonated in Swamiji's ear.

'We need to talk about Pallavi.' Without any preamble, Swamiji said flatly.

'What happened to Pallavi? Something serious? I spoke to her only yesterday; she did not say anything to me. What is it and what made you so concerned, I am just curious?' Rajkumar was both anxious as well as irritated that Amrit was poking his nose probably unnecessarily.

Swamiji could guess Rajkumar's sentiment and decided that the time had come when he needed to straighten his friend out a bit. Else, his way of approaching the issue at hand might not happen and the desired result might not be satisfactory.

Swamiji composed his thoughts and in an authoritative and crisp voice said, 'Rajendra, when you landed up at my Ashram unannounced early in the morning, a couple of days ago and started insinuating that my godson has something to do with your *muh-boli beti*, we gave it a patient hearing because you are my friend. You had called up a large number of respectable people on various pretexts in Mumbai to find out about Rabindranath and all of them are getting in touch with the hapless young man. Still I kept my calm, as we are friends. Now when I am calling you, why are you getting irritated? Is this what friendship is all about? Just being a yes-man and a one-way street? What happened to you, Rajendra? Have you lost everything? Why have you become so possessive about that girl?'

For a long time there was no answer. After some poignant pause Rajkumar said, 'Sorry. My mistake. Tell me what to do?'

The ever composed Swamiji said, 'Rabindranath might have traced Munia's father. No. Don't get panicky or overjoyed. Please keep your cool.'

'Roy? Munia's father? When? How?' Rajkumar's queries were rapid-fire, staccato.

'I told you to hold your horses. Else, it will not work over a long distance call. I will ask you a few more questions. If you know the answers, please let me know. First: is Munia a Bedia girl? What are they called ... Bedni?'

'Yes.' In a barely audible voice Rajkumar answered. Swamiji showed a thumbs-up to Roy.

'Just to reconfirm and refresh my memory, what you had shared with me a long time ago – that Munia's mother's name was Munni Bai and she was murdered by her clan people, supposedly?'

'Yes.' Rajkumar replied in the same hushed tone. Swamiji did another thumbs-up sign.

'Munni Bai was from Bhind district of Chambal valley, right?'

'Yes! She was from Bhind but some of her relatives were in Ambe, Mirpura and Morena. Munia was moved through various remote villages in her early childhood so that she could not be traced.'

Thumbs up, Swamiji calmly asked the last question, 'Who is Sushila Bai, what was her relation with Munni and where did they reside in Bombay?'

Rajkumar replied very patiently, 'Sushila Bai is a Madam. She used to run her mehfil from Compound. Munni used to work there. Why the question? Has Roy found this piece of information too?'

'Yes, he did, Rajendra. Rabindranath knows who the father is.'

'That story of The Prince and the Dancing Girl ... right? I am such a bloody fool ... it had stuck me once but very lightly ... what a bloody fool I am.' Rajkumar's voice sounded very hoarse.

There was again a very long silence. Swamiji could understand the turmoil inside his friend's heart. He said softly, 'Let her go, Rajendra. Let her fly. You need to be with Ayesha. She needs you and you need her. Concentrate my friend. Give me your permission to take this forward. You be in the US. Don't rush back. That would be foolish. You will lose Ayesha forever, and in all fairness, Munia too has to go. Let everyone fly. Whoever is yours, will return to you. Let all choose their respective nests.' Swamiji closed his eyes and prayed to his Guruji for Rajendra to have the strength.

'Please take care of her. She is a very nice girl; fought alone with the whole world to survive.' Rajkumar Mallik started weeping uncontrollably.

'Rajendra! Focus! Rajendra! We are executing the philosophy that you thought of, embraced and nurtured for so long. It needs courage and you have it. Focus, my friend. Don't become emotional now. One last request, please don't say anything to Munia at all right now. We need to see Munia's father's reaction. We will get back to you within the next forty-eight hours. If you want to talk, or communicate anything, call me anytime.'

'Who is her father?' Rajkumar asked, more composed now.

'Rajendra, at this point, that is irrelevant. Frankly speaking, with your kind of temper and emotion I wouldn't trust you with the name. You might blast the poor guy off. Oh! Can you trust me with Munia's mobile number? In case we need to contact her in an emergency. Is there anyone who stays with her?'

'Take down Munia's number. Yes. Madhuri Bai – the lady who bought her, Sushila Bai's daughter, she stays with her. Don't let her know anything. These people are still capable of viciousness. You never know, they might throw acid to disfigure her or will hide her inside a remote corner of Chambal, or could even murder her.'

'Rajendra Kumar Mallik, we have traversed a long way. Be at peace. In this fight too, I am with you. So is Rabindranath. Give my regards to Mr Mistri. One more thing, I would like to speak to Ayesha very soon. Please make sure it happens. Take care Rajendra,' Swamiji spoke resolutely and slowly replaced the receiver on the cradle of the telephone.

Extending the Argument

Amritananda was unusually quiet, immersed in his thoughts. He had hardly spoken to anyone and kept himself confined to his office and prayer room. Martha had enquired twice with Chinmayananda about him and was informed that Swamiji was in meditation and couldn't be disturbed. Roy was deliberating within himself whether he should discuss Pallavi with Ma, but ultimately decided against it. He wanted to think through more thoroughly. He thought of speaking to Kumudini. He had initially requested for a week's leave and the week would be over tomorrow. He looked at his watch, Kumudini would be in office by now and the weekend edit meeting was yet to start. He decided to walk till the main road and give Kumudini a call.

'Hello, Kumudini. Can we talk for a few moments, please?' Roy asked when Kumudini picked up her mobile.

'Roy! Hi! How is your Mom?' Kumudini enquired with genuine concern.

'She is okay now. Needs rest. Her blood pressure is slightly on the higher side. Loneliness and exhaustion, should be alright soon. How are you holding?'

'Well. It's cool. Balu and Freny want to leave.'

'Really? How come?' Roy was surprised.

'I suppose, not fitting into the regimented structure and the team effort we spoke of. In fact, your article helped me a great deal to make them understand what real passion to our profession can achieve; instead of a simple by-line grabbing attitude that lacks depth.'

'Thank you for your compliment. It is you who motivated me to write such an article.' Roy too was genuine in his submission.

'But you did it,' Kumudini smiled fondly which Roy couldn't see but could feel because of the way the sentiment was conveyed over the phone. Had he been present in front of Kumudini, he would have realised that her fondness for him had grown considerably in the last one week. 'When can you be in office Roy? I need you. I know your mother might want you to stay for sometime and I appreciate it, but I need you here too,' Kumudini said softly.

Roy thought for a while and said, 'Will it be alright if I am present during next week's weekly edit meeting?'

Kumudini took a deep breath and said, 'One more week?' She paused. 'Okay Roy. See you in a week.' As an afterthought she said, 'I know you are attending to your ailing mother. But you can at least call me some time. Your mobile is never available since the time you have left Mumbai. Bye Roy.'

'Bye Kumudini. Thank you for granting extension of my leave,' Roy replied earnestly.

Was she angry? Disappointed? Did he hear a tone of subdued hurt? Concern? Empathy? Love?

Before the Sunday morning prayer, Swamiji had sent word through Chinmayananda to Roy for him to stay back after the prayer and to meet him in his office.

When Roy entered Swamiji's office, he was seen pacing the breadth of the room holding his hands behind him in a thoughtful manner. 'Sit down Rabindranath,' he said, without breaking the rhythm of his walk. Once Roy sat on the couch placed at the side of the room, where the extension line of the telephone was kept, Swamiji looked at him and said, 'We need to discuss with Martha about Munia.'

'But what do you want to discuss Uncle?' Roy enquired.

'That I will send you as an emissary to her, so that you can organise a probable meeting with her father,' Swamiji said calmly.

'The father has to agree to the meeting, Uncle. We cannot force it upon him. We need to take Alok Singh and Mahendra Goradia into confidence to reach Prince Inder Kumar. Though I have got his address and other contact details through my Delhi sources but, I suppose it would be appropriate to reach him through his friends.'

'Yes. You are absolutely correct in your thinking. However, have you ever thought of a scenario that Goradia might have spoken out of turn? He might not even vaguely have thought of Munni producing an offspring of Inder Kumar. Has it ever occurred to you that he might not have remotely considered the option that someone may connect the dots, as you have said once? What would the implication then be?' Swamiji volleyed his question.

'A very valid point, Uncle. Okay, why wait then? Today is Sunday. Around lunch time, we can speak to Alok Singh and Mahendra Goradia when they will meet for their Sunday lunch. In the meantime, if you want and think it is absolutely necessary, kindly speak to Ma. I leave it to you how you place the issue. But Uncle, she should understand that I have not hidden anything from her purposely. Initially, I only thought that the time was not appropriate; and thereafter Rajendra Kumar Mallik's unplanned presence further complicated the issue.'

Swamiji nodded his head.

When Roy made the phone call to Alok Singh's residence, the lunch had just got over, and the four gentlemen were settling themselves into the living room to start their card game.

Bahadur picked up the call. He became excited on hearing Roy's voice, and as requested by Roy, called his master to the phone.

'Hello Roy. What a pleasant surprise. What can I do for you?' Mildly curious, Alok Singh said.

'Sir, I needed your permission to speak to Mr Goradia about Prince Inder Kumar and Munni Bai's daughter.' Without any preamble Roy came straight to the point.

Alok Singh was flabbergasted with the suddenness of the issue. He was hardly prepared to expect the totally unexpected. 'What did you say? Inder's daughter? Munni Bai? What?' he looked around at his friends sitting at the card table. They too looked back at him.

It took him sometime to absorb the impact of the information delivered over phone by Roy. And, when it did, the questions came like the rapid-fire round of a quiz programme. Roy was prepared to handle the situation and calmly said to his landlord, 'Sir, I suppose if you kindly request Mr Goradia to be on line, I can explain everything. Or perhaps you can put the phone on speaker and all of us can talk.'

The well-modulated voice of Mahendra Goradia resonated in Roy's ear over the surprisingly robust and clear telephone connection, 'Hello, Roy. Nice to hear from you. Alok did tell me that you want to discuss with me something about a supposed daughter of Inder. Is that right?' Courteous yet cautious, Mahendra Goradia, the eternal lawyer.

'Absolutely correct Sir, I am certain about the relationship and there is hardly any supposition in it.'

'Un huh ...' Goradia was deep in thought, and his very brief response made Roy critically aware of Swamiji's earlier comment of speaking 'out of turn.'

As was expected of him, Goradia asked Roy, 'How sure are you about your findings?'

'Very sure, Sir.' Roy replied very politely.

'What are the reasons for your being very sure of this fact? If I may ask?' Goradia was equally polite. However, Roy could make out that the person at the other end of the telephone was still deep in thought. He very judiciously narrated the steps that helped him come to the conclusion. Throughout his narration Mahendra Goradia did not, for even once, interrupt him. After Roy finished his recounting, he asked Roy, 'What motivated you to dig into Inder's story further? What possible gain did you expect out of it?'

Roy was not only astonished but extremely hurt by the tone of Mahendra Goradia's question. However, with his mature and calm thinking, he could understand Mahendra Goradia's awkward position and hence to ease the situation he said, with utmost honesty, that his only motive was to unite a daughter with her father. He even explained that he had neither spoken to the daughter nor contacted the father till now and was expecting Mahendra Goradia to guide him.

'Can you drop it?' Mahendra Goradia enquired softly.

'But why, Sir? Don't you want the daughter to know her father? Or, the father to at least know that he has a daughter?

Why are we presuming that what we are doing is not right?' Roy made his point at last.

'I need time to think through.' Mahendra Goradia said with finality.

'How much time, Sir?' Roy asked.

'I don't know, a few days probably. Moreover, I cannot discuss such a sensitive issue with Inder over phone. As I had said before, why make a private grief public?' Goradia sounded mildly agitated.

'Sir. You have interacted with me; do you think I want to sensationalise it? I want to discreetly try and create and if possible open a communication channel between the father and the daughter. You know me by now. You tell me what can be done? But kindly don't advise me to kill the prospect of the duo's meeting.' Roy spoke very passionately.

'I am still not very sure about the whole proposition, Roy. I need to ponder over it.' The forthright Mahendra Goradia, the mentor, Roy had met a few days ago was disturbed, and in his place a very cautious friend trying to guard the privacy and goodwill of another friend had emerged.

Roy knew that from Mahendra Goradia's standpoint he was correct. He could not fault or blame him at all. However, an inexplicable urge forced Roy to make up his mind. He knew that once he uttered his final position he would probably lose Mahendra Goradia as well as his landlord Alok Singh as his well-wishers. So he, with utmost politeness yet with a finality, stated to the senior counsel, 'Sir, I have a feeling that it would be difficult for you to discuss with Prince Inder Kumar what we have been debating so far. I think it would be appropriate for me to find an alternative approach to reach him. However, I assure you that I will never mention your name to him, and our current conversation will remain totally "off the record". I also want you to know that I respect you a lot. Have a great day.'

'Sure Roy. You too.' Mahendra Goradia, ever the gentleman, said with utmost politeness.

Roy kept the phone down.

'Did I behave rashly, Uncle?' he looked towards Swamiji and enquired.

'If you believe what you are doing is not to malign a person but as you said to honestly try to unite a daughter and her father, then I see no reason why you should be feeling guilty about it,' Swamiji said thoughtfully.

'Thank you, Uncle. I will call Inder Kumar on his mobile today evening from my mobile. So I will walk across to the main road. It would also give him an opportunity to have my mobile number on his phone book, in case he needed time to open up. I don't want to expose the Ashram's phone number to him as yet. Moreover, I don't want to disturb you before the Sunday prayer and evening discourse. Once I speak to him we would perhaps then contact Pallavi,' Roy made his plan of action known to Amritananda.

Comprehension

'Can I speak to Mr Inder Kumar, please?' Roy enquired.

'Yes. Speaking.'

'Good evening, Sir. I am Roy.'

'Good evening, Roy. I have received your text message; what is it that you want to discuss with me?' a deep and articulated voice replied.

'I want to meet you at your convenience within this week,' Roy put forward his request.

'What is this meeting all about? And wherefrom did you get my mobile number, if I may ask?' Inder Kumar enquired in a very reserved manner.

'Sir, I am a journalist. I have my sources. I really want to meet you in person and discuss.'

'Until you tell me the purpose of the meeting how do you expect me to agree Roy?' a very polite yet firm Inder Kumar replied.

'I have called to discuss a lady named Munni Bai, whom you had known about thirty years ago.' Roy was blunt as he could see no space for manoeuvring.

There was a momentary pause and then the recovery. Inder Kumar replied firmly, 'Why should I be interested to speak to you about this supposed lady you are referring to? What is this nonsense you are talking ?' However, the fact remained that Inder Kumar did not disconnect his phone line despite his thinking of the discussion as rubbish.

'No offence meant sir, but I have reason to believe that you have a daughter by this lady. I thought that I should inform you about her, in case you choose to meet her or want to know her. Nothing else.' Roy replied.

'I don't understand what you are talking,' ... the reply from the other end sounded genuine.

'Sir, you are a busy man and I would not like to keep you guessing. I want you to meet a girl who is your daughter.' Roy replied emphatically.

'Are you trying to threaten me or blackmail me?' The irritation was very evident but so was the caution in the voice.

Roy replied, 'Neither. No. I am not out to threaten you or blackmail you, sir. You have my mobile number. As I have said I am a journalist from a national English magazine—The India Post. I recently wrote an article for its 15th August issue, on Mumbai dance bars, and during my research I came across your daughter, a very nice girl. I thought possibly you will be delighted to know her, but I am sorry if I have intruded into your privacy and disturbed you. Good night, sir.' And he disconnected the phone.

The ploy was deliberate and well thought of on Roy's part. He knew that he could not force a reluctant father to meet his daughter when the relationship was illegitimate in nature and the father was a high profile businessman and an erstwhile Prince. What he thought of instead was to try and create a curiosity about the daughter in the father's mind as well as a sense of empathy towards her.

Moreover, he knew that Inder Kumar needed to have a positive opinion about him in order to be receptive to his views which he thought he would achieve with Mahendra Goradia's reference. Now that element being absent, he wanted to use his article and his profile as his reference. Hence he dropped the hint of his recent article to Inder Kumar.

He knew that he could do nothing else but wait for Inder Kumar to call him back, if at all, the love that was described by Mahendra Goradia was so powerful and enduring in Inder Kumar's life.

The phone call from Inder Kumar came the next day, in the late afternoon. Roy was heading towards the Ashram as he had gone out for a walk. Roy took the call as he ordered a cup of tea at the nearby teahouse and sat on its wooden bench.

'Good afternoon, Sir.' He replied very politely taking a sip of the piping hot tea.

'Good afternoon, Roy. Can we speak?' Prince Inder Kumar enquired cryptically.

'Of course, we can, sir. I am at a place where signals are not very reliable and the call may drop; so, kindly bear with me,' he explained.

'I know that you are in Hrishikesh visiting your mother. Mahendra told me. How is she now?' The ever polite Prince exuded genteelness.

'Oh. Thank you very much, she is recovering well,' Roy replied.

'Roy. I want to meet you. I have read your article. Spoke to Mahendra and Alok in detail as well. So we need to meet. I am in Delhi the whole week. When will it be convenient for you to meet me at my office?'

Roy thought for a while and said, 'Sir, I have to consult my mother and her Guruji Swami Amritananda as well. Can I let you know by tomorrow morning?'

'Yes. Please do. I can organise a ride for you from Hrishikesh. My company car can pick you up.'

'Thank you, Sir. But that won't be necessary. I will reach Delhi. I am really happy that you have agreed to meet me. Give me time till tomorrow morning and I will be in touch. Have a great evening, Sir.'

'I wish you the same, Roy.'

They had nothing in common, except their brilliant good looks and sharp minds. One had the princely background and the other was from the intelligentsia; one a bourgeois billionaire businessman and the other a middle-class Renaissance journalist; one in stylish jacket and trousers, the other in jeans and sneakers. Yet, both were keen to present their points of views fairly and squarely. Both wanted a resolution. The question was how to resolve the problem to everyone's satisfaction. Both were cordial to each other. However, polite conversation was not the intention because the issue at hand required hard talk.

Inder Kumar was very specific in his query. 'What interest do you have to find me a daughter?' he asked Roy very pointedly the moment they were left alone by his secretary, at his well-appointed office at Connaught Place in Lutyens' New Delhi.

'None to be precise. Only that a girl will get to know her biological father. I am sure she has her longings,' Roy replied in a polite yet confident tone.

'But how does it matter to you whether she will have a father or not?' Inder Kumar was persistent.

Roy looked at the man sitting slightly away from him – epitome of gracious politeness, yet very surprisingly behaving in a traditional mode. This could not have been the person who had the nerve to propose marriage to a mujrawali three decades ago, in a much more conservative social atmosphere. However, he needed to be cautious. He had thought long and hard on the issue. Inder Kumar could not be faulted and judged by him so quickly. He would have to be provided with more time for him to accept the situation. Roy opened his gambit in a very casual manner and tossed the question, 'Why did you call me back, sir? You had the option of not responding. I did not force you in any way.'

The Prince sitting away from him, crossed and uncrossed his legs, adorned by a pair of Seville Row trousers. He used his left palm to straighten the grey lock of hair that fell on his forehead. Thereafter, he replied in a contemplative manner, 'I wanted to meet you in person to request you to stop the inquisition. I thought you would be mature enough to understand my position.'

Roy sat still and spoke in a measured tone, 'Why are you using such words like inquisition, sir? Did I threaten you in any way?'

Inder Kumar leaned forward and replied, 'No you didn't. But why don't you understand that you have no jurisdiction on the matter. Who are you to gift me a daughter? What are you looking for?'

Roy put his hands up in a very friendly manner, flashed his most disarming smile and said, 'I am not qualified enough to read your thoughts though. But, with your permission, I would like to say that please do not look at me as an adversary. If you so want, I will leave your office at once and would never return to disturb you on this particular subject. But, the fact remains that it will not close the issue at hand. Your daughter will remain your daughter. Why don't you give her a chance to meet you?' Roy looked straight into Inder Kumar's eyes.

Inder Kumar was deep in thought. At long last he said, 'I cannot meet her. Neither am I ready to accept her as my daughter. I don't even know what kind of a creature we are discussing.'

Roy still wanted to reason with him. He could understand this man's plight. Follies of youth had returned to haunt him. Yet Roy felt that all was not lost. Very politely he said, 'I lost my father in a tragic accident a year ago. I still dream of him. Though I had my father beside me for three decades, yet I am unable to cover the void created by his untimely death. My mother could not accept the shock. Can you imagine a girl carrying the void for nearly three decades? She was not responsible for her birth. Two other people were. One died just after her birth and the other one was not even aware till about a day ago that he had a daughter. How do you think that the girl should behave? You give me the answer honestly and prudently and I will leave.' Roy stood up from his chair. 'Oh, by the way, I have met your daughter and that too in a crowded dance bar and in total for not more than a couple of hours. Still, I feel she deserves a chance.'

'How much?' in a very soft tone Inder Kumar said.

Roy was walking across the room to pick up the bottled water kept at a service table at a distance as he was feeling thirsty. He stopped short in his tracks, turned around and asked in an incredulous voice, 'Did you offer me money just now? Are you crazy, Mr Kumar? I thought of you as a very modern human being. But you are portraying yourself to be a very stereotyped feudal lord. Where is the question of money coming from? And how much money are you ready to spend to protect your so called goodwill?'

He walked back to the conference table and deliberately chose a chair next to Inder Kumar and sat down on it. In a very considerate tone with almost the disposition of a monk he said,

'Money will not be a solution. I don't need money. I earn some and my family has some. I am a happy person. So, it is Pallavi you are targeting. Oh, incidentally your daughter's name is Pallavi Singh. She is fairly comfortable financially, as far as I know. She used to earn a fairly handsome amount, come to think of it. So, where does your money lead you to? Okay, for a convoluted second, let's assume, that you will offer an obscene amount of money to us but what guarantee you have that we will still not sully your image thereafter.' Roy raised his eyebrows. 'What else can you offer?'

With a very immobile and inexpressive face, depicting a very foul mood Inder Kumar said, 'I can offer nothing else.'

'Not even a meeting with your daughter with absolute sworn secrecy and no strings attached?' Roy said very softly.

'But what guarantee do I have that I will not be blackmailed?' Inder Kumar asked. 'I run a billion dollar company. I cannot jeopardise its future and the future of my family; future of my brother, niece and nephew. One bloody leak and it would be disaster.'

Roy looked at the man and felt pity. A prince boxed inside a gilded cage, very happy and comfortable there. 'What kind of guarantee will make you comfortable? You want my personal guarantee; I am ready to sign an NDA. I doubt whether we should ask Pallavi to do so, the relationship then starts on a wrong note.'

'Let me consult my lawyers,' Inder Kumar said.

Roy could not take it anymore. He thought Rajkumar Mallik was a pompous ass. However, in comparison, Inder Kumar was a piece of art. He decided to be tough with him, 'Mr Kumar, there would be no guarantee. We will expect you in Mumbai tomorrow evening, at a place of your choice. Please be available by six o'clock in the evening. You can invite or bring in anyone you feel necessary. From her side, I think, it will only be Pallavi. You are simply being presumptive in your behaviour so far, as once your friend Mahendra Goradia said in a different context to me.' Roy took a pause and allowed the diktat to sink in. He was sure that Prince Inder Kumar was not used to being told what needed to be done. He resumed, 'I have not yet informed Pallavi. She does not know anything about you and this meeting. Should I inform her now, because the process will be irreversible? I need your cooperation. I feel that the father and daughter should simply talk. Will you give her and yourself a chance?' Roy stared steadily and volleyed the question to Inder Kumar.

The Prince nodded his head very reluctantly.

Inclusion

The journey was hectic. The schedule was killing – from Hrishikesh to Delhi to Mumbai. On top of all that, he had to organise numerous international and domestic tele-conferences and had to complete the meeting with the Prince. He also had to leave behind a worried mother and a concerned godfather. Why was he doing it? That he wanted a daughter to meet her father? Was that so simple? In his heart of hearts, he himself was in continuous search for the answer.

The plane had landed at Mumbai airport. He had to reach YMCA. Even before Alok Singh could put him on notice, Roy thought it prudent to book himself in YMCA for a fortnight. A disciple of Swamiji's from Delhi had organised it. He had already informed Alok Singh that he would collect his balance luggage the next day morning and move out. This could have ended otherwise. This should have ended otherwise. But, alas, it did not. And this was what life was all about. He was deeply engrossed in his thoughts. Was he correct in his approach to solve the issue? He was still searching for an answer.

He remembered that he had to call Pallavi.

By now Rajkumar Mallik must have spoken to Pallavi and informed her to expect a call from him within the next twenty-four hours. Prince Inder Kumar had confirmed to Roy that he would be present at Mahendra Goradia's office the next day at six o'clock in the evening.

The stage had been set.

Roy, with his rucksack slung across his shoulders, briskly came out of the airport concourse and hailed a black and yellow taxi. It was eleven o'clock at night. The roads were wet. Rain must have happened while Roy was airborne. The bright yellowish lights had amply illuminated the streets; the happy streets. Though it was barely over a couple of months that he was residing in this city, Roy had fallen in love with her. A few days absence had magnified it immensely. This was the city that embraced one and all; the city that provided hope to millions of people; created opportunities to succeed if you had the guts and merit; the city that would hold your hand lovingly if you faltered and would provide you with a second chance if you asked for it sincerely. Roy felt this was it – this was what life was all about.

It did not get registered into his consciousness. He was too engrossed introspecting. When it did, that a mobile was ringing, he took out his handset from the rucksack only to be aware of the fact that his phone was on the switched off mode. By then, the cabbie was talking on his mobile. He was blank for a moment and slowly realised that the cabbie and him, they both shared the same ringtone. He smiled to himself and switched on his phone. And, the moment he switched it on, the phone started ringing. Roy was bemused. He could not recognise the number. It was a landline number from Mumbai. He thought that in all likelihood it must be the YMCA reception checking out to see if he had landed in Mumbai and his probable time of reaching the youth hostel. He pressed the call receive button and said, 'Hello.' The moment a lady with a lilting voice responded from the other end he did not wait a bit and replied, 'I would be there in YMCA in sometime, Ma'am. I am on my way from the airport.'

The reply was instantaneous, 'Helloo. Why you always call me "Ma", you "Baba".... I told you earlier also. What wrong did I do to you?'

Roy was stunned.

'You disappeared that night to do whatever you wanted to do at *Round The Corner* and never returned. Are you still at it, mister?' That imperious, infectious and lively laughter resonated over Roy's mobile phone. 'Oh. I completely forgot ... congratulations on your story *Patrakarji*.' The mild curiosity expressed in that typical inimitable manner, just so subtly.

Suddenly Roy became alive. He had a reason to laugh. He did burst out into prolonged laughter.

The middle-aged cabbie for a fraction of a second wondered if his passenger had gone crazy. He looked through the rear-view mirror, saw him talking on his mobile and nodded his head in understanding ... *must be the girlfriend* he thought and went back to his driving.

Once Roy's laugh subsided, Pallavi asked in a soft voice, 'How is your mother?'

Roy, though mildly surprised by the question, replied truthfully, 'She is okay but requires some more time to get alright.'

However, the next question from Pallavi took Roy completely by surprise, 'Did you call her up to let her know that you have reached safely?'

Roy was silent. He thought but discarded the idea of fobbing her off with an inaccurate answer. He decided that the truth, as always, would liberate him and the truth should be told. 'No. I did not. Thought will call her tomorrow. She must be asleep by now.'

The very tender reply from the other end was so endearing, 'Try calling her now. You would be surprised. Call me back after you have spoken to her. Bye now.'

'Oh Sunny! Glad you called. I almost lost hope. So, have you reached Mumbai?'

'Yes Ma, I did,' Roy replied with a guilty feeling.

'Thank God. I was worried stiff. It was such a hectic journey. How was your meeting with the Prince?' Martha enquired.

'It was good, Ma,' Roy tried to keep the expectation level low considering Inder Kumar's behaviour.

'When is he meeting his daughter?' She asked.

'Tomorrow evening, Ma,' Roy replied again.

'You must be very tired. Check-in quickly and go off to sleep. And, you never know the call might drop. I will inform Amrit Maharaj first thing tomorrow morning. Take care love. We are all with you. Everything will be alright. Give that girl my best wishes. Good night, Sunny.' The eternal mother gave her blessings.

'Good night, Ma, and you be good. I need you in Mumbai very soon.'

On the very first ring Pallavi picked up the phone and without any prelude asked, 'Did you speak to your mother?'

Roy replied, 'Yes, I did.'

'Was she happy?'

'Yes indeed. Thank you very much.'

'Does she know about me, my father, our meeting?'

'Yes she does and so also our family Guruji. They have sent their best wishes.'

'Really? Or you are making it up?'

'Why should I make it up? In fact, Guruji is known to Mr Mallik,' Roy replied.

'I know that. They are childhood friends. Did you tell your mother that you forgot calling her and I reminded you?' she asked with a hint of mischievousness.

'No, I did not. I should have but I did not. It would have been a bit complicated issue to handle over long distance telephone call so late in the night,' Roy answered.

'Why are you behaving so honestly and openly now? Why didn't you do a *Round the Corner* trick with me this time?'

'I don't lie. That day I had no other option. I had to write the story and Mr Mallik could have created problems. Sorry.' Roy tried answering the question as truthfully as he could.

'Hmmmm. How far are you from your hotel?'

Roy was astonished. 'How do you know?'

'Rajababa told me everything. He and Swamiji had a very long conversation.'

Roy kept quiet. He digested the information. Tomorrow morning he needed to clarify with Swamiji what was the strategy behind disclosing everything.

'Are you there?' Pallavi asked very softly.

'Yes I am. But I have to go now. I have to check-in,' Roy replied politely.

'So, how are we meeting tomorrow?' She enquired.

'You tell me. What suits you?'

'Can we meet at the Tea Centre at Churchgate at 4:00 pm?' Pallavi asked.

'Oh! You know Tea Centre,' Roy was surprised but quickly recovered and said, 'Fantastic. But why at four? Our meeting is at six only?'

'I want to talk to you before that. Good night, Roy. Take care.'

'Bye Pallavi.'

Roy selected a cosy corner table, so that whatever Pallavi had to discuss could be done in relative privacy.

His mobile rang. Roy looked at it. He could see it was Pallavi as he had stored her cell-number provided by Swamiji before his journey to New Delhi. Yesterday, he was foxed as she had called from a landline, presumably from her home. 'Hello, Pallavi,' he replied.

'Why are you not picking up the call? Busy? Have you reached?' She volleyed a burst of questions.

'Yes, I am already at the Tea Centre. Where are you?' Roy asked evenly.

'Oh! I am parking the car close to the Churchgate station near that college. There is no parking space on the main road. I should be there in five minutes.' She disconnected the line.

She was in her formals. Roy was delightfully surprised. He could not have imagined that Pallavi would ever be in formals. But with her highly intuitive nature, Pallavi could understand Roy's surprise. 'Why? Don't you think I can carry myself off in formals? Only women executives can?' She mildly rebuked him.

Dressed in a pair of black trousers with a matching jacket, a pastel pink shirt and a pair of mid-stiletto-heel shoes, she looked ravishing. Her hair was pulled back tightly and tied at the back accentuating her features. Sans make-up with a faint hint of coffee-coloured lipstick, light blue mascara and her artistic long nails varnished with light silver coloured polish, a light gold chain adorning her neck and two small gold studs on her cute earlobes, she was a show-stopper. Roy was completely speechless.

'Won't you invite me in? Or are you going to keep me waiting at the steps?' She raised her eyebrows.

'Oh! Sure, please come in.' Roy held the door to the restaurant open for her, with a half bow.

'Thank you.' She complimented him. 'Nice place? Isn't it?' Pallavi looked at Roy while being seated.

'Yes indeed. Thank you. Credit goes to you. But, how did you know about this place?' Roy expressed curiosity.

'Why? Only because I dance in a bar I cannot know about your world, the world outside? Do you think we are dumb and lame? What do you think that we do not have ... what do you call it? Aha ... élan, style?' She paused, quickly looked around the table to see if anyone was paying attention to them and when she was satisfied that no one was overhearing their conversation she said, 'Okay. Raima suggested the place last night when I asked her where I should meet you. You know Raima, *na*? My duet partner. She is a nice girl. Studied in college and knows very good English. She has come to our line accidentally. Will you marry her?' with a very innocent face, Pallavi threw her first poser.

Roy was amused yet slightly irritated. At times it was very difficult to understand Pallavi. Not only a quick-wit, but her native intelligence was so highly honed. He simply smiled at her.

'So you will like to marry her? Why are you smiling? Hmmm.' She made a face.

'Did I say that?' Roy replied.

'Try marrying her. Try once. I will kill you.' She smiled and squeezed his hands which he had rested casually on the table. He practically jumped out of his chair. Thank God, not many customers were around. He was not used to physical contact and was not at all prepared for such behaviour from Pallavi.

'What happened?'

'Nothing. I am not used to such things from people whom I have not known for long,' he replied honestly.

'Oh! Is that so? Don't you have a girlfriend?' Pallavi asked, smiling mischievously.

'How is it related to having a girlfriend?' Roy asked to understand her thinking.

She clarified, 'At least, in that case you would be used to a young woman's touch.'

'No. I don't.'

'Never?'

'No. Never. I told you once before also, when you asked.'

'But why?' And suddenly she exclaimed, '*Hai meri Matarani*; so you never had sex, you mean to say? You are a virgin, *uuuiii Ammmaa*?' She clapped her hands silently. She bowed her head slightly, her right hand touched her forehead, some whispered intonations, possibly prayer offered to her Goddess. She opened her eyes and asked, '*Khabi idher-udher nahin gaya na? Ladki log ke pass?'* and made a gesture with her eyes enquiring if Roy ever solicited paid sex.

Roy was completely taken aback. He pushed his chair back and was ready to leave, 'What nonsense are you talking? I don't have time for all this.'

She reached across the table, held his hands tightly and smiled broadly, 'Please *yaar,* don't get angry and behave like a kid. You are my friend. I am just asking. Do you know I had marked you on the very first day? I had told Rajababa that I will leave the dance bar profession completely and settle down to a domesticated life, if you marry me. Rajababa was after my life since the last five years. Whenever he felt a customer might be suitable; he used to behave like mad. But I needed to like the person, *na*? The person had to be good like you, *na*? It is the question of our whole life. What do you think?' she looked straight into Roy's eyes; no inhibitions, no pretensions.

She was simply blabbering, Roy thought. He looked at the young woman sitting in front of him. So intelligent, so worldly-wise, yet she was like an innocent child. Once she had made up her mind she would be like *Ekalavya's arrow,* focused very specifically on her goal. 'I haven't thought of marrying you, honestly?' Roy wanted to make the record straight at the very outset. 'I had told you earlier also. Please don't discuss all such plans of yours,' he repeated once again in a matter-of-fact voice.

Pallavi released his hands and became argumentative, 'Then why did you visit my father? What right do you have?'

Roy deliberated. He started stroking his chin softly. When he would be deep in thought he did that mostly. He started drumming the fingers of his left hand on the table. At long last he said, 'I did it because I thought it is the right thing to do. It was by accident during my research for the article that I came to know about you, your mother and your father. I was researching about your community. I came to know how for ages crimes have been committed against the women of your community. Well, I thought someone needs to stand up to try and correct the situation. So I went to your father to let him know that he has a beautiful daughter waiting in Mumbai.'

'And, he has come to Mumbai to become my father? Correct?' She asked so very softly.

'I think so,' Roy replied.

'No, you should not think so. What you are talking is bullshit. What do you think I am? A stupid toy in your hand? Don't you feel obligated to discuss such things with me? It is my life we are talking about. When it comes to your marriage you have a firm opinion. Similarly, I am entitled to have an opinion about the issue related to my father.' She replied with a firm resolve.

Roy was unprepared for such gutsy behaviour and clarity of thought from Pallavi. He still tried defending himself, 'We had discussed everything with Mr Mallik and he said that he will in turn discuss with you.'

'You did? You and who else?' She asked.

'Swamiji—Amritanandaji, my father's friend and my mother's Guruji. We had long discussions even yesterday afternoon.'

'Where is your father?' She asked politely.

'Passed away. Last year. And before you start sympathising, it was a car accident and I am okay.' Roy just put up his hands in a defensive style and replied.

'Just look at yourself,' she said softly. 'Why are you mad at me? We are friends. Like you miss your father, I miss my father too. But when I hear that my father was reluctant to meet me and you have forced him to meet me for my happiness, I become sad. I feel that my father doesn't love me; else he would not have been reluctant. You can't force him to be my father. It has to come to him from within. I feel you love me more instead.' She extended her arms over the table top and caught hold of Roy's hands once again. She looked deeply into his eyes and said with very frank eyes and open face, 'You don't like me because I am a mujrawali. I am a girl with loose morals. You must have thought that I might have slept with a huge number of men. And, I don't have good values in life. Were those your discomforts?'

Roy thought of ditching the questions. Then he changed his mind. 'Yes you are correct. Moreover, my first discomfort is that Ma has an image of a girl who might become my wife. You are not fitting into the image because yes, you are correct, you are used to multiple sexual partners because of your profession and it is a known fact. So she might find it difficult to accept you. I am the only son. My duty is to protect my mother and her feelings.'

'Multiple ... hmmm. Don't you feel you have looked at me unfairly? Even, the so-called regular girls from your society could have multiple friends and be physically involved with them, but it is only a problem for me. Why?'

Roy was not really prepared to discuss this issue with Pallavi. He said, 'Frankly, when I am not considering marrying you, I should not really be bothered.'

Pallavi insisted, 'No. This needs to be discussed, and discussed openly, between you and me. Else, you should not have intruded into my life. What right do you have to step into my world and then deny me the opportunity of defending myself? You are being judgmental.'

Roy calmly said, 'I disagree with what you are saying. I have not intruded into your life.'

Pallavi without being defensive uttered, 'Yes. You did. And, please keep quiet and listen to what I am saying. I only had close physical relationships with two gentlemen; very wealthy and much more senior to me in age. One of them stayed with me for a long period. He was my pagadwala. You understand pagadwala, *na*? I couldn't protect myself because then I had to go against the wishes of my community elders, which I couldn't at that point of time. I had no financial strength or social security net to fall back upon. But once I consolidated my finances, became more mature and confidently started handling my own business affairs and payments with Adil seth, my community couldn't force anything on me anymore thereafter. Adil seth had helped me a lot to become the main dancer of Magnet. Rajababa told him to do so. Adil seth respects Rajababa and listens to him. It helped me. I earned a lot. There was no looking back. My community leaders and Madhuri Ma wanted money and I gave them a lot of it.'

'Look, I am not really interested.'

'Still, indulge me. Anything else that you find could be a shortcoming in me?'

'Parentage. Family. That would be important to Ma.'

'But now you know my parentage however illegitimate it is.' Pallavi replied very mildly again.

'It helps but it is not really an issue with me personally.' Roy gave a very straightforward reply.

'What is important to you? What would you be looking for in a person in case marriage is proposed?'

'Complete trust and truth in the relationship, no falsehood. I should be in love with the girl. Love first. Love second. Love third. I cannot marry and love. I need to be in love to be married. But look, I am not really bothered about such things currently.'

Roy for the rest of his life would not forget what Pallavi had uttered so softly yet surely at that very moment, 'Regardless of how everyone in this world might feel, I have the courage and the desire to become the woman you dream to be with. In the process, even if I lose my own identity I don't care, because at the end, the personality that I will emerge with will be so much more strong and enhanced that you will covet and love me for the rest of your life. It is never too late to be what you think you can be!'

Roy could ask only one question, 'Why are you doing this to yourself and me? '

Pallavi without even thinking for a second replied, 'Because I want to spend the rest of my life with you. I cannot imagine that you are not there besides me. I know Ma will like me. I can assure you that. Can we go tomorrow to meet Ma and Guruji?'

'But why? Why so suddenly?'

Pallavi started playing with Roy's robust hands. 'I have thought about it very deep for sometime now. No one does anything free for anyone in a place like Magnet. You did it for me. You traced my father for me and brought him to my doorstep. You knew I am a mujrawali, still you did. You have no idea the kind of happiness it gave me. That someone thought about me selflessly. You did not consider me only as flesh. You looked at my soul. At Magnet you never misbehaved with me, never ever hinted at anything objectionable. Not only to me, to any other girl. You have inherent respect ingrained in you for women, for anybody and everybody. You don't look at caste, creed, profession, nothing. Rajababa went to the Ashram in Hrishikesh chasing you, yet you gave him respect. You have kept your elders informed about all your activities. Rajababa highly praised you for your article. Above all, you are a very nice human being. Rajababa also told me that your father was a very nice man and a teacher. Your mother does charity work. You have an upbringing I dreamt of having. I want my children to have such upbringing. I am not a fool to let you go. Nevertheless, I have already spoken to Swami Amritanandaji Maharaj. Sorry *yaar*, if I have exceeded my limit. I will be visiting the Ashram soon.' She folded her hands seeking forgiveness and her eyes were twinkling and proposing a truce.

Roy was not prepared to be pursued so strongly. He was recoiling within himself with each of Pallavi's statements. Not because of any inhibition but he himself was not very clear of his own feelings. He was getting really angry, which was very unusual of him. He spoke to her in a calm voice though, 'When did you speak to Uncle Amrit about Hrishikesh?'

'Last night. Just before I called you to request you to call your mother, it was Swamiji's idea. He called me to find out if you had called me, because your mobile was coming switched off. Your mother was worried because you did not call her.' She made an apologetic face. 'Don't get angry. Can we just talk please?' Pallavi requested him.

'What else did you discuss with Uncle?' Roy persisted.

'Why should I tell you? You claim that he is your uncle, you ask him.' Pallavi made the comment, displaying mock anger.

Roy was in a dilemma. He kept messages in the Ashram twice since the early evening before boarding his flight from Delhi to Mumbai for Swamiji but he was yet to call back. Roy knew that a very large delegation from Germany had arrived and Swamiji must be busy with them. Roy did not want to involve his mother to communicate with Swamiji anymore on this issue as it might get complicated as far as his mother was concerned. So he had no other option but to keep quiet.

After a few agonising moments Pallavi said, 'Oh! He invited me to the Ashram and said I should come as soon as possible. Along with Niyati.'

'Who is Niyati?' Roy asked pointedly. He was also worried about what Uncle Amrit was up to.

'Your competitor.' Pallavi flashed her brilliant smile.

'Good. Get married to him.' Roy was just ready to leave and signalled to the waiter for the bill.

'What nonsense. You have lost your sense of humour or what? She is my daughter. I have adopted her. My cousin sister, Mukti, was her mother. She passed away. Niyati calls me Mommy.'

'Oh! I think I saw both of you in Dehradun. She fell from her cycle.' Roy made a dispassionate statement.

'You did?' She was astonished. 'You were in Dehradun that day? Why did you not get in touch with me at that time?' Pallavi leaned forward in her chair. '*Arre meri taraf to dekho aap*?' She cupped Roy's face in her palms and forced him to look at her. 'I will create a ruckus here if you leave now.' She enlarged and held her dazzling eyes wide open and looked directly into Roy's mystic eyes. She did not care for anyone anymore, except the person before her.

'Look, don't be dramatic. People are looking at us.' Roy felt uncomfortable with the sudden intimate gesture of this beautiful young woman. He purposefully looked at his watch; it was fifteen minutes to six. He indicated to Pallavi the inevitable, 'Time is up, baby. Daddy is waiting. You need to go.'

The waiter came. Pallavi snatched the bill from Roy's hand and cleared it making the statement, 'It is my treat. I had proposed the meeting.'

Roy kept his temper on check and once the bill was settled, he asked, 'Shall we go?'

Pallavi simply nodded her head. She also asked for Roy's phone. He was mildly curious yet he handed over the phone none-the-less. Pallavi went to the stored number panel of the phone book. She decided on a number, walked out of the restaurant with Roy following her in pursuit, and called that number.

The moment there was a response from the other end, she answered firmly in a polite voice, 'Saab, this is Munia Chhari. I am using Roy's phone because it had your number stored in it. My mother is Munni Chhari. I am told you are my father, but a reluctant father. So, I don't want to meet you because I cannot make you a father by forcing you to be one. I have lived my life so far without you, though of course, I constantly used to feel a void. But I cannot fill up that void by forcing you to be my father. It has to come from within. I know that Roy forced you to be here. I am apologising for that. It was not his fault. He did it for me. He had no other intentions. Please go home and be in peace. Your reputation will not be harmed; after all you are my father. I have no reason to hurt you. If anytime in future you feel like talking to me or want to be my father, please give a call on this number ... *Khamma Ghani Hukum* ...' Prince Inder Kumar being Rajput, the ever sensitive and highly intuitive Pallavi signed off in his language in her salutation to the man she acknowledged as her father ...

But, Roy was furious. 'What the hell were you saying just now? Why did you have to do that? This is unfair to him. I had invited him to Mumbai after it was discussed with Mr Mallik. No, sorry. I cannot be a party to it anymore. Excuse me, please. I have to go.' He turned around to leave.

Standing in the middle of the Tea Centre's open courtyard, without raising her voice a single decibel Pallavi said, 'Wait. Hear me out. After that you are free to go and I will not be coming after you, will not chase you or bother you.'

Roy turned around.

Pallavi continued looking unblinkingly at Roy, 'Can you tell me why you are getting upset unnecessarily? Only because I did something you thought is wrong? And you don't want to be with me? Look at the similarity – my father did exactly the same thing to me. He came to meet me reluctantly. He came to meet me because he was here to protect his name and not because he loves me. He was scared of you. I don't want to meet him under such circumstances. I don't want to see my father scared. If he ever feels for me, now that he knows, he will be in touch with you in the future. I will meet him then. What separates us from the rest of the ordinary souls is how courageously we can handle our misfortunes and can rise above them and rebuild our lives. Now, please tell me, am I wrong?'

Roy was amazed; he had to admit by saying so. 'No you are not wrong. But how do you know that he was meeting you reluctantly?'

Pallavi gave a mysterious smile and said, 'Someone who loves you and wants to protect you, told me. His logic behind telling me was that if my father tried insulting me as he insulted you, by offering money, I should not get upset with you. He was someone wise, who understands how the universe moves, and alerted me to that prospect. He said that you should not be misunderstood by me for my father's odd behaviour and reluctance, should I choose to meet him.'

Roy kept staring at the girl standing in front of him – the girl with the dazzling eyes. He thought that all through their current interaction she displayed strength of character and positive attitude towards life backed by impeccable arguments. Moreover, no one who was cunning, worldly-wise and opportunistic in nature would have behaved the way she did with her billionaire father. She behaved with utmost dignity. Roy was forced to accept that he was not dealing with an ordinary dance bar girl, a mujrawali; but with a highly intelligent, greatly intuitive, morally upright, emotionally robust girl. She was not just anyone, but an exceptionally extraordinary girl. Roy thought, loving this girl, after all, might not be so difficult.

Just to ease off the tension that was in the air because of his haughty behaviour he extended his right hand, smiled and said, 'Hey Munia Chhari, sorry for pushing you. By the way, I am Rabindranath Royce Chandrabhanu Kashyap. Nice meeting you.'

'Hey Roy ... *thuri* ... *thuri* ... Rabindranath! What a poetic name. Nice meeting you too and no offence taken.' She smiled back and shook his extended hand very firmly in a smart gesture. 'Now that we have enough time on our hands and there is a distinct possibility of an imminent shower, shall we go for a stroll around Marine Drive?' She looked at Roy for an affirmation. He interjected, 'But what about your car?'

'Oh! I can collect it later. In fact, I hardly use it. Mostly used by the lady who stays with me,' she said without any hesitation or rancour, in a very matter of fact tone. And then wistfully she added, 'You wouldn't believe; I haven't got drenched in the rain, ever. Especially with someone who cares for me.'

She looked at him with a very loving smile. Thereafter, she closed her eyes and murmured softly ...

'*O sun re mona, ghama, chona, saj devala,*
e hoi thommniata, biav'.

'What was that?' he asked.

'An ancient lore. Our hymn. A belief,' she replied earnestly.

They began walking together ...

Their souls transcended the waves of existence and transgressed the unacceptable. No one could prevent this impulse. It came from within. It called upon them to go further beyond in an unreasoning migration to the life anew. In their collective consciousness, they realised the fragrance of life without any prejudice.

It started to rain ...

Author's Note

Like every action of our society, evidences of situations narrated in this book can be found documented in bits and pieces, scattered over different media through the centuries; from the published memoirs of the British era, to the government records of our country, to study papers submitted by the scholars in the recent times, as well as news reports in various newspapers, magazines, electronic and other media. During my research for the book, I personally received first-hand information from numerous individuals and organisations as primary sources as well. I am indebted to each and every individual, organisation and document for enriching me with knowledge which, in turn, helped me in narrating the story.

I have referred to certain historical, social, and political events in the story as well, which were necessary for establishing the veracity of the theme. To borrow the words of Abraham Lincoln, this book is written, 'with malice toward none, with charity for all, with firmness in the right ...' Lastly, any resemblance with any person, living or dead, with any character of the book is not intentional and deliberate.

Furthermore, my sincere gratitude to: *The Hindu*, *The Times of India*, *The Telegraph*, *The Pioneer*, *Mid-Day*, *The Tribune*,

Outlook, NDTV, Rediff.com, Advocate Flavia Agnes, Dr Anuja Agrawal, Dr Mike Dash, Shri Ram Sanehi, Barrister Rustom Vachha, Shri Pratim Ranjan Bose, Shri Dilip D'Souza, Ms Malini Bhupta, Ms Swati Sucharita, Shri Kingshuk Nag, Shri Purnendu Shekhar Mitra, Shri Sekhar Basu Mallik, Prof Sudokshina Bhattacharyya and the Maharashtra State Archives, Government of Maharashtra, as well as to those lot many individuals who did not want to be identified.

To my wife Anjanaa and sons Dev and Dipayan, I say that without you I am incomplete. And, my sincere gratitude to all three of you for putting up with my mood swings, insecurity, anxiety and eccentric behaviour.